THE CONSPIRACY

THE
CONSPIRACY

a novel by
John Hersey

1972

ALFRED A. KNOPF
New York

THIS IS A BORZOI BOOK
PUBLISHED BY ALFRED A. KNOPF, INC.

ISBN: 0-394-47929-7
Library of Congress Catalog Card Number: 75-173775

Manufactured in the United States of America

To my good friend

Lillian Hellman

A NOTE ON THE TYPE

The text of this book is set in Electra, a typeface designed by W. A. Dwiggins for the Mergenthaler Linotype Company and first made available in 1935. Electra cannot be classified as either "modern" or "old style." It is not based on any historical model, and hence does not echo any particular period or style of type design. It avoids the extreme contrast between "thick" and "thin" elements that marks most modern faces, and is without eccentricities which catch the eye and interfere with reading. In general, Electra is a simple, readable typeface which attempts to give a feeling of fluidity, power, and speed.

ONE

64 A.D.

September 15

To TIGELLINUS, Co-Commander, Praetorian Guard, from PAENUS, Tribune of Secret Police

I have information. When can I see you?

To PAENUS, Tribune of Secret Police, from TIGELLINUS

Come to me after the baths.

September 16

To PAENUS, Tribune of Secret Police, from TIGELLINUS

This morning I told Himself about our talk. He has no fear of these people because, he said, they are men of thought, not of action. His advice was: Listen, gather, wait. The time to sharpen our scythes, he said, will come. I must add: Your informant is not well known to us. I was amazed again this morning, as I so often am, by Himself. Poppaea was in the room while we talked. Perhaps for her benefit, Himself joked about assassination. Think, Paenus, how the Caesars have died—three out of five violently; four if, as some people say, Tiberius was smothered in his bed. Yet Himself clapped me on the shoulder and said, "How will I go, Tigellinus? Will you be the one to let the air out of me?"

I have an uncouth soul, I laughed like a drunk when he said that. I thank my stars that after I began laughing he did, too. Also the Empress—a bit too heartily, I thought.

To cover ourselves, we need a full report on the dinner at Piso's. Have it done.

To TIGELLINUS from PAENUS, Tribune of Secret Police
The report has been ordered. The informant, as I told you, is a certain Curtius Marsus. He is more or less a poet, morbidly ambitious, about twenty years old, recently taken up by Piso on recommendation of Bassus. It seems that he is willing to reach fame by any ladder that offers itself; he obviously hopes that his work as an informer will bring him to the attention of the most eminent poet of all. His immense crushed nose, which seems to have been imprinted with great pressure on his face—no doubt at birth, because there could scarcely have been passageway for both him and it to come into the world at the same time—describes curves left and right as it plunges down his long face and is, I am told, larger than his talent. He has become a curiosity among the intellectuals, however, not on account of his nearly beautiful ugliness but because he has a freak memory which, like one of those cloaks of black Leuconian wool, picks up every bit of lint that floats in the air and will not let it go. I will cull his report. I will also set a watch on his reliability.

To PAENUS, Tribune of Secret Police, from TIGELLINUS
Enough about snouts. You put them in every report.

To CELER, Office of Planning and Construction, from TIGELLINUS
Prepare me a barge. I want it for an occasion on the Lake of the Golden House. It should hold about fifty persons at a

time and should delight all who board it. One principal chamber and several alcoves, with hangings. Bulkheads, pillars, and doors of rare woods inlaid with gold, ivory, copper, tin, lead, and silver. Place a high throne for Himself near the bow, facing forward. Illumination. And as to illumination, a warning. Watch out for fire hazard. Himself is presently capable of becoming dangerously irritable at the smallest lamp that licks or flickers. Banners. Also, for the shores, numerous booths. Prepare their separate walls in secrecy at a distance, so they can be assembled by the lake at the last moment. Colored gauze hangings for the open side of each, to face the lake. Brilliant lights within.

You have a month.

To CANUS, Imperial Household, from TIGELLINUS

Procure, for an occasion on the Lake of the Golden House, various animals, birds, and monsters.

Flamingos from the Nile, guinea fowl from Numidia, pheasants from the Phasis and Macedonia. Particular care to have pheasants of many colors.

Domesticated leopards, elephants, apes, to walk naturally in the gardens among the guests.

At least two hippopotamuses, some freshwater serpents, water monsters as discovered.

And above all, a difficult task, the successful outcome of which will win you much favor with Himself. It will be—*must* be—a surprise to him. Procure one thousand swans. Have made for them body harnesses of brilliant colors with long cords attached to them, which will be used for the towing of a barge. A gold collar for the neck of each swan, a long colored ribbon, of lightest weight, as a rein; a system of consolidation of the reins so that one pair of final ribbons can be held by Himself at a conning throne. Small gilded boats to guide the mass of swans. Rehearse this at a distance and in secrecy.

You have a month.

To AMMIANA, Imperial Household, from TIGELLINUS

Be warned of an occasion for special foods for about four hundred persons in one month. Send now for apples and pears from Ameria; persimmons from Judaea; figs, dates, plums, and pomegranates from Damascus and Alexandria.

Let us discuss what will be served. You of all people, Ammiana, know how in bad times pleasure eats pleasure, how tired our tongues become of scandal and condiments, how wide the net must be thrown for things that are new.

To TIGELLINUS from PAENUS, Tribune of Secret Police

About my insistence upon noses: I suppose it comes from the fact that my only competence is putting mine in other people's business. But wait till you see this one belonging to the informant, Curtius Marsus. We should have Sulpicius Castor carve a likeness of it. I would suggest the veined pink marble from Numidia.

September 19

To TIGELLINUS from PAENUS, Tribune of Secret Police

Herewith the report from Curtius Marsus on the dinner at Piso's—or, rather, parts of it. I have cut out some passages that are diverting but not to the purpose. Some of what I have left in may seem irrelevant at first glance but may prove useful in procuring informants, suborning, blackmailing, etc.

From here on, words of Curtius (who, by the way, seems to be neither especially reliable nor especially unreliable, as yet, for he is too raw, too ungainly, too ambitious, and too mediocre to be judged by the highest standards either of danger or of literary criticism; seems, anyway, to have a memory; makes no mention of his nose, so I will not either):

"An 'intimate' dinner at Piso's. Twenty-seven guests, all of the moment. After Beneventum, where I have been recently, the Roman women seem breathtaking to me. Piso's wife Atria reclines next to me, her black hair in tiers of curls arched by a vulgar diadem, her forehead and arms chalked, her cheeks and lips glowing with lees of wine, her eyelids shadowed with powdered antimony—but the cosmetics cannot hide either her young ripeness or her restless dissatisfaction. You probably know that she is lowborn. She is slack in her duties as hostess, and she seems to melt and actually to lose physical strength when flattered—not by me, but by Natalis on her other side. I detected eye signs of a growing understanding between them. . . .

"The dinner starts out sedately—one of Piso's usual evenings for literati and their admirers. The important thing to remember is that the men at the dinner are serious. Worried, proud, and unafraid. In love with the *idea* of Rome. Notorious, some of them—but without exception these men are scornful of notoriety; do not need false supports. They are dangerous because they are complacent.

"I give you, for example, Scaevinus. Here he reclines between two beauties. He seems, as he always seems, drowsy, as if the heavy dregs of dream years of excruciating delights have settled in his thick eyelids and in the bold veins of the whites of his eyes. He drinks more than most of these men. I saw Scaevinus one day at the palestra of the baths at the Field of Mars, playing snatchball, looking half drunk and three quarters asleep, yet I was astonished at his agility, feints, dodges, bursts of speed, while what must have been nearly pure wine cascaded from his pink pores. His mind, too, has agility, no matter how much he drinks; one must not be taken in by the stupid nodding, the sticky eyes, the hanging lower lip. Here at this dinner I overhear him expound, with a facility of tongue and depth of knowledge that are dazzling, on bee-keeping, on the management of the grain supply at Ostia, on the method of stiffening lawn cloth, on the mechanics of earthquakes. He is Piso's best friend. . . .

"There is a current of expectancy. I have heard beforehand that Lucan is going to read a new passage from his long poem. The prospect, however, is not as promising as it might be. Lucan, at the place of honor at the uppermost table, is in one of his distant moods, staring. He will speak to no one. Piso tries to stir him with questions, one of which is: 'Lucan, why did Seneca refuse to come tonight?' No answer. Lucan gazes blankly at his own hands. He may get up and walk out and go home without a word, as I gather he often does—leaving his superb Polla, by the way, to temptations that are surely pressed on her the moment her husband trails his mysterious preoccupation out with him.

"MYSELF (I am new to this, a new little carp caught in the gauze net): How does he dare do these readings?

"ATRIA: This is not publication. We are in a private house.

"MYSELF: Yes, but can you trust all your guests?

"ATRIA: Trust? My husband says all you can hope of a guest is that he will enjoy himself while he is in your house.

"Piso is to me a disconcerting host. He is one of the most popular men in Rome. I know that. It is clear that he knows it. When I first approached him this evening he appeared to be thinking very hard about some household detail; he was raising his arm and twiddling his fingers to summon a freed-man when my face swam into focus in his eyes. One saw the instantaneous lighting of an interior lantern, one heard a tempestuous clacking of the tablets of a file in his head, and then, his face composed, his tall frame canted forward, his expression rather bleak and unkind, he said he was delighted to have me in his house; he had met my mother once when he argued a case of a cousin of hers in the courts; he remembered her expert knowledge of cameos cut from ivory and mother-of-pearl. This was extraordinary. The case of my aunt Aemelia was eight years ago. His exchange of chitchat with my mother must have been brief and most casual, and must have come when he had pressing legal matters on his mind. Yet this feat gave me no pleasure. Water is water: I love the baths, I take no great pleasure in the display of fountains. He gave me, besides, the distinct feeling he had decided, after having invited me to the dinner, that it had been a mistake to invite me. I had a sense that he had made the crudest and cruelest of literary judgments—that which is made, not on the basis of reading or hearing a man's work, but on the basis of gossip.

"The dinner proceeds. The food is overspiced to appease the love of sensation of writers. Not love. Need. Craving in the false name of art. Lucan remains immobile. He suddenly stirs to eat; wolfs a small amount of food with twisted face and violent chewing; then as suddenly subsides and reassumes a face of wax.

"Polla, at another group of tables, vivacious to the point of being silly as if to compensate for her husband's lugubrious silence, occasionally glances at him. She plays the dutiful wife to perfection. Her face is never in repose. Even when no one is speaking to her or looking at her, she wears an attentive mask, with a vaporous smile hovering on her lips like a frail morning mist on a pond.

"The gossip on our couch was all about Lucan. Two women in his life. The first, this Polla. Atria says: 1) Polla is in love, not with prickly Lucan, but with being great Lucan's wife; 2) she leaves things—a purse, a necklace, a comb, a shawl— at other people's houses, as a way of laying a claim on their premises; 3) men say she is unbearably beautiful, women say

she has blue veins on her legs; 4) she is desperate to entertain
the newest 'arrival,' particularly any young writer to whom the
Emperor has decided to nod his head; 5) her curiosity over-
powers her, and she will walk into a friend's house unan-
nounced the morning after a dinner, perhaps coming after
something she has left or on a flimsy errand of solicitude,
penetrating right to the bedroom, where she will finger the
material of a gown or without leave lift the cover of a box
and inspect her friend's jewels; 6) whatever her curiosity dis-
covers she retails in gossip, but she often gets things mixed
up, sometimes to the detriment of reputations; 7) she herself
has a reputation of being an angel of kindness, sympathy,
understanding, charity, connubial fidelity—a reputation which
the pursed lips of Atria, speaking of it, seem to belie. It is my
conclusion, watching Polla's tense and self-conscious 'ease,'
that she is half crazy from the effort of keeping this bubble
from bursting in her face.

"Natalis does not think Polla knows about Lucan's other
woman. Since Natalis lays claim to a full catalogue of all
Roman indiscretion, his knowing and her not knowing does
not seem odd to him. This second woman is a certain Epicharis, the mistress of Lucan's father, Mela. What a strange,
perverse tangle! Mela has abandoned his wife—Lucan's
mother—in Rome. He lives near Misenum with this Epicharis, who is twenty years younger than he is—and ten years
older than Lucan; but it seems she is a remarkable natural
actress who wears age lightly and changeably, as if it were
clothing to be chosen for the occasions of each day. She is a
by-the-way daughter of an Eastern slave and a Roman Senator. She has, Natalis says, tawny beauty and a nervous, demon-
strative warmth which teeters always on the edge of anger.
When she shows anger she glows with an almost irresistible lambent seductiveness; she is a tempting fruit then for
the male senses of touch and taste. Natalis says she loves

every hurt thing on earth and nourishes sufferers with a fierce
and challenging gift of provocation—stirs up anger (but not
at her) and desire (for her and for a vague, abstract idealism)
in those for whom she is sorry. Little pink resentful Lucan is
her perfect suitor. Lucan goes off often on mysterious trips,
Natalis says—where but to Misenum, to distance himself
from a mother he loathes and bitterly to cuckold a father he
loves with this ripe persimmon? . . .

"It takes only one sentence from Piso, saying it is time for
the reading, to bring Lucan out of his trance. The poet moves
languidly to the center of the room, with the nine couches in
a semicircle around him. A reading stand has been set up, but
the poet recites from memory. The first lines of a new book
of the vast poem. His voice is resonant, and I am shaken by
it. All evening I have seen this man sunk in a daze of unnatural meditation—unnatural because it has been at the heart
of a cheerful dinner party—and now the passionate trembling
of his deep voice is startling, for one senses a vibrancy that
must have been caged until now in that impassivity, a fever
of intense emotion.

"The passage describes a visit of Julius Caesar, newly arrived in Egypt, to the tomb of Alexander. It is the scathing
portrait of Alexander that opens the dam of Lucan's feelings
—and that unlocks much else this evening. At the phrase
'madman offspring of Philip,' one senses a deep waiting
silence in the room. There follow other words and phrases
like flashes of fateful lightning. 'Pellaean robber,' the limbs
in the sarcophagus that 'should be scattered over the earth,'
'these tyrant days.' Then the lines:

> For if the world were once set free again
> All men would mock the dust of one who taught
> The evil lesson that many lands can serve
> One master. . . .

" 'Plunging his sword through peoples.' 'Curse of all earth.' And finally tears well in Lucan's eyes as he pronounces slowly the phrase 'the madman king.'

"He is finished. There is no applause. A silence in which everyone seems to be holding his breath. Then:

"PISO, in a low voice: You have a lot of anger in you, Lucan.

"LUCAN: Anger is the food of love. A man without anger cannot be a poet.

"PISO: Of love? I heard only hatred in that passage.

"LUCAN: I have that, too. You should know that, Piso. You have it. Who here does not have it?

"No one answers. A long, long wait for an answer. Then Lucan returns to his place on the couch. There follows a period of general conversation, flattery of Lucan. . . .

"But soon the connection is made—to Nero Caesar, though the name is never mentioned. It is Natalis, on my couch beyond Atria, who starts it. Natalis is a man on the razor's edge of fashion. He is also, as we have seen, a gossip. He is also very close to Piso and, as I conjecture, getting a little too close to his dear friend Piso's wife—and thus a tricky man not to be trusted by you, either, Paenus. . . . His first remark is rather innocuous, but it is spoken out in a pause and is heard by all the company:

"NATALIS: I wonder how a certain personage would like this new section of your poem, Lucan.

"VARILLA (wife of Scaevinus, fat hen pheasant) tactlessly: He *used* to like your work.

"Lucan glances at this silly woman in a fury.

"Scaevinus, who nodded all through the reading but obviously heard it all, trying now to cover his wife's lapse of taste, spews out a worse one, which opens the door to all that follows. Out of the blue he says that 'this personage' was born 'ass first.' There are a few embarrassed titters at mention of this bad omen. He goes on, affecting to be bored with what he is saying:

"SCAEVINUS: Yes. Didn't you know that? A breech. Oh, certainly. Agrippina never forgave him for backing into the world.

"There is cautious laughter all around.

"Now there ensues, Paenus, a total loss of control. One member of the company after another pours out some sarcasm, some anecdote of denigration. It is as if they have all been biting their tongues for months to keep from saying these things. The worst are Lucan, Natalis, and Scaevinus. Apart from one comment, which I will note, Piso remains rather restrained and indeed makes some efforts to hush the worst offenders. Please note that two of the most distinguished writers present, Caesius Bassus and Servilius Nonianus, remain silent throughout, do not laugh much, are circumspect—but neither do they protest even the most egregious slanders. . . .

"*Item*. Natalis mocks the personage's musicianship. Tells of the time the personage had Terpnus come and sing to him to teach him 'the tricks,' as if music were something a trained bear could learn in an afternoon.

"*Item*. Afranius Quintianus agrees. This effeminate manikin waves his arms and the little pink flags of his hands flutter along after. He tells of a time when the personage walked with a company on the Palatine and said (the effect of the man's sibilant, flutey voice quoting the personage's roar is not lost on the company): ' "Did you know that cut leeks are marvelous for the high tones? I eat no fruit. One exercise that is very good for singing is to lie on your back with a lead plate on your chest—deepens your breath. Fruit is bad, makes your throat raspy. I cut out bread every fourth day." ' Much laughter.

"*Item*. Piso recalls that the theater at Naples collapsed right after the certain man performed in it.

"PISO: Even the stones laughed till they fell down.

"Gradually it gets worse. This is a malign atmosphere, Paenus. What is appalling is the headlong quality of the slander. One after another pours out his gall, not caring what the slaves and freedmen hear. . . .

"Now we hear from Scaevinus, who says that the personage wrestles every day, that he has the ambition of competing with the athletes at Olympia, and that he has the absolute delusion that whatever is done, he can do best.

"Now from Glitius Gallus we have mention of the matricide. Not done 'best.' What a clumsy artifice, says Gallus, to build a vessel with a ceiling that is supposed to collapse spontaneously!

"And now follows Natalis, describing the personage's mock marriage to his eunuch, the freedman Sporus, at a party given by Tigellinus (at the pronunciation of whose name Natalis makes as if to vomit). Natalis says he was present at the 'wedding.' Bridal veil. The party rabble witnessing everything— ceremony, dower, couch, nuptial torches, fond kisses, and worse and worse, a show of pederasty. Atria whispers to me that it would have been good for all of us if the personage's father, Domitius, had had a eunuch for a wife.

"I will not describe to you in writing the filth that comes next. Much to prove that the wedding to Sporus was an aberration from the norm of the personage's appetites. Much raucous laughter. Let us pass to a relatively innocuous line (after this sewage) lisped by Afranius Quintianus—to the effect that the personage 'is the first who has needed another man's eloquence.' By 'the first' he clearly means the first Emperor of Rome who has had such a need.

"It is this obvious reference to Lucan's uncle Seneca that touches off a tirade by the poet, who talks—or raves—his wildness seems the more unrestrained because of his earlier muteness—about the heartless way the personage has treated the philosopher who tutored him, who did indeed write for him the noble words of the early years of his 'influence,' who might have helped him to be 'as noble as Augustus' if he had had even a few shreds of greatness in him. Frequent mention of the 'coarse,' 'brutalizing,' and 'vulgar' influence of Tigellinus. Lucan describes, with scorn run riot, a dinner for poets given by the personage shortly before Lucan was proscribed. A scurrilous portrait: 'Look at him! The neck of a farm ox rising out of a woman's dinner gown of the sort we men are supposed to wear only during the Saturnalia, of mauve silk. He wears no belt, no sandals. There are spots of dissipation on his skin. His arms are unfinished oak timbers jutting from that lady-silk, and they are raised to hold a scroll because he has not been able to memorize even his own words, if they *are* his. His hair is arranged in tiers of curls that look like a plowed hillside. His eyes are a milky blue, enraptured by the sound of his own words, if they *are* his. His lower lip sticks out in the willful pout of the son of a tyrannical whore.' Lucan mimics, with palpable sarcasm, the delivery by the Emperor of a flat couplet:

> *Sounding in the dappled shade*
> *The hollow woe of doves.*

" 'He is a creature,' Lucan shouts, 'in whose mind "shade" is *always* "dappled," "woe of doves" is *always* "hollow." ' "

"Lucan's performance strikes me as a catastrophic artistic anticlimax, for his reading of the excoriation of Alexander said the same things (about 'the personage,' by metaphor) within the discipline of poetry, and therefore far more movingly. Now he is ranting.

"But Lucan's outpouring transforms the occasion. No more

loud laughter. Now the listeners exchange significant looks, nod, raise their hands in gestures of desperation. There is a quiet, grim, dangerous air in the room. Piso claps his hands and orders wine. Red like blood. All drink in silence. . . .

"A few words in summation, Paenus. As you see, nothing overtly threatening was spoken at the dinner. I fear I must confess that I have previously heard whispered in various places most of the slander and filth that came out here. But take note of: The general outpouring. The breaking of a dam of some kind. The assumption of a common mind all round. Everyone talking as if no secret police could possibly be present. I was haunted by a feeling that there was some kind of *readiness*. Forgive me if I am telling you much that is either useless or that you already know. . . .

"If you could speak to T. about the possibility of an introduction at court during some literary occasion, I would not only be grateful, I would be your apt pupil in the writing of documents of this kind. . . ."

September 21

To TIGELLINUS from CELER, Office of Planning and Construction

I have a design for the barge. It will seem to float on clouds—a vessel in a strange dream. But I have one demurrer to your command. Dacian gold and ivory from the Syrtes and Mauretania are in plentiful supply; enough silver I can easily get from Spain. But tin in sufficient amounts is not to be found here just now and must come all the way from the Cassiterides. There is not time.

To TIGELLINUS from CANUS, Imperial Household

I hasten to report that for your occasion I have found two novelties. First, a game of lion and rabbit. A lion has been trained to pursue and catch a rabbit without hurting it and to run to the feet of a guest of honor, to kneel there, and to open its mouth and let out the rabbit, which by now is trembling with fear and disbelief and cannot run away. A living satire, Tigellinus, on that most unnatural of man's vices, mercy. And second, an elephant that has been taught to write in the dust with its trunk. It has a large vocabulary. Even the keeper never knows what it will write.

We are training the swans and expect a good result.

To PAENUS, Tribune of Secret Police, from TIGELLINUS

I have read the report of the dinner at Piso's.

I am suspicious of this informant. Could you not see his ill-concealed enjoyment of the filthy slanders of the effete company he describes? Notice how he says that Lucan's reading of the Alexander passage was more "moving" than his later overt libels. Notice his savoring at length of Lucan's sketch of Himself at a reading. There is a smirk behind this report, Paenus. If you are to use this young man, set a closer watch on him. No introductions to Himself until you can give me better proofs of his usefulness.

As to the substance of what he reports, it turns my stomach. These arrogant literati have not, the whole pack of them, a tenth of the energy, the versatility, the love of life, and yes, the sheer genius of the man they mock, long may you and I protect him. They are crab lice in the pubic hair of Rome. They would not recognize culture if it were pushed in their pus-pocked faces. They have no sense of pride in the greatness of Nero's realm, in its vigor, its manliness, its *originality*.

But your task, Paenus, is the security of the person of Himself. You cannot excite yourself over every wisp of unpleasantness that drifts past your nostrils. What you have to do—it takes a strong nose and a leather stomach—is to sniff carefully over every stink for the special odor of the putrefaction of treachery. It is a faint but unique smell, like that of distant carrion. Let me tell you what I smell in this report.

Not much. We are witness to the bravado of weak men.

Let me take the principal ones your informant cites.

Caius Calpurnius PISO, the host. Your young man misjudges the "mildness" of Piso. Already extremely powerful. Favored in every way. Leading member of the Calpurnian family—unassailable. Intolerably (to us) rich; his place at Baiae makes our mouths water. Face of an angel. Cultured. Sweet manners to all, despite the "unkind" expression your informant saw—will see, Paenus, on the face of every man who patronizes his rambling nose. Now I have mentioned the overmentioned object, may dogs eat your balls. Piso did himself no harm by stealing another man's wife, lowborn at that—an immensely shrewd woman; you saw how she made this ugly young man think her "restless." Piso is munificent toward young poets and orators on the rise: gives them money, praise, entertainment, hope, and the greatest literary prize of all—a sense of being in the inner circle of culture. But there is something flaccid in Piso's character. He lacks the resolution of a great Roman. Perhaps he has been partly dissolved by the lickspittle of pretentious intellectuals. I don't worry my head over Piso, and you must not. It is, however, shocking that men could act as if there were no secret police at his lavish parties. Place some among his slaves. But do not put Piso under special watch. That can wait.

The poet LUCAN. This little worm puzzles me. One has no trouble finding the cause of his bitterness, yet he does love Rome and I have a stubborn theory that in spite of everything he still loves Himself—not in *that* way, you understand, but with the icy love of a spurned fellow artist and patriot. I may be wrong. I want to know. I will discuss him with Himself. Work me up a full file on Lucan, and put the man under the most tactful but alert surveillance. Also, get me the complete text of the passage he read at the dinner.

Antonius NATALIS, the one who was on the couch with our informant and Piso's wife, and who gossiped about Lucan's women. Lives on rents of country estates valued at six million sesterces. Close friend, as your informant notes, to Piso. Formidable learning, but of a superficial kind, in Greek literature. Record of service to the state paltry. Makes it his business to know what and who is in fashion, and aggrandizes socially on that knowledge. We have enough information on what he does with his restless hands to blackmail him twenty times over. Nothing to worry about with this piece of scum.

Flavius SCAEVINUS. Sleepy-Eyes is another matter. Far more dissolute than Natalis, but by the same measure more discreet. Has covered his tracks well. A Senator, and not a bad one. Fortune of more than eight million. Quick, facile mind. His few speeches at the Capitol have been of the soft-spined sort. For example, supported Seneca in the move to charge the City Prefect with receiving and investigating complaints by slaves against the injustice of their masters. Also close to Piso. I cannot say exactly why, but my nose gets a whiff here of something turning rotten. Put this drowsy spider under surveillance.

Afranius QUINTIANUS. Here is an interesting case: an egregious pederast who is quietly loved by several manifestly heterosexual men—loved, I mean, as companion and mental equal. Hates Himself for good reason. You may remember the hilarious lampoon Himself wrote on the intrepid explorer of the nates of Rome; it was passed around the court at the top of everyone's voice that his model was Quintianus, and Quintianus has been heard grinding his pretty pearly teeth over it. But wait on this one. We can easily get to him in due course by way of his failing.

Get me information on the woman EPICHARIS, about whose

"provocations" Natalis spoke. Her "tawny beauty" and anger pique my curiosity. What did Natalis mean by her stirring up anger and desire in "sufferers"?

To CANUS, Imperial Household, from TIGELLINUS

Limit yourself to the carrying out of instructions as given. We cannot afford to expose Himself to an unpredictable outburst of rage from a wild beast having been humiliated into behaving like a human being. Think what a shrewd and furious elephant might write! It is bad enough that Himself is constantly surrounded by human beings who are driven to behave, without needing to be trained to it, like goats, tigers, pythons, toads, and buzzards.

To CELER, Office of Planning and Construction, from TIGELLINUS

Take the tin from a temple.

September 23

To TIGELLINUS from THE COLLEGE OF AUGURS

For the Emperor, *at your discretion.*

You may already have heard that a comet has been seen on the three successive nights just past.

We need not emphasize to you the danger to the highest persons signified by this apparition. We address this irregular notice to you because of a conjunction of other unfavorable portents during the days separated by these same nights. In view of the recent great disaster, we consider that sober thought, preparatory acts of propitiation, and above all discretion would be advisable in the interpretation of these portents to the Emperor.

The two most noteworthy of these conjoined portents are:

Item. At the sacrifice of a pregnant ewe at the Altar of

Peace, an unborn lamb was discovered with two heads, ill-formed, showing signs of premature mortification.

Item. In the Placentia district, close beside the public road, a calf was delivered with its head firmly attached to its leg.

Our preliminary interpretation, prepared in haste:

A second "head" is coming among us. Its power will be limited; it will, however, be known, notable, seen, morbid, and dangerous.

We leave to your discretion the means of conveying to the Emperor these unhappy indications.

To THE COLLEGE OF AUGURS from TIGELLINUS

Give us better divination. I mean clearer. And I mean more favorable. I know I shock you with these commands. This is no time to raise alarms.

To BALBILLUS, Astrologer, from TIGELLINUS

Be so kind as to prepare, for highest eyes, horoscopes taking into account the comet presently visible. I would appreciate your avoiding technical language. We are sick of cusps, ascendancies, influences. Reduce your recommendations to the clearest, simplest, and *most efficacious* terms. Urgent.

September 24

To SECRETARIAT from TIGELLINUS

Send the following to Lists III and IV, and also to these persons: C. C. Piso, A. Natalis, A. Quintianus, F. Scaevinus, M. A. Lucan, G. Gallus, C. Bassus, S. Nonianus, A. Mela, ... and wives:

From Sofonius Tigellinus, Prefect of the Praetorian Guard, cordial greetings. In honor of Nero Claudius Caesar Drusus Germanicus, Emperor, and on the occasion of the inauguration of the new gardens of the Lake of the Golden House, a festive occasion on the Ides of October, beginning at the tenth hour. Refreshment, diversions, works of art, voyages, wonderful creatures. Be present.

To PAENUS, Tribune of Secret Police, from TIGELLINUS
On the Ides of October I will be host to approximately four hundred at an occasion at the Lake of the Golden House. Please arrange special security precautions. I am purposely inviting, besides Lists III and IV, a small number of "doubtfuls," including those mentioned in the information of Curtius Marsus as having been audible at the Piso dinner, and some others (list enclosed). Assign agents individually to these people for 1) protection of the Person, 2) elicitation of incriminating material, either on the spot or later through developed relationships. In other words, Paenus, set some of your nice little snares. Authorize methods according to the special capabilities of each agent. Extreme discretion.

To ABASCANTUS, Imperial Treasury, from TIGELLINUS
Set aside fifty-five thousand ($\overline{LV}$) sesterces for the expenses of inauguration of the new gardens at the Lake of the Golden House. Funds to be administered by me in person.

September 25
To TIGELLINUS from PAENUS, Tribune of Secret Police
You asked for information on EPICHARIS, the mistress of Mela, described by Natalis at the Piso dinner as Lucan's "second woman":
This is a woman known in the entire district around Misenum for her powerful and meddlesome energy. While we use the word "meddlesome," we must make it clear that the woman is much loved by the impoverished artisans and farmers of the area, and by slaves, because this fierce vitality of

hers is put exclusively to the service of the poor and of slaves. Mela's neighbors consider her a great nuisance. We will come back to this matter of her "provocations."

Epicharis is the bastard daughter of an Eastern slave woman by Apicius Marcellus, Senator. Natalis did not do justice to her face and figure—"ripe persimmon"! She is a woman in whom a peppery strength and a yielding wish to please are not in tension but in balance, and accordingly her body seems always perfectly at ease; they say that one *sees* feelings stir in her, like smoke lazily drifting in warm, still air; one can read the messages of her responsiveness on her skin. She has huge brown eyes like those of a doe. Natalis was right about the anger. When it flares she seems to become, oddly, even softer than usual. Her forehead and cheeks are wide, and when she is aroused there is a delicate glistening in exceptionally small pores; she has a melting look of one who has suffered and learned both to endure and to act; her mouth looks as soft as the inner petals of a rose.

Though she was brought up on a free status in the Apicius household and enjoys a noblewoman's prerogatives in Mela's, she apparently builds her life around her maternal origins— slavery. She presides over Mela's house, but she regularly performs the most menial and even bestial tasks of the household, laboring in rotation side by side and one by one with Mela's female slaves. She does not draw back even from recovering night soil from the slaves' latrines. She seems to want to demonstrate that she came—that in remote ways we have all come—from humble sources, that the strata of society and the whims of fortune are arbitrary, capricious, and perhaps even changeable.

This, then, is the nature of her "provocations." It seems that a fierce sense of justice burns in her, and the reason Mela's neighbors despise her is that she takes her symbolic gestures out of the house and onto the streets and into the marketplace. She is often to be seen in public in earnest conversation with slaves, sometimes males, frequently showing the seductive signs of her anger. She will go a mile out of her way to share a market burden with an old female slave. She is attracted to the squabbles of the street booths, and she always takes the part of the slave or the poor against the merchant. She often risks infection and the dangers of excessive gratitude by nursing and bathing sick beggars—in public, in full view of passers-by. On account of these activities she has two reputations in the district—as a pure, kind heart, if you listen to slaves; or, if you listen to masters, as a busybody with a need to share her anger at a world that made her the mistress rather than the wife of a Roman knight.

Mela seems oblivious to this side of Epicharis. He is a mild and decent man, who, unlike his brothers Seneca and Gallio, is totally without ambition. Epicharis firmly manages him but gives him an illusion of his supremacy. He seems an exceptionally happy scholar-farmer.

Now, careful investigations, including a thorough penetration of the Mela slave quarters, do not offer corroboration of Natalis's suggestion that Lucan and Epicharis have tied a knot behind Mela's back. Lucan does visit his father's house from time to time, and he and Epicharis go for long walks in the countryside, but no one thinks that she is anything to him but a sympathetic ear. He, like the slaves and beggars and impoverished free artisans she comforts and "stirs up," is tortured and confused, these people say, and she gives him courage to inflate his vanity, and that is all. It may be that Natalis's love of scandal has led him into invention; it may be that Mela's slaves protect Epicharis, out of loyalty and gratitude; or it may be, of course, that Lucan and Epicharis are more discreet and ingenious than most lovers are. One does wonder whether mild Mela can assuage the enormous sensual energy of this woman. At any rate, Epicharis has a reputation on her home ground for physical integrity.

To IPPOLITE, Imperial Household, from TIGELLINUS
Discretion and secrecy.

Secure the agreement of about twenty women of most noble families and greatest wealth to pretend to be prostitutes in booths on the banks of the Lake of the Golden House on an occasion three weeks from now. Each must be led to think herself a particular choice of Himself. About one third must agree to remain naked behind gauze hangings for a number of hours. Suitably enticing sheer gowns for the others. Teach them soliciting movements and obscene gestures, if they do not already know them. Mix in three or four real whores for piquancy's sake. Special discretion: I have reason to believe it would give Himself particular pleasure if you could assure me that the knight Annaeus Mela's mistress Epicharis would be one of these women, naked if possible. While Epicharis may not qualify for this privilege on grounds of social standing, she has other riches that interest Himself. Mela lives at Misenum. I wish you well. Employ only the most trusted go-betweens. Coordinate with Paenus, who may have use for some of these women.

To TIGELLINUS from BALBILLUS, Astrologer
I will try to be straightforward, as you asked me to be. There are some matters, Tigellinus, that cannot be reduced to street language without distorting them. So be it, I will try.

Extreme danger to the highest power in the relationship of this comet to the constellation of the bear. I would advise —as I think you *knew* I would advise—*a large-scale sacrifice of the lives of persons of great influence and consequence.*

There is no other path to safety.

To IPPOLITE, Imperial Household, from TIGELLINUS
Another task.

That scoundrel Licinius Crispus has proposed for my occasion by the lake something that would amuse us. A foot race of hunchbacks. Arrange it.

September 27

To TIGELLINUS from PAENUS, Tribune of Secret Police

Herewith the passage that Lucan read at the Piso dinner. You will see that my informant extracted the meat from the nut in the quotations he offered. We now realize that they amounted to a brilliant act of culling by memory after one hearing. I think you are hard on this young man.

Enclosure: Draft, *Pharsalia*, Book X, Lines 1–60.

While picking off this passage in Lucan's library, our alert agent found there an unfinished letter from Lucan to Seneca, and made a copy. Although the letter contains nothing overtly incriminating, its tone is worth noting at this moment, and it contains a reference to the Piso dinner. I send forward to you some excerpts.

". . . I miss you, dear Seca. You told me once that I called you that when I was very small. We have not always seen eye to eye. I have been rude to you, a bad nephew. I am driven to rudeness, to quarrels, I hope you know that; then I am driven to regrets. I feel the need these days of your presence. I wish I could talk with you. What are the responsibilities of a writer? My famous nerves are raw, I wake up and stumble around in my room at night. I see monstrosities, dear Seca, Seca, and it is not easy for me to keep myself close to my great work. The idea of art sometimes nauseates me when I think of what is happening in Rome in broad daylight. . . .

"I write in a void. To write is to reach out in agony to other souls. But I am cut off. If I read a few lines at a dinner at Piso's, I am like a musician hired to play the flute. The guests are drunk. My passion, my anger—they fly past those ears to the walls and fall with shattered wings to the floor. Write to me, Seca. What I remember best about you, now that we are separated, is your great calm. What can a writer do? . . ."

September 28

To PAENUS, Tribune of Secret Police, from TIGELLINUS

Today discussed with Himself the question of Lucan. Himself says Lucan is not dangerous. He believes Lucan's famous outbursts, his boldness of speech, his truculence are all signs not of manly force but of childishness. This childishness is, in Himself's view, the secret of Lucan's impressive talent. "We see genius when we see, as the windows of a supreme intelligence, the wide-open eyes of a child." Not that Lucan is a genius. He is, rather, according to Himself, a "phenomenon." Himself has read this new passage on Alexander from the *Pharsalia*, and, after a laughing comparison of it with the truckling adulation that Lucan put into the first book of the poem, when he was licking up favors—"Ah, Tigellinus, I was the charioteer of the Sun, then, he wanted me to shine forever over Rome, I was his muse!"—after this comparison, he said seriously that he *admired* this passage. Alexander, he said, was indeed a monster—"because of the narrowness of his ambition." As to the obvious thrust of the passage toward his own person, as to the increasing republicanism of the poem, he is rather pitying than angry.

But if Lucan's uncle is involved in these rumblings, whatever they may mean, *that*, he says, is quite another matter. It is strange, Paenus: The most powerful man on earth still has for this feeble old scribbler the awe of an unprepared pupil toward his stern master. He is, besides, still very angry at Seneca for his withdrawal to Nomentum after the fire, his pretending to be sick, shutting himself up, as if—this is what angers Himself—*as if disapproving everything*.

I know that you already have Seneca under surveillance. Redouble it. Extra care.

September 29

To TIGELLINUS from IPPOLITE, Imperial Household

Ask me to suborn a hundred proud women to a charade of prostitution, or to the thing itself, *two* hundred, but do not ask me to approach Mela's Epicharis on this errand. I have diligently inquired about her, and it is clear that she is far removed from the bored and disenchanted circle here in Rome in which we can confidently fish for beauties for this game. I feel sure that she would *never* accede. But there is more than that. I do not address this to you on my own behalf. Not only does this woman hold her head very high, but there is this: The son of her patron is Lucan, a poet of genius who has reason to be resentful. You will expose yourself—and Himself —to powerful satires.

To TIGELLINUS from PAENUS, Tribune of Secret Police

You will be glad to know that for some time we have been making efforts, now promising fruit, to soften—never mind how—Seneca's freedman Cleonicus, who is the philosopher's most trusted servant and his messenger in the delivery of his moral epistles to his friend Lucilius Junior in Naples. About four months ago we received information from a slave of Seneca's that besides the letters Seneca has been sending Lucilius, he has also been writing more personal letters to others, including Lucan, which Cleonicus has carried, concealed in some way not yet clear to us—letters which may well tell us much that we want to know about Seneca's present attitude toward Himself. I expect to be able to send you some of the harvest of this effort soon. This will have been a remarkable feat of confidence, and we must be prepared to give a suitable reward to the beautiful young man— I will reveal only that much of the how—who will have pulled it off.

The Lucan file is ready.

To GEMINUS, Imperial Household, from TIGELLINUS
For an occasion at the Lake of the Golden House, assemble trumpeters, zither players, flutists, cymbalists, foot-cymbalists, and singers. Sensuous music.

You have two weeks.

To BALBILLUS, Astrologer, from TIGELLINUS
You will have to send forward other and better advice about propitiation of the comet. Idiot, this is not a time when we can afford to slaughter popular men. Do you not remember the riots after the divorce of Octavia? Are you not aware of the mood of the people since the fire? Even you should realize that this has not been a good year. Send alternative means of propitiation. Take note, Balbillus. This is a command.

To IPPOLITE, Imperial Household, from TIGELLINUS
Get her.

September 30
To PAENUS, Tribune of Secret Police, from TIGELLINUS
I have been having some thoughts, stirred up perhaps by

the report on the Piso dinner, on how to deal with writers, with artists in general—this side of extreme measures.

Their principal weakness is their self-importance. They think that the world cares about their opinions. Some even think they change the world! Lucan speaks of a writer's "responsibilities." A writer has no responsibilities, for responsibilities are the burden of power. He is, at best, an entertainer, like that trained bear we saw nodding its head and catching apples in its mouth the other evening. At less than best, he is an oaf who lets farts at both ends.

The second weakness of artists is their love of sniffing *each other's* farts. Unlike other egoists, creators of works of art really believe that they are superior not only as individuals but also as a class. For this reason they are extremely jealous of each other's credentials. They believe they have a sort of priesthood. They delight therefore in cutting down others of their kind, believing they are keeping the priesthood pure and strong.

Now, how play on these weaknesses? One way—used by Himself all the time—is to aggravate the first weakness, by praise and the giving of honors, in order that the second weakness may be intensified to the point where they denounce and even inform on each other. Another way is to intrigue with them, in response to the second weakness, for the destruction of undesirables among them. Another way is to undermine their sense of their importance by ridicule, name-calling, and vulgar attacks, which, though these may tend to unite them superficially, will nevertheless creep under their skins, for they are, of all men, the most vain, sensitive, and needful of praise. If you overstate by threefold your criticism of them, and if they half believe what you say, you will have accomplished a beginning of their demoralization. Another method is by sexual entrapment into blackmail. You will say all men are vulnerable in this respect. No, these people are more so, because their active imaginations make both the possibilities and the consequences of action vivid in their minds far beyond reality.

If these means fail, it is always possible, Paenus, as you know better than I, to knock them over the head and drop them in the Tiber.

October 1

To TIGELLINUS from BALBILLUS, Astrologer

I cannot move the stars. The Emperor, with all his power, cannot move the stars. You are an upstart. You would do well to heed the warnings of the augurs and of Balbillus, who loves Rome, knows science, and has no fear of upstarts, who come and go.

To PAENUS, Tribune of Secret Police, from TIGELLINUS
Urgent.

Do you know anything that would compromise Balbillus, the astrologer?

Send me the Lucan file.

To TIGELLINUS from PAENUS, Tribune of Secret Police
Urgent.

Balbillus—untouchable. Be careful.

To FAENUS RUFUS, Co-Commander, Praetorian Guard, from TIGELLINUS

Confidential.

Would this not be a good time, esteemed colleague, for a discreet but *ruthless* check on the loyalty of the officers and men in the ranks of the Guard? We are in a delicate period. The great Guard is like a mechanism, let's say, for the closing

of a sluice. One faulty cog on one key gear and the floodgate
is breached at the moment of danger. I believe it would
give Himself much comfort if you would supervise the investigation yourself.

October 3

To TIGELLINUS from FAENUS RUFUS, Co-Commander,
Praetorian Guard
Confidential.

If this is indeed a "delicate period," it seems to me that a
"ruthless" purge—that is what you are suggesting, is it not?—
would be a calamitous mistake. Letting some of its blood
would shatter the morale of the Guard—make every Guardsman's loyalty rest on his fear of the sword at the neck. Such
slaughter would be widely reported throughout the city, which
is so surfeited with punishments that, as you know, even the
followers of the Eastern superstitions, the Jews and the adherents of Cristus, are now objects of pity rather than, as before, contempt and loathing.

Better, I would suggest, build the loyalty of the Guard
than enforce it. It has been a long time since Himself gave the
Guard a donative.

To FAENUS RUFUS, Co-Commander, Praetorian Guard,
from TIGELLINUS
Confidential.

A donative is out of the question. You should know, dear
colleague, that the Imperial Treasury is severely strained by
the reconstruction of the city. Himself today requested me
to see that the check of Praetorian loyalties is made. He would
be grateful if you would see to it. In view of your expressed
doubts about this measure, Himself requested prompt word
from you that you will not be halfhearted in its execution.

To *TIGELLINUS from FAENUS RUFUS, Co-Commander,*
   Praetorian Guard
   I am a soldier. I am never fainthearted in the carrying out
of orders.

Confidential
THE LUCAN FILE

❪ MARCUS ANNAEUS LUCANUS

❪ *For recognition:* Lucan is of moderate stature, but he gives
the impression of being small. He seems shrunken into himself; this is a matter partly of his bearing, which is flaccid and
all pulled down, partly of his introverted personality, and
partly of the odd shape of his torso, which has a low bulge
front and back—it is a jug, a pear, a young onion. His complexion is pink, except during bouts of melancholy, when it is
marble pale or sometimes livid. A charming face made up of
undistinguished features—large blue eyes resting on puffy
cushions; weak chin and mouth; protruding ears. Curly blond
hair. Notably expressive hands, lissome gestures. Physical
summation: a picture of compactness, intensity, heat, erratic
power.

❪ Born November 3, third year Caligula, in Cordoba—cele-
brates his twenty-fifth birthday next month. Grandfather:
Seneca the Elder, the rhetorician. Father: Annaeus Mela.
Uncles: L. Annaeus Seneca, the philosopher, and M. Annaeus
Novatus Gallio, formerly Proconsul in Achaea.

❪ Conversation between Seneca and Lucan, on the subject
of their common Spanish origins, one month after the latter's
return from Greece six years ago, at Seneca's villa at Lake

Albanus, as overheard, recorded, and submitted shortly afterward by Seneca's slave Ajax Minor:

S.: We are not Romans, you and I, my dear. To have been
highborn in the patrician colony of Cordoba is like having
been left a grand villa in a will of doubtful validity.

L.: It seems to me it matters more to whom you were born,
than where.

S.: If one must be provincial, it matters where. Those born
in Germany are like leather—tough, useful, and apt for cruel
purposes. In Britain, weak in the lungs, and cerebral. In
France, bibulous, argumentative. But we from Spain—we
know the sun, we are shrewd people, we easily laugh and cry.
We hold on.

L.: It must have helped to have come from a man like
Grandfather. Father told me once that Grandfather could
repeat ten thousand names in the right order, without a
mistake, after hearing the list read just once. Is that true?

S.: Listen to what I am saying. You and I are from Spain.
We can imitate, but never be, "old Romans." We have the
advantage of tenacity, but the weakness of never being quite
authentic. Yes, my dear, your grandfather had a frighteningly
capacious mind, and you and I are fortunate to own a few
odd rags and pennants out of it. But do you follow what I
am saying?

L.: Yes, Uncle. You are saying: Take a tight grip and keep
looking around.

S.: Good pupil.

⟨[Lucan was brought to Rome by Mela at age eight months.
Tutored in grammar and in Greek and Latin literature by
Arcturus, a slave; endless appetite for Virgil and Ovid, could
not stomach Horace. Later studied Stoic philosophy under
Cornutus.

⟨ The poet Persius, five years Lucan's elder and his close friend up until Persius's untimely death, once gave this account (to a Senator who happened to be one of our agents) of Lucan's early education: "This boy was so facile—I watched his lessons often, Cornutus was also my teacher—so devilish, so swift and sinuous of mind, that one could not say which came first, the self-confidence or the universal applause, the applause or the assurance. Each fed the other, until the boy, not yet fourteen, was insufferably arrogant. What made the arrogance insupportable was the fact that it was so fully warranted. In the end, the arrogance became a kind of charm. During 'controversies' he would stand on one leg, twisted, gloomy-looking, forehead wrinkled and perspiring like a cloth being wrung out, with mischief flashing from his eyes and wit from his tongue. Half the time Cornutus had his hand over his mouth to hide his laughter."

⟨ Introduced at court, age fifteen, by Seneca. Minute by the late Burrus: "Lucan introduced. Two years younger than N. Rude young man. Played on N.'s delight in verbal abuse. Set on this dubious course by his uncle? Must discuss with Seneca."

⟨ At eighteen went to Greece; considerable success in contests. Recalled late the next year to Rome and to the court by the Emperor. Received public recognition with his reading of "Praise of Nero" at first Neronia. Two public readings the next year of passages from early books of the *Pharsalia*. Named to Emperor's Circle of Friends. Awarded Quaestorship four years before normal age of twenty-five. Appointed the next year a Priest of the College of Augurs.

⟨ Quaestorship. This was in the year of Nero's fourth consulship, and it was clearly and only as the Emperor's "assistant" that Lucan served. The Emperor's co-consul, Cornelius Cossus, reports confidentially: "Of the twenty Quaestors, Lucan did the least. This could not have been otherwise, since he did nothing. He was never to be seen either at the Capitol or at the Temple of Saturn. He contributed nothing toward the paving of roads. He contributed nothing for gladiatorial games. If he made a contribution toward the support of the first Neronian Quinquennial Games, it must have been directly into the Emperor's palm. I have no knowledge of a single act of his on behalf of Rome."

⟨ Augurship. In his first year as Augur, Lucan conducted one auspice: defined his templum at midnight on the crest of one of the Alban hills near Seneca's villa, pitched his tent, sat in its open side facing south—and drank wine all the rest of the night; saw not a single sign, was very drunk by morning. That was his one and only undertaking as an Augur. Has never memorized the manual of ritual; seems never even to have read the anthology of answers. Yet he does not hesitate in his vanity to wear the priest's toga, which he greatly fancies because of its scarlet stripes and purple border.

⟨ From Frontinus Portius, member of the Circle of Friends who came to know Lucan intimately during the period after L.'s recall from Greece: "The man is unpredictable. At times he will sit like a stone through an entire evening; at other times his animation, wit, and charm, though perverse, are overpowering. Even when in high spirits, however, he can be blunt with those he loves most. He forever contradicts, and always says with a fierce shake of his head, 'I already *know* that,' or, 'Beh, you are mistaken.' His egoism, even considering that he is a writer, dwarfs Vesuvius. He experiences vivid forewarnings and forebodings, which frighten him. A strange face in the street will remind him of a long-absent friend, whom he is sure he will see shortly; he trembles with terror until, he says, he always does in fact encounter that friend within an hour or two; he is then flooded with relief, though for several days he carries an after-ache of vague disquiet. He is very much afraid of the number seventeen. On occasion he will abruptly take up with a second-rate and vulgar person, a total stranger, and be full of schemes, pranks, whispering. Eats little, gulps that little. I never knew him to sleep yet never saw him sleepy. Loathes exercise and often mocks the Emperor's mania for musculature. Has a quality of enthusiasm that shines in his poetry. He writes mostly late at night at the speed of the wind in a tempest."

❡ The volume of his literary output has indeed been almost unbelievable. Before his twenty-fifth birthday he has written: Ten books of lyrics, panegyrics, and pastorals, mostly in hexameters but also some hendecasyllabics and many Sapphics, Alcaics. The *Iliacon*, an epic of the siege of Troy. The *Catachthonion*, a descent into Hades. The "Praise of Nero." An *Orpheus*. A delicious *Adlocutio* to his wife Polla Argentaria. A *Saturnalia*. Epigrams by the cartload; they say he even feeds them to old Seneca. And, of course, as of this date, more than seven thousand five hundred hexameters of his capstone work, the *Pharsalia*. I have heard he is also working on an account of the fire, and that he has an unfinished draft of a tragedy of Medea.

❡ Many perversities are joyously described in his *Saturnalia*, but he himself is reported to be inflexibly heterosexual. In general, outwardly chaste. In utmost confidence: According to a member of the Circle (not Frontinus), L. rebuffed approaches by Himself on several occasions. Far from angering Himself, this was said to have further inflamed him. L.'s circumspection thought to be mainly instinct for survival; he was undoubtedly trained to prudence by Seneca.

⟨[Lucan's pride and self-esteem are such that he has no fear
or awe of persons in authority. Witness this report by an
agent (obviously, you will see, a woman) of a conversation
with Agrippina, shortly after Lucan's return from Greece and
only a few months before Agrippina's death. You and I,
Tigellinus, remember what an overpowering personage the
Emperor's mother was. The meeting took place one morning
in the lower cypress garden of the Palatinate palace. There,
according to the informant, "in the needle-scented autumn
clarity strolls Agrippina with two Senators' wives and a bad-
tempered chatterbox of a male dwarf who amuses her. Four
Praetorian Guardsmen follow with drawn swords at a 'discreet' distance, a leap and a slash away. Here stands in the
path an awkward young man. The dowager Empress recognizes him at once.

" 'This must be Lucan.'

"Obeisance. 'I am Lucan.'

" 'Are you the one?—I think so—he likes you. I hope not
too much.'

"The young man laughs. 'Spare your nerves, I am not that
way. Is your son that way?'

"Agrippina's smile is like lampshine, bright but smoky—
artificial light. 'He is all ways,' she says. 'You have had great
successes in Greece. My son loves everything Greek. You are
good for him.'

" 'He should go there and see with his own eyes that this
everything he loves is humdrum. Your son can be foolish.'

" 'How shrewd. What a delightful young man! Where can
we find you?'

" 'I am staying with my uncle.'

" 'Ah. My son tells me you are beginning a long poem
about the civil war.'

" 'I didn't know he knew. I don't talk about my work until
it is ready to be read.'

" 'We have ways of knowing things. . . . You are wise to dream and write about the past.'

" 'In which the present was gestating.'

" 'Do not disguise my son in your work. In any way. Ever.'

" 'He has enrolled me in the Circle. I am promised great delights. Why would I "disguise" him?'

" 'Fuh, you're a poet. Poets don't make good loyalists—or even good friends, for that matter.'

" 'Poets don't lend themselves to such silly generalizations as that.'

" 'Poets and emperors both believe the universe belongs to them. Poets are just as ruthless as emperors. A poet reduces every aspect of real life to negotiable fabrications. His craft is lying.'

" 'Poetry survives. Emperors do not.'

" 'You had better write fast.' A divine pink glow suffuses Agrippina's cheek. She obviously adores this young man even as she threatens him. 'You've been in Greece too long. In Rome it doesn't pay to be clever.'

" 'Who is this limpcock?' the dwarf snorts. The exquisite mother emits a relaxed laugh and caresses the young man's arm."

⟨ Lucan's ingenuity in mockery knows no bounds; on this fault he will some day trip himself. In the year of his return from Greece he wrote a vicious lampoon of the courts, using the form of two skillful briefs—on both sides of the Octavius Sagitta case. To remind you: Octavius, a wealthy tribune, persuaded Pontia, a married woman, to leave her husband and marry him. Once divorced, however, she met a richer man than Octavius and began to dandle him, driving him wild by her vacillation. He pleaded and menaced; she teased. At last he begged for the gift of one final night with her, which he said would enable him to break the wild spirit of his desire and put a harness on it for the future. She agreed. She had a trusted female slave prepare a room. Octavius entered with a freedman. The servants retired. Alone together, the two violently quarreled (apparently their accustomed mode of mutual stimulation), and their strife ripened into a consummation on a couch. Later she was found stabbed to death on that same couch. The next day the freedman said that he had murdered Pontia because of her tormenting of his patron. The slave girl had also been wounded that night, and when she recovered she accused Octavius of having stabbed Pontia and of having wounded her when she intervened to help her mistress. (At the end of his tribuneship, Octavius was in fact sentenced to death by the Senate.) One of Lucan's briefs imputed the crime to Octavius; the other maintained that the freedman and the slave girl had murdered Pontia and had arranged between them to have the freedman gain the honor of defending his patron and to have the slave girl then place the blame on the innocent Octavius. It is a brilliant and scandalous work, this double brief, casting doubt on many aspects of our judicial system.

⟨ Extremely confidential. From Statius Spurinnus, member of the Circle, formerly close to L.: "The Poet's Poet—that is what some of us called him—we meant by that, Nero's Poet—accompanied us one night on one of N.'s street raids. We had to tease him for a long time to persuade him to join us. He has (or then had) a horror of anything athletic, and he had imagined the raids to consist of action for the arena. At any rate, he came.

"We started out about midnight and went down to the area around the Milvian bridge. Threw a pair of drunks in the Tiber. Robbed a vendor. N. was in particularly high spirits, in my opinion because L. was with us. L. rather subdued, disapproving.

"Eventually we went to the alleys near the house of a Senator, Frontinus Sulpicer, where we heard there was a banquet under way. We were well disguised as usual. We waited for the guests to emerge.

"First came that fat imbecile Senator Trebius and his pretty wife, followed by two male slaves. We swooped on them, caught and held Trebius and the slaves, and N. threw the wife to the ground, stripped her naked, except for her many jewels, and then removed the jewels one by one and put them on Himself, saying *this* was the sort of pendant he had always dreamed of having, *this* was a delicious earring!

"The second couple that came out, with slaves, happened to be Licinius Afer, the man who some years ago spread the story that Seneca had committed adultery with N.'s sister Julia, and who may indeed have been responsible for Seneca's being sent into exile; and Licinius's young wife, his third, whom he had only recently married. Lucan, recognizing Licinius as he came out of the gate in the light of torches, whispered to N. that he wanted the privilege of dealing with the two. N. consented.

"Good. We swooped, trapped the males. L. then danced about in front of the young wife, and he put on the most unusual show. He knew a great deal of slimy gossip about Licinius, which he must have heard from a vengeful Seneca years before, and mimicking Licinius with wicked accuracy, both as to voice and gesture, he poured out a stream of filth for the ears of the young wife that must surely have cut the heart out of whatever relationship she may have had with the old man. What made Lucan's performance so shocking was that without touching the young woman, with tongue alone, he managed a masterpiece of rape long remembered by all the raiders as more subtle, keen, effective, and brutal, as a more wicked statement of the abasement of all virtue which was—if anything was—the point of our raids, than any act N. ever

managed before or after. And we had thought L. so fastidi-
ous, so censorious! It is true that he did this from a motive
of loyalty to his uncle."

❨ Stormy relationships with and between his parents. Source
Sulpicio, a freedman of Lucan's: "Lucan's mother Atilla is a
chestnut burr, or perhaps rather a nettle. Do not touch:
prickles and stings. She has an agile mind and an infuriating
habit of anticipating what you intend to say and of scornfully
finishing your sentences for you before you can get them out,
as if to suggest that she has known your thoughts all along
and has judged them trivial. She looks at your lips rather
than your eyes, and her expression is haughty and disapproving. Mela, Lucan's father, moved to a comfortable villa over-
looking the sea at Misenum to get away from her. Living
with Mela there is Epicharis, his mistress, a woman with large
brown eyes and a satin skin, who dusts the house beside the
slaves. Lucan can scarcely talk to either his father or his
mother. His father's calm self-containment drives Lucan wild.
Lucan has a full measure of his mother's sharp points, little
of his father's melancholy serenity. Lucan has developed a
warm fondness for Epicharis, and when he visits his father's
villa he walks endlessly in the garden, and sometimes outside,
with her." So much for Sulpicio. We have not developed anything new so far on Lucan's "fondness" for Epicharis but
have set a watch on it.

❨ Lucan's *Adlocutio* to Polla. Again from Frontinus Portius:
"Polla works day and night at being Lucan's wife. Her endless
entertainments are particularly revealing. She began by inviting anyone and everyone who might be useful to Lucan—
influential men, carefully selected poets and artists whose
presence in Lucan's house would color his reputation with
tones reflecting their various special gifts; but her greed for

him and basically for herself gradually dulled her critical taste, and she ended by inviting simply anyone and everyone. The result is that the poet's house is nightly crowded by cultural leeches, creaky poetical praying mantises, cockroaches of state, moths where once great butterflies swarmed. Especially since Lucan's proscription many of the best men prudently stay away. All who do come tell Polla that she is beautiful, dutiful, and talented (she writes nauseating tragedies). Indiscriminate praise has made her indiscriminating. Lucan knows very well who these people are. He is in a rage every night, yet he does not put an end to the ritual, which revolves, after all, around him. This by way of background for his transparent *Adlocutio* to his wife.

"The poem takes the form of an address to her by him at the end of an evening of revelry in their home. He praises her with clashing salutes, but it is clear (to everyone, one supposes, but Polla) that the cymbals are made of tin. One sees in this poem that Lucan has begun to realize that he married a pale shade of his terrible mother. The flattery grinds on, one almost hears the son–husband gnash his teeth in writing it, and at the end of the poem it is obvious that the poet and his wife are now to retire to the couch together for embraces of ambiguous passion, each wishing the partner were someone else."

⟨ From his freedman Sulpicio: "Lucan is totally lacking in senses of orientation and recognition. He can stand in front of the Capitol and ask the direction to the Capitoline Hill. I have often been sent out late at night to find him, and I have often found him turning away from his own gate to look for his own gate. He has a lightning memory, but faces are to him like empty plates, he cannot tell one from another unless there is, so to speak, food on one and not on the other. He frequently insults old acquaintances by not recognizing them."

❲ His greatest weakness is his compulsion to quarrel with those he loves. Again from Sulpicio: "I can tell six hours beforehand when he is going to get into a quarrel. He is at that point agreeable but emits from time to time a quick, raucous laugh disproportionate to the humor that caused it; his hands tremble, as if with eagerness; he drops things on the floor and curses them, as if they had willfully tricked him; sends slaves on a hundred invented errands; and is exceptionally forgetful. Then, as the evening comes on, you can see him work up to it. He seems to have selected his adversary long in advance. In a crowd he seeks the company of this person, talks with him soberly and with hooded eyes, looking downward. Then he begins to interrupt, to correct 'errors' which are often not errors at all. He becomes formal. 'Please excuse me, but you are grossly mistaken.' He is positive. The friend defends his veracity, sometimes his honor. It ends with shouting. Lucan's aim—at the very core of his adversary's most tender uncertainty—is terrifying. The next day he is rueful. Keeps saying he had too much to drink the night before."

❲ A delicate relationship between Lucan and Seneca. The conceited poet thinks himself superior to the philosopher. The philosopher, though famous for his "modesty," must find this attitude insufferable. Yet it is clear that Lucan, who is unstable, depends heavily on the old man's steadiness and equanimity. At the same time these very qualities in Seneca— of evenness, fidelity, staunchness—are to Lucan tiresome and boring. The tie here, despite the friction, is very strong. Seneca never had a son, and Lucan's mild father has always kept his distance from a son who knew how to hurt him. Without Lucan, Seneca would be sad; without Seneca, Lucan would through folly and headlong impulsiveness destroy himself.

❨ Through a sensitive series of interventions by discreet persons we procured the following most important commentary on the *Pharsalia,* delivered to a close friend by the poet Caesius Bassus, who was at the Piso dinner and remains on good but not intimate terms—in other words, terms of mutual envy—with Lucan:

"The change in tone of the poem is notorious. One way of putting this is that the epic has three heroes: Caesar, Pompey, and Cato; and as the poem goes forward Cato, the Republican, emerges as the figure Lucan really loves and admires. His praises of Pompey one can write off as stemming from the traditional allegiance of Cordobans to Pompey. But the feeling for Cato is another matter—and if you look at that feeling closely and think about what has happened in Lucan's relationship with the present Caesar, you will find very dark thoughts indeed lurking in the poem. I would cite, for example, Cato's speech in the desert, in the last book before the one Lucan is now writing. Stripped to its bones, the speech says that the crossing of the desert is to be the test of his soldiers' 'virtue'; only by suffering and then fighting can true patriots recover liberty for Rome; the choice is death or freedom, and those who choose the easy way, avoiding hardship and danger, deserve to live a suffocating life under a tyrant. This is strong stuff, my dear friend. And there are other things —the speech of Vulteius on suicide: Death is the brave man's only choice when his liberty is taken from him. And—in strictest confidence—I went to a banquet last month at which Lucan read a new passage, containing an attack on Alexander that was like an assault in a dream. Do you know how figures in a dream wear evanescent masks which fade, or can be torn away by hard thought, revealing other, 'truer' faces? Strip off the Alexander mask in that passage, and you find the face of Julius Caesar. Strip off the mask of Julius Caesar, then, and you find—but, my dear friend, one cannot speak of such things. . . ."

❡ This year, shortly before the fire, a contest of poets was announced. Himself was enrolled early on the roster of competitors, which mostly consisted of submissive young poets and poetasters who wanted nothing more than the honor of reading from the same stage as Himself. Enters Lucan, proclaiming with his usual assurance that he will read the finest poem he has ever written. The contest. The judges award the prize to Lucan. (The three judges, as you know, presently reside on three different distant rocky islands.)

❡ Two weeks later, Lucan has the effrontery to announce a solo public reading, at which the final piece is to be the poem that beat the Emperor. Himself is present as Lucan begins. Suddenly, while Lucan is reciting, Himself orders in a loud voice an immediate meeting of the Senate, and gets up and leaves, taking with him more than half the audience.

❡ For five days Lucan circulates in the city, denouncing the convening of the Senate, the only purpose of which, says Lucan, was to throw cold water on his performance.

❡ On the sixth day, the Emperor hands down the following order: "To the Censors. From Nero Claudius Caesar Drusus Germanicus, Emperor. M. Annaeus Lucanus is henceforth and forever proscribed from poetical or literary production or publication, and is forbidden to plead causes or cases or to participate in readings, forensic contests, competitions, games, or public occasions of any sort whatsoever."

❡ Lucan is bound by this order to silence as to recital, but this does not stop him from much ill-mannered behavior. His rage breaks out in public baths, at receptions, in the streets.

He is both out of control and under control, because he uses, in his wild outbursts, the most subtle innuendo and indirection—not a word that is overtly libelous or actionable.

⟦ *Summary and assessment:*

After the death of Persius, Lucan remained uncontestably the foremost poet of Rome. It is my considered conclusion, Tigellinus, that Lucan's warped mind has led him to believe that being Rome's best poet is more important than being Rome's Emperor. (Remember Agrippina's insight.) If this conclusion is correct, he is more pitiable than dangerous. Still, we must keep a close watch on him. There seems to be no question that he has harbored more and more republican ideas, though of the most ingenuous and soft-headed sort— less products of thought and conviction than of his contumacious personality. Nothing criminal or actionably subversive in his record as yet. His weaknesses are his vanity and his quarrelsome temper. Sexual approaches will be futile. Can possibly be trapped into provocative rudeness of an actionable sort. May be vulnerable from the direction of his ambitious wife. Something mysterious and possibly exploitable in his relationship with Epicharis. Cut the thread that ties him to Seneca and you will have set him adrift. We can handle this man.

October 5

To TIGELLINUS from IPPOLITE, Imperial Household

I am doing my best, but we are having the trouble I expected with Epicharis. We worked out with great care a prudent avenue to her, through Racilia, wife of the Senator Tuscus. He has a seaside place, which he and Racilia visit often, near Misenum, and they are friendly with Mela. Racilia, a woman till now irreproachably correct, modest, and virtuous, agreed to our surprise and delight (superb work by Tuscus's sister-in-law Claudia Larcia) to the charade of prostitution; not only that, she has developed a kind of fever of mischievous anticipation of this prank, as she regards it. It was she who approached Epicharis, suggesting that they do this thing in each other's company, for the sensation of it. I assume that you know that Epicharis has a local reputation as a somewhat showy doer of good works among poor freedmen and slaves. Racilia believes, however, that Epicharis is not exempt from the gnawing ambition so often seen in slave-born bastards and freedwomen, that she is hotly curious about high social life in Rome, and that she feels cut off from the excitements of the capital in this back-eddy with dull Mela. Racilia intuited that Epicharis was in her secret self greatly excited by an idea that on the surface seemed so out of character for her. Racilia apparently has not told her husband about this naughty game; she plans to deal Tuscus a bit of a surprise that evening. But it seems that Epicharis, though she controls Mela in every way, is inclined to discuss each decision of their lives with him. Racilia planned to keep after Epicharis, fanning the obscure and perverse ember of restlessness she thought she saw in her. But apparently Mela has put an end to this possibility. Epicharis has now suddenly cut off the relationship with Racilia; refuses to see her. I am inclined to doubt whether Mela will even honor your command to be present that night.

I still think this is a futile and risky gamble to take, but because you have ordered it, will keep trying.

To IPPOLITE, Imperial Household, from TIGELLINUS

Mela will be present at the occasion at the lake. He would dare to refuse, but remember that he is the brother of Seneca and father of Lucan: curiosity will not let him stay away. You will see. Keep after her. Get her. Get her.

To BALBILLUS, Astrologer, from TIGELLINUS

Having had time to reflect, I consider your advice as to propitiation of the comet to have been sound. Excuse my rough language. A soldier's tongue gets to be like a wood file. We will find a way to let some good blood, though it may take time. Will delay matter?

October 6

To TIGELLINUS from BALBILLUS, Astrologer

You were wise to acknowledge your effrontery. It does not matter when the sacrifices are made. The delay should not be too great, however.

October 7

To TIGELLINUS from IPPOLITE, Imperial Household

I have found and enlisted some hunchbacks for the foot race by the lake. Would it not be amusing to mix in a few dwarfs? Their short bow legs running for a prize would be delicious.

To IPPOLITE, Imperial Household, from TIGELLINUS

Yes, good work, get a few dwarfs. Those with most monstrous heads. Tell them and the hunchbacks that their prize will be to take a beautiful Senator's wife before an audience that will include the Senator.

October 8

To TIGELLINUS from PAENUS, Tribune of Secret Police

First fruit of our new surveillance of Lucan. We have developed an alert plant in the heart of his household, and this agent has found and copied a letter from Seneca to Lucan; the first paragraphs of a reply by Lucan; and what appears to be part of a letter to a woman—no salutation. It is not clear whether Lucan intended or intends to finish his answer to Seneca and send it; he may have thought better of it. I draw your urgent attention to the last paragraph of this drafted fragment of Lucan's.

"Seneca to Lucan, greetings:

"It gives me joy, dear nephew, to hold in my hands a letter from you. I feel, when I do, that I am taking you by the shoulders and looking you in the face. This letter I have just received, however, also makes me thoughtful; the look that I see in your eyes, so to speak, is sad and even frenzied. I hasten to write.

"What, you ask, is a writer's responsibility?

"The responsibility of a writer is to avoid frenzy. This applies whether he be a writer of philosophy, poetry, or tragedy. I can only speculate as to the cause of your 'raw nerves.' As you say, we have not always been in tune with each other. Besides, I am on the downward slope of life, you have scarcely begun the climb. Nevertheless I will send some words of counsel, a philosopher's message of admonition and consolation. I call to you from great distances—from the far reaches of old age, from the quiet horizon of retirement, from the haze-dimmed hilltop of philosophy. Forgive me if I presume to know you better than you know yourself.

"A writer—no, rather let me take you again by the shoulders and say: You, Lucan, dear Lucan—should not run away from life, but neither should you run at it quite so headlong. Your nerves are raw because of your inability to hold back. One week you rush to Baiae where you witness, perhaps even you may join, groups of revelers moving along the beach with the doubly strange gait of drunken walkers in sand, or where you will be invited on licentious sailing parties and rousting outdoor banquets in groves on the hills, with singing, lounging, and too much wit. The next week will find you in the city at the games, where in the morning they throw criminals or political prisoners to the bears and lions, and at noon desperate men are put in combat in the newest fashion of voluptuous brutality—with swords but with neither helmets nor shields to fend off death; in your ears ring the roars of the spectators demanding that the man who has just succeeded in butchering his fellow face another who will succeed in butchering him. You never exercise with the bladder ball or hop ball. You go to dinner parties where Senators kiss the hands of other men's slaves, 'delicates' and 'smooths,' who have been kept beardless by having the hair plucked out and who have been trained to remain boys with graceful gestures even into manhood. You eat too fast. You steep yourself in hot baths alongside women who know no shame. You lose your temper daily. You associate with men who are glutted with power and who take the cross, the rack, the hook, and the stake for granted, and the pairs of chariots that tear human limbs apart by driving in opposite directions, and the vest interwoven and smeared with inflammable agents. And all the while you tell yourself that these experiences are the food on which your writing lives, and you converse with men who are extremely clever and who delight in stretching possibilities until they are torn just like men under torture: ' "Mouse" is a syllable; mice eat cheese; therefore syllables eat cheese.'

"This life, dear nephew, is not a proper basis for writing. Thought is the only ground upon which writing can stand. You have no time for thought. You have no time even to read anything but what is in fashion. Look to Zeno, to Cleanthes, to Epicurus for counsel. Epicurus says something you should heed, my dearest nephew: 'Ungoverned anger begets madness.' Run until you are warm, take cold baths. Eat a piece of bread and some dried figs. Drink from a spring. Remember always that drunkenness is nothing but a condition of insanity purposely assumed. Turn your eyes away from the cruelty of powerful men. Do not deliberately provoke the anger of the most powerful man of all; no, put your helm over, steer away, just as the wise pilot avoids choppy currents and skirts around squalls.

"Indeed, writers should never approach too close to power. They long to have reality approach the level of art, and they give impossible advice. Better to dream and write about the past, as you are doing in your *Pharsalia*.

"Epicurus once again (it is strange, in my retirement I find myself turning more to Epicurus than to 'our' teachers): 'Think about death.' In saying this he bids us think about freedom. You know how Cato died; I am sure you will write superbly about his leap to freedom. Do you know how Scipio died, the father-in-law of Pompey? His ship was driven onto the lee shore of Africa by a headwind and he saw that it was going to fall into the hands of his enemies, so he stabbed himself, and when they asked where the commander was, he answered, 'All is well with the commander.' It was, for he had conquered more than an enemy, he had conquered death and escaped tyranny, and he was a free man.

"Farewell."

"Lucan to Seneca, greetings:
"Having hungered for your advice, I devoured your letter, but as soon as I had finished it I had to put a feather in the throat of my mind. I had to vomit out all that overrich fat meat and heavy oil. You give me the urge to be a Suilius, to charge you with fatuous and self-serving inconsistencies. 'Writers should never approach too close to power.' This from *you?*

"I do not wish to be free and dead. I wish to be free and alive. The same is true of you—why else have you pulled away to the solitude and security of Nomentum? I think your talk about dying bravely is bluster. You are as much afraid of the inevitable mystery as any other man. Eat figs, you say. I remember all too well the kind of table you knew how to set here in the city.

"I want to be *alive*! I am a poet. I do not wish to run until my body is warm. I want to exercise not my muscles but my senses until they are hot, hot, hot. My anger is at the center of my sanity. It goes out through my mouth, and I am purged and in good health.

"Who said my *Pharsalia* is about the past? Not I. A writer is not responsible to the past, he must answer to the future. And therefore he cannot pretend that the present does not exist.

"I need better advice than you can give me, old man. Where can I turn? Where can I turn? . . ."

The draft breaks off at this point. We will try to ascertain whether the letter has been, or is to be, completed and sent.

The fragment of a letter by Lucan intended for a nameless woman has, as noted above, no name on it. Is it meant for Epicharis? We can only guess. If it is, Lucan's feelings for her seem to go beyond "fondness."

(No salutation.)
"We were interrupted, dear one, just as we began to open our hearts to each other. I will come again as soon as I can.

"I have found the dyes you wanted, and some others, compact promises in little alabaster jars of the beauty those silks will finally have when your arms, your shoulders, your cheeks, your eyes bring the colors to life. I found soapwort and nut gall, salt of tartar and woad and madder, saffron and archil. I am still looking for reseda, which makes a good yellowish green. I will bring them all when I come. I dream of the day when your body sets free the meaning of the tints.

> *Iridescent down the mist-green caverns*
> *Shimmers a trail from Apollo's burning mantle.*
> *Pale! Pale! He begs for clouds to hide his car,*
> *Seeing his sunset shamed by your subtler radiance.*

"Polla got on my nerves last night. She carries on about plans, plans. . . ."

October 9

To TIGELLINUS from PAENUS, Tribune of Secret Police

I am humiliated by having to report to you that your instinct was right about young Curtius Marsus, he of the vagrant nose, the fledgling informant who gave us the account of the Piso dinner. He has been too free with his hopes for fame as a poet, to be achieved by other means than by mere writing. He has been overheard by a reliable agent telling Piso's friend Natalis, "in confidence," that you, Tigellinus, intended to persuade Himself to find a pretext to send Piso into exile in order to confiscate his estates, particularly the one at Baiae. Curtius must have made this up, but, as you will have to admit, his fantasy was all too plausible. I am sorry, because I had entertained some hopes of developing a useful source of solid information where it is hardest to get—from among writers.

To PAENUS, Tribune of Secret Police, from TIGELLINUS

Concerning Curtius Marsus: Get rid of him. Report the means of his disposal.

October 10

To TIGELLINUS from IPPOLITE, Imperial Household

You may find it hard to believe, but beautiful rich young married women of sound reputation are now applying to me to be allowed to be "prostitutes" at your gala. I have made every effort to keep this matter secret, but our finest females apparently cannot refrain from acting as volunteer agents of your most pungent dreams. I am now in a position to say that we will assuredly have fifty of Rome's proudest beauties for this game. One thing I am sure of: None of them intends to tell her husband. Come the evening, you will see some splendid chagrin. Some men will put a good face on their surprise —will pretend they have known all along; others will be complacent for another reason—will be delighted to take other men's wives about whom they have been speculating for some time.

I have, however, failed with Mela's Epicharis. Banish me from Rome if you will, but no man could have done more. Mela will attend; you were right. He has ordered Epicharis to stay at home. Upon a possibility that she is angry at being sequestered that evening rests one last chance to "get her," as you keep putting it. I think this outcome most unlikely. Epicharis is too proud.

To TIGELLINUS from CELER, Office of Planning and Construction

The barge is ready. It is an artifact from a tender dream. I have found for it, besides much else, some perfect Baltic amber and some vivid coral from India. Even you will be astonished by the array of swans. The booths are ready to assemble.

October 11

To TIGELLINUS from PAENUS, Tribune of Secret Police

Concerning Curtius Marsus, the young informer-gone-wrong:

Late last night he was set upon at the foot of the Aventine, where he had been dining with friends, by a gang of cutpurses, who inadvertently, striking blows in haste, knocked the young man's head against a wall and broke his skull. They stole his purse and left him dead. I understand that the cutpurses were pursued by police but escaped.

Tell me, Tigellinus, am I not something of a poet of action? Hail and farewell, finest nose in Rome!

October 12

To TIGELLINUS from PAENUS, Tribune of Secret Police

You commanded surveillance of Flavius Scaevinus, Sleepy-Eyes as you called him, who talked too freely at Piso's dinner.

This is to report that a close watch has been established. First results meager.

Persistent reports of one quality that may prove useful to us: Extreme vanity. Scaevinus spends two to three hours each morning under the hands of his barber, a slave named Paliarchus, who works with a whole squad of helpers. Scaevinus sits before a large three-leafed mirror, which allows him to watch, with slight shifts of his eyes and apparently with the greatest satisfaction, his full face and both profiles. He sits there with a gown of cambric over his clothes and sighs with pleasure as Paliarchus piles on the curls with a hot iron. He is very proud that he does not copy, as so many do, the style of tiered curls that Himself has set. His are half-curls, completely "natural," and casually disposed. But not so casually made. He has been known to spend half an hour making sure that a single curl is in the right place. The drowsy look, as I think you suspected, is an affectation. He rehearses it before the three-faced mirror. It is true that he leads an exceptionally luxurious and dissipated life, but his physique must be superb. Never complains of a headache or nausea after a night of heavy drinking. Always seems fresh-skinned, though he often has gilded plaster spots put on his face to make it appear that the hard life he leads causes the blemishes other men suffer. There is his vanity for you: Everything simulates the "natural"—his curls, his weary, drooping eyes, his pseudo-pimples.

At the same time, let us not forget he is a substantial man, with a brilliant mind crackling with the most various kinds of knowledge. And as shrewd as a vintner from Campania.

October 14

To CELER, Office of Planning and Construction
To CANUS, IPPOLITE, AMMIANA, GEMINUS, Imperial
Household
To PAENUS, Tribune of Secret Police
from TIGELLINUS

Is everything ready for tomorrow afternoon and evening?

To TIGELLINUS from CELER, Office of Planning and Construction

Your eyes will give you testimony of my barge that your mind will refuse to believe.

At what time do you want us to begin assembling the booths? We have estimated two hours only will be needed to put them together, from start to finish.

To TIGELLINUS from CANUS, Imperial Household

The beasts are collected, well fed, sleek, and strange. There is no danger. You will have all the living earth within the walls of a single garden.

To TIGELLINUS from GEMINUS, Imperial Household
Yes, there will be trembling music.

To TIGELLINUS from AMMIANA, Imperial Household
Keep yourself hungry until you get there, my powerful friend.

To TIGELLINUS from IPPOLITE, Imperial Household
I believe I must excuse myself from the occasion. Failure with Epicharis. I have tried four separate approaches, each of irresistible respectability. She is rooted to her refusal like a live-oak tree to a hill. I await your displeasure.

To TIGELLINUS from PAENUS, Tribune of Secret Police
Security will be tight, and our snares are prepared. The twigs are limed, the pits are disguised, the nets are strung, the weirs are set. We will have a fine bag of wretches for Himself and for you.

A word on behalf of Ippolite. He feels that he has done an extraordinary piece of procurement for you and that all is spoiled because you have pressed him too hard on an impossible mission. You know how brilliant and sensitive (and inwardly raging) he is; he is one of the most powerful freedmen in Rome, but he never forgets his days of slavery to a mediocre merchant down by the warehouses on the river. He is prepared to open his veins. But he will do so, Tigellinus, if you order it—you have always said you want me to be honest with you—with the conviction that your motive in insisting so long on this one errand was not the greatest good of the Person but your own concupiscence. He has not even whispered any such thought to me. I read it in his wounded-deer eyes. I can testify to the unwavering accuracy of his aim in going after some but not others of our proudest beauties for this charade, and to the amazing web of confidence and secrecy he has woven, and I must say that he has made my own task far, far easier. Write him a comforting message, won't you?

To FAENUS RUFUS, Co-Commander, Praetorian Guard, from TIGELLINUS

Urgent.

This is to countermand, on behalf of Himself, the order for the purge of the Praetorian Guard. In strictest confidence, such an action had been deemed necessary in order to find sacrifices sufficient to propitiate the recent comet; we believe we are now on the threshold of uncovering certain crimes of opinion, the punishment of which, I am confident, will provide ample propitiation.

To CELER, Office of Planning and Construction, from TIGELLINUS

The guests are commanded to come at the tenth hour. Begin assembling the booths after they have arrived but during daylight hours. Make a delightful and mysterious little pantomime of these constructions. Dress the slaves who do the work in colored gauzes and give them caps of gilded paper, cocked with pheasant feathers. Tell them to prance and turn cartwheels at their labor.

To TIGELLINUS from FAENUS RUFUS, Co-Commander, Praetorian Guard

Wise decision. Our preliminary checks found, as far as we had gone, loyalty unwavering in the Guard, and morale high. Not so high that a donative would not elevate it even more, but I gather, dear colleague, that this will have to wait until

after such necessary expenditures as those for your imminent
gala by the lake.

*To FAENUS RUFUS, Co-Commander, Praetorian Guard,
    from TIGELLINUS*
   You are dutiful and also sarcastic, as a good soldier should
be. A donative is out of the question.

To IPPOLITE, Imperial Household, from TIGELLINUS
   Come to the lake tomorrow and be honored, dear Ippolite.
Choose for your taking, before the Emperor Himself chooses,
the beauty of beauties from among all your charming catches.

To TIGELLINUS from IPPOLITE, Imperial Household
   You take prudent care of those who are useful to you.
My thanks. I did the best I could. I will be there, but you
forget: I am chaste and always will be.

To IPPOLITE, Imperial Household, from TIGELLINUS
   I forgive you even your chastity.

TWO

October 16

To *TIGELLINUS* from *PAENUS, Tribune of Secret Police*
First report, in haste.

I am led to believe that the Piso–Lucan affair may be much
more serious than we had thought.

I have nothing to tell you. Not one useful word. All our
preparations went to nothing.

From the entrapments set for the other groups of "doubtfuls," we have many positive results, a good strong harvest of
information which I shall send to you separately. But Piso,
Lucan, Natalis, Scaevinus, Quintianus, Gallus, Bassus, Nonianus, Mela—unanimous discretion of the most impeccable
sort.

In the moments of wildest abandon—the rush for the
booths when the torches had been lit, the third "voyage" on
the barge, the crowd at the race of grotesques, the scene
surrounding the booth where Baba and Isio took the Senator
Gatrialus's wife and each other all together—in even those
moments this group was a solid squad of propriety. To each
was assigned, on that frenzied third "voyage," a woman (to

Quintianus a boy) of thrilling beauty and shrewdness—in at
least three cases, women we had had reason to think the men
had been trying for months to seduce; but no result. No result. Nothing. Stiff and decent courtesies, no more. No man
among those eight drank a single cup of wine all evening
long. Not a scrap of revealing conversation. We have not
been able to discover from all our agents put together the
tiniest crack in the wall around this group.

In such a fevered setting, with every restraint dissolved, in
a mob of people abandoned to the pleasure closest at hand,
their solidarity, the absolute uniformity of their decorousness,
the clamping of their tongues between their teeth as if by a
shared set of jaw muscles—these could not have been coinci-
dental. They must have decided together beforehand on this
line of action. There was even a kind of effrontery in their
uniform prudence.

I will write more later when I have gathered my wits—I
confess a slight headache—and have combed the agents again.

By the way, the occasion was your greatest triumph. I salute
you, Tigellinus. You are a genius in the theater of the voluptuous.

To PAENUS, Tribune of Secret Police, from TIGELLINUS
Hasty response to your hasty preliminary report. I, too,
have what you call a slight headache.

I am sure it will have occurred to you that the Piso–Lucan
circle may simply have had a dull evening. May not like that
sort of caper. May be entirely innocent. If they are *not*, then
I think Himself was right; the crack will show itself sooner or
later.

I must admit I am well satisfied with how the occasion
came off. Himself—"slight headache" notwithstanding—tells
me over and over that he never enjoyed himself more. There

were times, during the first assault on the booths and especially during the third "voyage" when everyone rushed to the one side to watch the fleet-footed hunchback tup his reluctant prize, that frightened me; I was afraid we might have a disaster on our hands. Also, an indiscreet act by Vestinus, the Consul-Elect, about which I will tell you in due course. But all turned out well. Congratulations of Himself are pouring in, and he is acknowledging them with a comical modesty.

To ABASCANTUS, Imperial Treasury, from TIGELLINUS
Gifts of honor, fifty thousand sesterces each, to Celer and Ippolite; twenty thousand sesterces each, to Ammiana, Canus, Germinus, Paenus. The Emperor's message to each recipient: "The tree of pleasure blooms again in Rome."

To VEIANUS NIGER, Tribune of the Praetorian Guard, from TIGELLINUS
Consult with Paenus, and seize four estates in Campania, upon establishment of appropriate guilts of their owners, and give the estates, in order of value, to Paenus, Celer, Ippolite, Canus. Portal inscriptions: SERVICE TO ROME.

To TULLIUS SEVERUS, Senator, from TIGELLINUS
Something came up at the gala last night about which I need confidential advice. You are held by Himself to be a particularly intimate and trusted friend, and perhaps you can judge the import of what I am to tell you, always in strictest secrecy. Perhaps you noticed some of this yourself.

As you know, Atticus Vestinus, who has also enjoyed great intimacy with Himself, is to become Co-Consul at the new year, only a few weeks from now. Did you see his behavior last night?

First, his arrival. He came into the gardens, with that

haughty air of his, surrounded by a party of his lovely lithe slaves. As you may know, these beautiful young men, who are Parthians, of pale silken skin, are all said to be within two weeks of each other in age, presently just over nineteen. Vestinus has trained a bodyguard of them in the most exquisite dance-like paramilitary maneuvers, so that they flow around him as he walks, like the many folds of an ample, hooded cloak in a light breeze. He had the audacity to present them armed at the gate. Of course their weapons were taken away from them. But throughout the gala they clung like lovely cloth around Vestinus, even in his several approaches to Himself.

But there was worse. You know Vestinus's high spirits and bluff manner. His banter entertains Himself, but at the same time, some of his sarcastic teasing is a bit too closely constructed of bricks of fact. Two recent actions of Vestinus have especially galled Himself: that Vestinus had the temerity, two months ago, to marry Statilia Messalina while she was still at the height of Himself's favor, and that in preparation for his consulship Vestinus has built and lives in such a virtual fortress right over the Forum, on the shoulder of the Palatine.

To my great chagrin, it turned out that Vestinus knew something that I had not known—that Himself has a specific and isolated, but acute, fear of apes. I had thought him perfectly at home with wild beasts of all kinds; have seen him stroke lions and tigers. While Himself was walking from booth to booth, before the torches were lit to signal come-one-come-all, taking his time choosing the two or three noble ladies whose cunts he might rent, Vestinus and his beautiful convoy came swooping up. Vestinus had a large tame ape by the hand, one of the animals that had been moving freely among the guests. Mind you, I am virtually certain that Vestinus *knew* about the Emperor's panic at the sight of these creatures. He walked right up to the Presence hand in hand with the hairy one. His complaisant companion now and again grinned the knowing grin of apes; held its long, hispid arm up in a military salute. Vestinus said, "May I have the honor, dear friend, to present my cousin, Fabius Vestinus? He's just turned nineteen. I was wondering, would Your Gracious Eminence be willing, when I become Consul, to waive the usual consideration of age and appoint him a Quaestor?"

I saw the blood drain from Himself's face. He hastily said he wanted once more to board the barge. The terror Himself must have felt in those moments, dear Tullius, is surely why he did not, after all, avail Himself all night of any one of the distinguished women who were quite prepared to be at his service. I had known nothing of this fear. How little we know our most beloved friends—never guessing the peculiar terrors that lurk behind their composed and even radiant faces.

I am worried, Tullius. Vestinus is to be Consul. Himself has been deeply fond of this reckless, hearty man. I have observed that if a relationship wilts, Himself turns with special bitterness against men who have been his most intimate friends. You know how it has gone with Lucan. But Lucan is not, will not be, a Consul. (And by the way, Vestinus *must* know that the only time Nero has waived the age requirement for the quaestorship was when he did it in favor of Lucan; thus does Vestinus subtly tread on toes.) Have you any advice? Can you influence Vestinus to refrain from this teasing that cuts so deep? We must avoid explosions, Tullius, you will understand that. I would be grateful for any help you can give me on this *most confidential* matter.

To CANUS, Imperial Household, from TIGELLINUS

For the future: Whenever wild beasts are introduced to the

Presence, make sure that there are no apes or monkeys among them.

To PAENUS, Tribune of Secret Police, from TIGELLINUS
Already, before the seventh hour, we have received more than three hundred messages of congratulations to Himself on the entertainments at the lake. Some masterpieces among them from husbands of ladies who had offered themselves for hire and had proved rather proficient in the unaccustomed trade. From the Piso–Lucan group we have responses, cast in conventional terms, from Bassus and Nonianus. *No word from any of the others.*
Urgent:
Tullius Severus is trustworthy, is he not? Let me know within an hour if there is anything new on him that is unfavorable. I have written him an important letter and want to get it off.

To TIGELLINUS from PAENUS, Tribune of Secret Police
TULLIUS SEVERUS: Up to now, as far as we know, clean as a tunic almost worn out with washing. I need not remind you that Himself remains grateful to Severus even now for his help, when Himself was newly Emperor and just seventeen years old, in setting up Himself's affair with Acte.

To TIGELLINUS from PAENUS, Tribune of Secret Police
On the Piso–Lucan group at the gala, still nothing. I cannot dig up the slightest fragment. Not a single agent succeeded in arranging later meetings. Nothing. Nothing. I do not like the smell of it.
On your hypothesis that all these men just happened to be bored: impossible. Several of them know very well how to enjoy themselves: Piso, Scaevinus, Natalis, and Quintianus

not the least. No, Tigellinus, they were unanimous and they were resistant. I am prepared to accept the idea that the writers Bassus and Nonianus—who, you say, have written to thank Himself, and who, you remember, were silent at the Piso banquet—must be thought to have had somewhat different motives for their behavior from the rest.

October 17

To TIGELLINUS from TULLIUS SEVERUS, Senator

The Consul-Elect Vestinus is not easily subject to influence, but I will do what I can with him. As you know, he is headstrong and proud of his roughness that wears an epicene mask, and I am not certain I can persuade him to be circumspect. I will try.

To TIGELLINUS from PAENUS, Tribune of Secret Police

A scrap, at least, at last. Nothing incriminating, but a very strange account and, to my mind, a significant one.

This comes from Valerius Flavus, with whose talents as an informer you are well acquainted. He was not engaged for surveillance that night—one does not "engage" such a powerful man as he has become—but simply attended as a guest. Today he volunteered this bit. I took the trouble to have a stenographer present at our interview, and we have the following exact transcript of what he said:

"You know, Paenus, I always keep my eyes open. Something about Lucan caught my attention. At the moment when every other man was on the verge of orgasm, or of apoplexy, or of choking to death on laughter, he stood aloof. He was pale. He looked haunted. He looked gray—like a wavering column of thin smoke. I stayed near him without his knowing it. The moment when he betrayed himself was at the race of dwarfs and hunchbacks. The crowd crushed close beside the

improvised racetrack, you remember. Lucan had drifted into
the midst of the pack, obviously unaware of what was to take
place. A certain woman, whom I can name, lightly clad, one
of those delicious volunteers, started pressing herself against
Lucan, trying to excite him. He pushed her away and cursed
her. Then I caught the moment at which he realized what
was now to be exhibited. A foot race of monsters. His face,
Paenus! As on a scroll was written there: *I, too, am a monster.
What are they doing to you, fellow monsters? Brothers,
brothers, what are they doing to us?* You will remember that
Tigellinus roared out to the crowd an announcement of the
prize for the race, and dropped the flag, and those creatures
began to run, spurred by lust, and—you remember this, Paenus—about a hundred paces from the start the fools Isio and
Baba darted out from the crowd and together tripped the
hunchback who happened then to be quite far in the lead,
and one saw on the face of the falling racer an instantaneous
flash of disbelief and rage because the soft prize he was already covering in his mind had suddenly been snatched from
him. There was all this while a perfect tumult of laughter.
Lucan lunged forward. His face was contorted with another
sort of disbelief and rage. I think he would have strangled
Isio and Baba, one with each hand, but for the fact that the
crowd was too tightly compressed. He could not break free.
Then, Paenus, I saw tears running down his face. There were
tears on many faces—from laughter. His were different. The
laughing faces were ruddy. Hectic and crimson. His was white
as alabaster. His head was turning slowly from side to side.
He was looking at the roaring mouths in the crowd around
him. He was weeping like a woman. Anyone else might not
have noticed this, Paenus. This might simply have been a
young man who was very drunk. Don't you know, Paenus,
how sometimes a man who is very drunk will think he is

laughing but be crying instead? But that was not Lucan's case. He is a deranged person, Paenus. All poets are mad, but he is dangerous. He is capable of believing he is a hunchback. That can lead to no good outcome. I tell you: Beware of Lucan."

October 18

To PAENUS, Tribune of Secret Police, from TIGELLINUS
Do not let yourself be too elated by the report on Lucan by Valerius. I personally have gone a bit sour on Valerius's information; though Himself, I must admit, still has confidence in him. First of all, remember his origins. He was born of a shoemaker and grew up in the squalor of a cobbler's shop. His ugly face, his short, twisted body, leaning to one side over a shriveled right leg, and his gross wit, so very swift, led to his introduction at court in the first place under Caligula as a fool, a butt. But then he began to whisper scandal in the ears of influential persons, and he began to get little rewards, hunks of gristle thrown to a watchdog, and the gobbets grew bigger as the scandal he reported became more shocking—and here we now are with that sorry, contorted shoemaker's son as one of the richest, most influential, and most destructive men in Rome. He can afford to put on provincial gladiatorial shows! He must love to watch strong men cut each other down. Do you not think it somewhat hard, Paenus, to accept at face value the report by a man with a misshapen body of a straight-bodied man's reaction to a foot race of men with misshapen bodies? I would make you a good wager that Lucan with his brusque manner has at some point snubbed Valerius.

To TIGELLINUS from PAENUS, Tribune of Secret Police
You will have to agree that the Valerius report on Lucan has a true ring.

To PAENUS, Tribune of Secret Police, from TIGELLINUS
Valerius on Lucan: Believable yes. Actionable, no.

October 27

To TIGELLINUS from PAENUS, Tribune of Secret Police
Apparently Lucan did send to Seneca the rude letter of which we found the first fragment. Our agent among Lucan's slaves now brings us from his master's writing room a copy of Seneca's reply. This begins to be interesting. I think you will agree that this letter merits being sent in full.

"Seneca to Lucan, greetings:

"Your intemperate letter, dear nephew, hurt me, not because I took your reproaches to heart but because I feel I must have neglected you somehow over the years, must have failed you. How could such an abyss suddenly open between you and me? I have been up all night talking with Paulina about this bitter communication from you.

"You ask how I, of all people, could write the sentence, 'Writers should never approach too close to power.'

"Education does not end with lessons in rhetoric, Lucan. Give me credit for having learned something in my older years. Yes, this sentence is the fruit of my heavy years —years, I might say, of disillusionment; years, *you* might say, of clinging to vanity, folly, and some mad hope of advantage.

"I did what I did—I *thought* I did what I did—for Rome. I tutored Nero when he was a boy, and I advised him when he became a man. I knew from his youngest years his beautiful animal power, and I knew the evil in him. Burrus and I turned his course for a few years to the good side. This seemed to me a valuable thing for a writer to be doing.

"Yes, a writer. I was, am, will be a writer. And so your letter—because you know what a benign influence I exerted for so long, but more importantly because you are a critic I respect, even though you are a very young man—your letter has kept me up all night, trying to find in the company of my dear wife the basis for your scorn, your terrible contempt.

"I am afraid I know. I scooped out the innermost snail meat from my heart before Paulina in the early morning hours, and now I humble myself before you.

"In these hours I recalled three proofs in my writings of the sentence, 'Writers should never approach too close to power.' I have written much that I think will live in the eyes of men, but I have written three things that I wish I could erase, and never can.

"First, the groveling in 'To Polybius,' in which, begging so abjectly to be allowed to come home from my exile, I tied myself, without realizing it, to a desire for power. To Nero's mother. Agrippina must have seen that piece of sniveling and decided to make me her creature, one of her tools in her ambition to bring her son to power. She got Claudius to pardon me and appointed me Nero's tutor as soon as I reached home, and as his tutor I witnessed—and rode, as if in a litter—Agrippina's inexorable campaign to have her son substituted for Claudius's natural heir Britannicus. I confess to you, Lucan, in the face of your scorn, that I watched Agrippina's mastery of Claudius not simply as one watching a spider entrap, lull with venom, and bind a bumblebee, but with a little too much pleasure in the watching, in gazing at the exquisite web, its geometry of avarice pearled with innocent dew, and at the sensuous, darting dance of the web tender on the trembling threads of her treachery. How could I not have known that all the time I was entangled myself?

"Second, the funeral oration on Claudius, after Agrippina murdered him, which I wrote for Nero's mouth. The Senators knew I had written that gem of hypocrisy, and they openly laughed at it. What the Senators did not know was the depth of the hypocrisy—that I had known beforehand

that Agrippina had hired Locusta to poison the mushrooms for
Claudius's last meal. Soon afterwards I compounded my
hypocrisy, in her eyes as in my own, by reading in public my
'Pumpkinification of Claudius,' in which, with self-betraying
tardiness, I joined the general laughter at the murdered man.

"And third, five years later, my apology for the murder
of Agrippina herself. This was the worst. Again, I had known
a few hours beforehand that Nero was trying to kill his
mother; I had, by my unwillingness or inability to prevent the
murder, become very nearly an accomplice. That death may
have been a relief for many of us, and especially for me, so
long Agrippina's pawn, but I made the crime of matricide
seem like a heroic deed, a blessing for Rome, a deliverance.

"You know about these lapses, Lucan; I suppose everyone knows about them. They are at the center of the humility
I have finally grown into. I care nothing about the accusation
of adultery with Julia that sent me into exile, or for the gossip
that Agrippina seduced me years ago, for Suilius's gibes at my
wealth, for the charges of usury. I am not ashamed of my life.
In my actions I have been, by and large, a Stoic man, a strong
man; a man for humanity, a man with men and with women.
But in my mind, and in yours, I am sure, it is the writing that
counts for me and against me.

"I have written much that recommends me, even to a
severe critic like you. I believe the first five years of Nero's
reign, when I was hand in hand with noble Burrus in guiding
Nero, were the best Rome has had, certainly since the Republic, and I wrote all the great words of those great years. You
know my private works. I have been a force for honor. The
body of my work is sound. You know that.

"But you know of the slippages, too.

"Those three pieces of writing gnaw at my liver. I am
not sure after all this time that I understand power. I do

understand that power is dangerous to a writer, and that my long proximity to unlimited power adulterated my writings. In the taste I developed for that proximity lay the one great flaw in my Stoic apparatus.

"One can say that a writer, if he be anything like a sage, is indifferent to wealth and is unchanged by either having it or not having it; but it cannot be said that he is unaffected by power. Power nourishes. Power makes a man more himself. All that is creative and all that is malign in him stands larger and more fully rounded when he has others at his mercy. How much larger than life Nero has become—that feather-stuffed leather ball of a rascal I once tutored, a monster now. Burrus and I had the illusion that under our influence the good in Nero would grow and the evil would shrivel and mortify. What happened, instead, to us, the teachers? I know that I came to harbor murder in my heart. Stoic! Stoic! Could cold baths wash away such secrets? I tried three years ago to retire. Nero refused permission. Now I have finally managed to withdraw altogether from the region of power.

"You will say, Lucan, that I am still very rich. That wealth is power. But a writer does not sleep better on a couch stuffed with down, the finest product of luxury; or worse on a pallet in the slums, a jag of hay for a pillow, under him a crude mattress with its stuffing of rags tumbling out through torn places. What difference to me whether I live in a palace or a hovel? As no general trusts peace enough to be unready for war, so no writer, at least no wise writer, will allow himself, once wealthy, to become unequipped for beggary. Let that man enjoy the present who faces with composure any future.

"There is no hypocrisy in that, Lucan. I face the ultimate poverty, death, with evening calm. It seems that no one, not even you, will believe that.

"Farewell."

November 1

To PAENUS, Tribune of Secret Police, from TIGELLINUS

Once again I have discussed with Himself the implications of the Piso dinner, and we went over what you and I have discovered since then, and what we have not discovered.

Himself came forward with one of his characteristically perverse ideas, which worries me, and on which I need your soberest judgment.

He proposes a literary evening, for which he wishes to command the presence of, among others, all our principals: Lucan, Bassus, Nonianus, Piso, Quintianus, Natalis, Gallus. He would also pull Seneca and Columella all the way in from Nomentum. Wants Petronius, who, as you know, despises Seneca and Lucan. A certain quarrel. Wants Celsus, Calpurnius, Vagellius, Antistius, Curtius Montanus. In other words, all the brightest lights, from encyclopedists to tragedians.

He does not say—I cannot pry out of him—what he would order done that night, but I can well imagine that it would be something foolhardy and deliberately risky, an attempt of some kind to draw the conspirators, if there are conspirators, out into the open. Himself was mischievous, cuffing my shoulders with awkward but forceful blows like those of a lion cub at play, as he threw this idea out to me; his eyes sparkled. At moments I thought he was simply teasing me—teasing *us*, Paenus, because he thinks we jump at shadows in the dark.

But I think he is serious about having such an evening. It is like him to make a bull's run at danger. Tell me what you think. This is urgent.

To TIGELLINUS from PAENUS, Tribune of Secret Police
Urgent.
I am fearful of the literary evening.

It is true that we know nothing for sure. But I am still shaken by the meagerness of the harvest from the gala by the lake. This business may be farther along than we think. It is like Himself to dangle a perfect opportunity before desperate men. If they were to prove almost but not quite ready, then his game might succeed where many trained agents at my disposal have failed. But if they were ready—no, it would be much too dangerous to offer such an opportunity.

We cannot flood a literary banquet, as we can almost any other social occasion, with strong men, bodyguards. Someone like Lucan would be sure to ask about one of our knuckle-boys, "Who is this one? Let's have him read us a little lyric."

No, Tigellinus, tell Himself not to play games with assassins.

November 2

To PAENUS, Tribune of Secret Police, from TIGELLINUS

Your reply confirmed my instinct about the literary evening. This morning I put our judgment to Himself in the strongest terms. He thought a few moments, then set a date and gave me a list of people to invite.

Apropos:

Later in the day Himself decided on a whim to visit the Temple of Saturn, saying he wished to meditate there. (What he did there, in fact, was to enter the vaults of the Treasury, where he gazed fixedly at silver ingots for an hour with a rapt expression, as of a priest.) As the cortege moved homeward up the Sacra Via, my litter preceding his as usual, a commoner, a leathery old gaffer with a face wrinkled into radiance by years of laughter, came forward to the flanking Guardsmen saying he was a carver of ivory and begging permission to give the Emperor a gift. The Tribune Veianus Niger, in our escort, taken with the benign face of the old craftsman, reported the petition to me. I interviewed the supplicant and was amused by his antics; and I descended from my litter and walked with him to Himself's litter, where the gift was given with good cheer and laughter all around.

The gift was an exquisite ivory figurine of a girl. The old man said that this girl had a singular power: she could ward off plots. Upon the carver's saying this, Himself, thinking perhaps of my talk with him a few hours earlier about our literary friends, gave me a buffoon's look of heavy significance, and broke out in coarse laughter.

But when we got back to the Golden House he ordered a little shrine made for her in his bedchamber, and he burned a sacrifice to her, just as if she were a statue of a divinity.

November 4

To TIGELLINUS from PAENUS, Tribune of Secret Police

One more item—a rather frail one, I fear—from the gala at the lake. A Senator's wife whom we assigned to Natalis reports, after repeated questioning, that she thought she intercepted significant glances between Natalis and Scaevinus. This is, as I say, flimsy stuff, but it has a measure of weight in that the woman assigned to Natalis did not know that Sleepy-Eyes was another suspected person.

I have felt all along that your complacency about Natalis, in your first analysis of the report of the Piso dinner, was not fully justified. I have taken the liberty of setting a light watch on him.

To PAENUS, Tribune of Secret Police, from TIGELLINUS

Remove the surveillance from Natalis at once. A man in a position to learn as much as you must have learned about fellow citizens sometimes forgets himself. Knowledge of other men's weaknesses dulls one's perception of his own. Look in a mirror, Paenus. Watch your lips closely as you say out loud to yourself, "Obedience is the first duty of a secret policeman."

November 5

To TIGELLINUS from PAENUS, Tribune of Secret Police
Natalis flies free as the summer hawk. Perhaps it was this man's pleasing nose, arched at the top and then suddenly going flat, with wide horselike nostrils, that led me into indiscretion. Laugh as you forgive me.

November 15

To TIGELLINUS from PAENUS, Tribune of Secret Police
A draft of a sylvan poem, or part of one, "borrowed" from Lucan's desk for copying by our agent in his house. For the eyes of Epicharis? One important clue: the seashore. Misenum? A memory of one of the "walks in the countryside" Lucan is reported to take from time to time with Epicharis? An encoded message? At any rate, here it is:

> *The south wind guesses in the pines above the dunes,*
> *And shadows and flecks of sunlight shift on the path*
> *That nymphs have made running up from the surf*
> *With sea foam on their thighs to share the wine*
> *And salt the lips of the Hill-gods, mindless of time;*
> *You are here, and I am here, and the sun*
> *Of a single day is high, and our time is short.*
> *I take your hand in mine. I touch the silver*
> *Brooch at your shoulder that holds you imprisoned*
>   *in silk,*
> *And now, and now—the waves, the roar of the waves,*
> *Time will not pause for you and me; the drumming*
> *Of tides grinds rocks into sand, and does not end.*

In the same haul, this letter from Lucan to Seneca. Mentions the feared crime. As to the means of acquisition of the poem and of this letter, some bad news within the letter itself —bad news in general about the conduct of our agents.

"Lucan to Seneca, greetings:

"Oh, Seca, I am so depressed and angry all the time. Only two or three years ago there was no better company in Rome than mine. I had my moods, but I could be a fountain of laughter, too. Don't you remember? Your letter, rather than soothing the irritation I had felt toward you earlier, only made me feel heavy and in exile—cut off, that is, from an especially dear one and therefore somehow from everything dear.

"It was terrible that you felt a need to abase yourself before me. But worse than that, considering your letter as further comment on my question, 'What is a writer's responsibility?', it seemed to say something very bleak to me— namely, that it is a writer's responsibility to keep his nose clean.

"I see terrible things happening. I have been driven nearly out of my mind by an odious gala N. gave recently. You may have heard about it. The occasion was the opening of an artificial lake N. has had built in the natural basin between the Esquiline and Palatine hills, in the gardens of the Golden House. A sad marriage has taken place in our Rome, Seca, between superb taste and grossest vulgarity. A vessel had been built by Celer, who, as you know, has an eye, and this ship, which had nowhere to go, was a sweet toy for Neptune himself; it was towed around the pond, if you can believe it, by a great multitude of white swans harnessed in brilliant ribbons. What a conception! And what a scene this lovely ship became, shortly after midnight, of lasciviousness, of total abandonment of shame on the part of the leaders of Rome.

Nero, Nero, to think that you were my best friend! All around
the lake were booths, in which the noble ladies of the capital
offered themselves for money to Senators, to knights, to other
women, to Praetorian Guardsmen, to freedmen, and even to
slaves into whose hands masters out of a jaded sense of mischief slipped the privileged sums these women were asking.
And loathsome exhibitions—multiple couplings, a fifteen-
year-old girl mounted by a large dog. I cannot bring myself to
write you some of what I saw.

"But the sight that shocked me most, Seca, was that of
a foot race of cripples for a prize of copulation with a noble
Roman woman. Hunchbacks and dwarfs. One old soldier,
both of whose legs had been cut off below the knees in battle,
who raced on all fours and almost won. The faces of those
poor creatures, Seca—devoid of any sense of their degradation,
that was the worst of it. Glowing with hope, trembling with
helpless fear. Those wounded beings had been totally corrupted by visions of a reward beyond their dreams. Ears deaf
to the laughter of those who had corrupted them. I wake up
at night tortured by the burning memory of those happy
frightened faces at the starting line. They spoke to me, still
speak to me, of the meaning of tyranny. Where consent is
achieved through corruption and fear, the absolute power of
Augustus inevitably becomes the absolute power of Nero.

"Absolute power can keep absolute power only by
repression. The controls these days are so crude that they
clank like actual fetters. I suppose a man like Tigellinus sin-
cerely believes that he protects the Emperor by making everyone aware that disloyalty means gross punishment, by keeping the threats out in the open. But it is all so flagrant. The
surveillance hangs in the air around one like a fishmarket
stink. That hideous lopsided footpad Valerius clung to me
like a grape to the stem at the gala at N.'s lake last month,
and all the while he looked so like a small boy playing cen-

turion, as if he really believed I was unaware of his watching me. The writings on my desk are being gone through almost every night. I know where every scroll and tablet lies when I leave my desk; my things are continually combed. The palace tried to bring foul pressure on Epicharis, of all people, before the gala, to be one of the "whores" there. Every time I go to see my friend Piso I am followed in the streets. I don't care any more. I could teach these stupid secret policemen a bit of finesse—but perhaps they *want* to be seen, in order to remind.

"But I will tell you what they are on the point of doing, Seca. They are going to force us into what their diseased minds have imagined. We are innocent, if desperate. They need the guilt of others. They are going to drive us to it. I feel like a figure in someone else's nightmare.

"*This* is why I need to know what a writer's duty is. I know his duty is to his art—that he must stretch his gifts to the tearing point with every line he writes. But can there be a distinction, in times like these, between aesthetic achievement and vital action? You said that writers should stay away from power because they are forever wishing that reality could reach the level of art. I wonder, seeing reality so formless, so chaotic, so mad, whether this is not a reason why writers—artists in general—should not indeed approach very close to power through their works. To me the ideal of a work of art is that each man should be able, in contemplating it, to see himself as he really is. Thus art and reality meet. This is the great healing strength of art, this is the power of art, which is greater than the power of emperors. Emperors try to keep themselves in power with secret policemen and with arms, and still they are assassinated. Art's power, which nothing can challenge, is the blinding light of recognition.

"I can write these words to you, Seca, and believe them, but I am still at a loss as to what a writer as a man should *do*—that is, what *I* should do in the actual situation in which I find myself. Somewhere in my relationship with Nero, and therefore with power, the puzzle lies for me.

"Could he be influenced, if I were still his friend? Or have we no hope of bringing him to his senses? You know him better than I. Is our headlong rush toward infamy—the descent into primeval slime that was so vividly exemplified by that race of the cripples—is this all to be laid at Nero's feet? He has the power. Must we hold him responsible for what is happening to us? Or is he, too, being swept along as if by a current of the river of our time? Are we all responsible together? You know Nero better than anyone in Rome, Seca. Advise me. Help me, help me, before it is too late.

"Farewell."

To PAENUS, Tribune of Secret Police, from TIGELLINUS

I have just been sniffing this shit of Lucan's. Fugh! Very bad. You ought to be put to the sword, Paenus. If everything your agents and informers do is as transparent and clumsy as Lucan makes his surveillance seem, then we have built walls of muslin and made shields of eggshells to protect Himself. I hate to admit that this little peacock feather of a poet has frightened me, but he has. You will have to undertake a complete review of training methods. Do not panic and haul your wooden-thumbed agents off Lucan's back. At the stage of recklessness he has reached, we cannot afford to take the risk of a pause of even a few days, or the worse risk of replacing wooden thumbs with leaden thumbs, which would very likely be the case. But Paenus, you have work to do.

November 26

To TIGELLINUS from FLACCUS VALENS, Praetor

Word has come to me from officials of the town of Farentum, which I feel I must pass on to you.

Farentum, as you probably know, is a prosperous colonial town in the Etruscan hills, a day's forced march or two comfortable days' journey from the capital. I have family in the town, and for this reason a delegation of officials, including a cousin of mine, came to me in great agitation today to tell of a strange incident that had disturbed them.

There is in Farentum a rather important temple, that of Fortune; at least, the citizens of the town regard it as important because of a series of omens and signs associated with it: For example, its altar was blackened by a bolt of lightning last year on the day before the start of the great fire here. One day last week a priest of the temple noticed that a dagger, consecrated to the safety of public officials and suspended in its scabbard against a wall at one side of the main altar, had been stolen. The dagger has a straight steel two-edged blade the length of a man's hand, and a handle made of laminations of olive wood bound with bronze and pricked with gold, with tiny shapes of wolves and deer. No one knows its history. The only persons who are permitted under normal circumstances in the area of the temple where the dagger hung are the priests. Extended questioning of them—no result. There is so much awe and fear associated with the altar that it seems (to the officials) certain that the theft was not the act of a citizen of Farentum. Farentum is off the main roads. No one recalls having seen strangers. I tell you of this incident because of the specific consecration of the dagger.

To FLACCUS VALENS, Praetor, from TIGELLINUS

Thank you for your valuable communication. But I am curious. Why did you, a newly installed Praetor, report to me about the theft of the dagger, instead of going through the normal channels to the Consuls?

To PAENUS, Tribune of Secret Police, from TIGELLINUS
Urgent.

Alert every agent you have: Be on the lookout for a dagger stolen from the Temple of Fortune in Farentum, which *must* be recovered.

Description: steel blade, double-sharpened, length of a man's hand; handle of layered olive wood, bronze-fastened, decorations of gold in small designs of wolf and stag.

Have all pawnshops and knife peddlers' stalls searched discreetly, as if by customers. Have all agents who are assigned to "doubtfuls" be on special lookout.

To TIGELLINUS from PAENUS, Tribune of Secret Police
You urge me to remain calm. Then you throw at me two commands that seem rattled in themselves and are certainly calculated to rattle me. First, remake the secret service from top to bottom. Second, marked "urgent," search Rome for a provincial paring knife.

To TIGELLINUS from FLACCUS VALENS, Praetor
I wrote to you rather than the Consuls about the dagger because many people hate you.

To PAENUS, Tribune of Secret Police, from TIGELLINUS
Stop your whining. Find the dagger. This is a particular dagger. It lusts for important flesh. Perhaps, Paenus, for yours. Then, you will ask, why should you find it? Because it may yearn for mine. Or for far more important flesh than yours or mine. Spare no pains.

To SILIUS NERVA and ATTICUS VESTINUS, Consuls, from TIGELLINUS
In my previous memoranda to you as new Consuls, I have outlined certain concerns of the Emperor under the headings

of public safety, dealings with foreign ambassadors, conduct of public ceremonies, and procedure of the Senate. This letter concerns security of the Imperial Person, Office, Palace, and Treasury.

You are of course aware that an apparatus exists for the purpose of ensuring these aspects of security. I am sure you are also sensitive to the extremely delicate relationships between the civil structure, which you represent, the Praetorian Guard, which Faenus Rufus and I command, and the secret service, which the Emperor has put under my charge. The fact that the Emperor has entrusted this last care to a Co-Commander of the Praetorian Guard should make it clear to you that the secret service is essentially an instrument of the armed strength of the ruler.

Translating this clarification into procedure, you should instruct all civil authorities under your jurisdiction to refer information bearing on security directly to me rather than moving through their normal civil channels. I beg you to understand this as a wish of the Emperor and not an interference on my part with your regular chains of authority. I think you will be able to see that the risk of leaks and of delay would be very great if we were to depend upon normal channels for the transmission of dangerous information.

You have come to office, as I am sure you are aware, in a period of extreme sensitivity, from the point of view of Imperial security. The hysteria, public clamor, and variable sense of personal loss stemming from the fire have not abated, even though several months have now passed. It is clear that the utmost alertness is in order.

I append to this general statement two relatively minor yet rather important matters:

The first, Vestinus, concerns your bodyguard. While the Emperor, like everyone else, admires the clever drills of your handsome young slaves, he does not regard it as seemly, now that you have been sworn as Consul, that a high public official should be seen at the Capitol or in the Forum with a private, as distinguished from a regularly provided, bodyguard. I am sure that you will understand my conveying this to you in a memorandum addressed jointly to the Consuls, rather than in a private note to you, as expressive of a principle rather than as a personal matter.

And second, *confidentially*, I have had indications of an ambiguous attitude on the part of the Praetor Flaccus Valens. Would you kindly give me your estimate of his reliability?

November 28

To TIGELLINUS from SILIUS NERVA, Consul

Answering your esteemed memorandum:

1. The Emperor's command, as to channels for security, noted and acted on.

2. I write on behalf of Vestinus. You have cut him to the bone. His bodyguard is so close to the center of his total persona that stripping him of it would be like stripping him of his toga and asking him to preside over the Senate in his undertunic. This is a cruel order. Surely those effeminate young men are a threat to no one. I urge you to urge the Emperor to relent on this point.

3. Flaccus Valens is ambitious. This means that at every move he will keep an alternate path open. But do not worry yourself about him. He is stupid.

To PAENUS, Tribune of Secret Police, from TIGELLINUS

Begin surveillance of Flaccus Valens, Praetor. He has a reputation for stupidity. This means that you must use one of your shrewdest and most intelligent agents. Men with a reputation of being stupid are often the most elusive. Have you noticed that?

To SILIUS NERVA, Consul, from TIGELLINUS

As a comment on your plea on behalf of Vestinus and his little dance of guards, the Emperor was pleased to shrug his shoulders. I would suggest that you tell your colleague about that shrug. Let him understand it any way he wants.

December 3

To TIGELLINUS from PAENUS, Tribune of Secret Police

And now, Tigellinus, I *am* excited. We have our first intercept of Cleonicus, Seneca's freedman and courier, yielding a covert exchange with Lucan, both parts of which I send forward in full.

You will measure Seneca's trust in Cleonicus by his abandonment of the most fundamental precautions in this deeply compromising letter.

As for Lucan's end of the business, he has come, as you noted earlier, to a stage of recklessness that certainly puts us on our mettle. Thanks to the cooperation of Cleonicus, I need no longer depend on the agent in Lucan's household whose methods Lucan criticized. I attribute Lucan's awareness that he was being watched to his rampant vanity and irascibility; he is a touchy instrument. Have you ever noticed his eyes when a loud noise is heard nearby? One suddenly sees a glittering, searing look of suspicion; it is as if there were vials of molten brass in his eyeballs. This is not to deny the need for new training in the service; it is only to suggest that Lucan is a cat in human skin. I would like permission to reward this very agent whom Lucan found so disturbing. After all, he did give us much valuable material. I would like to keep him on the job, for there may be more.

But to the treasures from Cleonicus:

"Seneca to Lucan, greetings:

"This is bad news, my dear Lucan, that you send me from the capital. Two correspondents besides yourself who were present at this appalling entertainment of Nero's have written me about it, and I gather that this gala surpassed all his previous follies in its debauchery and wasteful magnificence. I assume that that supreme vulgarian Tigellinus was the dark genius of these revels, but Nero, alas, was at the heart of them. The splendor of Imperial displays is nothing new to me. I remember a naval battle Claudius staged on Lake Fucinus, twelve years ago, when the tunnel through the mountain between Fucinus and the river Liris had been finished—four-banked galleys, marines on decked vessels, Praetorian cavalry on a huge raft, nineteen thousand men out on the water really trying to kill each other, or at least trying to slaughter a large number of condemned criminals among them; an enormous mass of people from Rome and from the whole countryside on the banks all around, right up to the tops of the mountains that formed a great theater for the battle. I sat next to Nero that day. He was wearing a Praetorian cloak; he was a handsome, slender youth of fifteen, not long adopted by Claudius; my pupil, a quite different person from the creature we see today. But that sort of display, bloody as it was, had a theme at least of valor, of pride, of Rome's magnificence. This new, squalid debauch of Nero's, designed not to delight the mass of the people but only to glut the eyes and swell the stomachs and ease the groins of a handful of the inner circle—and coming so soon after the horrible fire that reduced so many wretched Romans to rags— this had no theme, except perhaps the false new theme, corrupting the Epicurean ideal, that indulgence in sensuous pleasure somehow opens out the mind.

"You ask me, and I ask myself: Can we hold Nero personally responsible for what is happening to dear Rome?

"He has the power, as you say. We have developed a misconception of power. The institutions of war and slavery subtly pervade all our human relationships; and we have come to this: The aim of power is to keep power. The only real and lasting power, it should be clear, is that of character, that which obliges others to follow because of admiration and love. Augustus knew this. I tried to teach Nero this. There was a time when I really believed he could surpass noble Augustus. Look at him now. Uffa! Look, and try to control your nausea. He has had, to our sorrow, other teachers besides your Seca.

"The change in Nero, when I began to lose influence over him, came quickly and dramatically after he murdered his mother, six years ago, nearly seven. It was then that we saw the beginning of his excesses.

"It was then that his night outings in the city turned from youthful pranks into criminal raids: He would go out into the alleys late at night with a few companions, all disguised as slaves, and they would play at cutpurse and tavern-robber and rapist, terrorizing proprietors, knocking innocent people on the head, violating decent women. When it became known that the Emperor of Rome played these games, not only every shabby outlaw but also many noble youths imitated him. Our city streets became a nightmare. It was as if Rome had fallen in war to a cruel enemy.

"It was then, too, that Nero began to put himself on public display. It started in the Circus; whereas formerly he had watched hidden by a curtain, he now sat in broad view, openly enjoying the games along with the rabble. He took up driving a four-horse chariot. Burrus and I arranged to have a space in the Vatican valley enclosed by a high wall where he could play with his horses without its becoming a public scandal, but he began inviting first his friends, then a huge crowd of people at large; and finally we saw him in the Circus, a common charioteer of the Green team.

"He sang with a lyre, first at private dinners, saying

that this was a royal custom among ancient chiefs, and finally before all Rome in theaters. He was shameless in his solicitation of praise and applause. Once he saw a group of young men from Alexandria applauding in a theater in their rhythmic styles, which they called 'bee hum,' 'sound of roof tiles,' 'bricks clacking,' and he then enlisted a large corps of young men to be present and applaud in these ways whenever he performed; they would shout in unison that Nero was divine, until Nero believed them. I saw him once mincing in the part of Niobe, singing falsetto, and I wept. The parts he chose! *Canace in Labor*—about the daughter of an Etruscan king, pregnant by her own brother; all Rome snickered behind its hand about Nero 'groaning in childbirth.' *Orestes the Matricide*—think of his choosing to sing that role! *The Blinding of Oedipus. The Frenzy of Hercules.* No one was allowed to leave a theater while he sang—and once a certain Senator went to the length of pretending to die so he could be carried out.

"As you are all too aware, Nero also began to imagine that he was a poet; you know the type of mediocre young tinkers and cobblers of poetry he drew around himself at first for his games of extemporization. Then he began to think himself the equal of such as you and Persius and Bassus. You took part in the first of the Neronia, you saw how he put on Greek dress and read poems and orated in the competitions before the entire populace, and you heard the announcement that he was victorious. Everyone but he knew that the judgments were farcical. It sickened me to see him 'humble' in the face of the verdicts—the way, when they offered him the prize for lyre-playing, he knelt before it and asked that it be placed at the feet of the statue of Augustus.

"The bad year, dear Lucan, was three years ago. Everything has gone disastrously downhill since then. The year

opened with signs of the suppression of all dissidence—the
revival of the Law of High Treason; the banishment of the
Praetor Antistius Sosianus and of Fabricius Vaiento; a public
burning of books that mocked authority. Next Burrus, my
beloved ally in the effort to keep alive the better side of Nero,
died ostensibly of an abscess of the throat; I would say he
died of sadness. I sometimes wish I had—a soldier could die
of sadness, somehow a philosopher could not. Nero then replaced Burrus with the one man who above all others has
brought ruin to Rome: Sofonius Tigellinus.

"Then troubles fell like hail. Nero's old enemies Plau-
tus and Sulla were murdered in exile. The corn ships were
wrecked in that terrible storm in Ostia. Nero divorced Octavia,
married Poppaea, murdered Octavia. There were riots. Persius
with his lovely poetic talent died, and you turned bitter.
Suilius denounced me—I now wonder if he was hired to do it.
I tried to retire to this place, offering Nero all my worldly
goods, but he made me a long false speech about how much
he needed me. In fact I no longer offered advice and, for that
matter, was no longer asked for it. Tigellinus had taken into his
calloused paws Nero's ear, mouth, penis, eyes, anus, fingertips,
legs, paunch—his all, body and mind.

"Before long Rome will regret the day Tigellinus was
born—in a hovel in southern Sicily, Lucan. He was so destructive and vicious as a youth that he was sent into exile, and he
lived several years as a fisherman in Achaea. Then he was
pardoned and became a horse breeder in the harsh upper
pasturage of Apulia and Calabria. Nero bought chariot horses
from him, admired his swagger and aped his foul mouth, and
brought him to Rome and gave him the post for which he
surely had the greatest talent—Prefect of Police. And when
Burrus died we got this delinquent in his place, this outlaw
still stinking of fish and venality, a tough of the tracks, a

born alleyway policeman, vulgar, cruel for the sake of cruelty, gifted however to our sorrow with a vivid imagination and quick to learn the patterns of so-called elegance without taking in a shred of culture. I will tell you what he has been able to do: He has been able to make me hate Nero, whom once I loved.

"Have the disgraces of this triennium been Nero's 'fault'? There is a subtle interplay between the comportment of a ruler and the temper of his people. Each influences the other. But the ruler, who is like a father, must remember at every moment that others will follow his example. I tried to din this into Nero, who had to try to act the father when he was only seventeen years old. But alas, Nero had other teachers who taught him the easier lessons of power: frighten, corrupt, divide, exploit, enjoy, dominate, dominate, dominate. Caligula, Claudius, Agrippina, Poppaea, Tigellinus above all.

"You ask if he could be influenced for the better. I used to think so. For five years Burrus and I influenced him for the good of Rome. But for the last three years, Nero has been without Burrus, without Seneca.

"I am afraid I have not answered your urgent questions very well, Lucan. I understand your suffering, and I share it. Write to me what you think about all this. Destroy this letter as soon as you have read it.

"Farewell."

"Lucan to Seneca, greetings:
"I will take advantage of Cleonicus's return.
"You certainly have *not* answered my questions very well. What conceit! I asked big questions—whether Nero should be held to account for ruining all of us, or all of us for ruining Nero and Rome. And what do you reply? That Nero has gone bad for want of Seneca's tutelage! I *know* all that

story of the night raids—I went on one. One should try to think about possibilities of charm, magnetism, very great attractiveness in people whose ideas one loathes. One can like, perhaps love, some of those with whom one disagrees on important matters. What a beautiful organism Nero still is! Even Tigellinus has a punch, a vitality, a horseman's humor. I used to have *a good time* with Nero and Tigellinus and the Circle. You are above reproach; I find your company boring and gloomy. One must face unpleasant thoughts once in a while, Seca.

"What about Nero's member? He more than once tried to put it in my asshole. I wish you had given me your observations on *this* side of Nero—particularly his strange dealings with women. This business of reaching a long arm all the way to Misenum to drag Epicharis into whoredom— peculiar, extremely peculiar, since the category of women chosen for that humiliation (which so many Roman women embraced!) was that of high society, to which Epicharis does not belong.

"Seca, Seca, you do not seem to understand how desperate I am—we are. You must know that I am not alone in my desperation.

"Farewell."

December 5

To PAENUS, Tribune of Secret Police, from TIGELLINUS

Congratulations on the Cleonicus intercepts. If we get our hands on a few more such letters from Seneca we will be in a position at last to step on that old beetle as if by accident and hear his hard old shell crack. Good work, Paenus. Reward the pretty boy who pulled it off.

And yes, you may give a reward, but a modest one, to the agent in Lucan's household, and you may keep him there—but under tight rein. Maybe he will have helped us to catch a rat, or perhaps I should say a mouse.

December 6

To TIGELLINUS from PAENUS, Tribune of Secret Police
Getting praise from you is like finding pomegranate meat in a walnut. One faints—but is it from the sweet taste on the tongue or the strange fear in the heart? What next?

To PAENUS, Tribune of Secret Police, from TIGELLINUS
When you have come out of your swoon get busy with the repairs on your lamentable service.

December 9

To TIGELLINUS from PAENUS, Tribune of Secret Police
After Piso's banquet you ordered me to infiltrate agents into his household but not to put him under close watch. These were somewhat self-contradictory commands, but I have tried with every scruple to follow them ("the first duty of a secret policeman . . ."). It is inevitable that some reports on their master would come from these new slaves—with whose proficiency in domestic work, by the way, Piso is said to be extremely pleased. I hope you will not consider this unauthorized "surveillance," and that you will construe what comes of it, whatever it may be, as worth reporting.

The one recurring item of some importance to us is this: Even now that the weather has suddenly turned colder, Piso takes walks in his garden several times a week, each time alone with one person; and very often the person is one of three of our doubtfuls—Lucan most frequently of all, droopy-eyed Scaevinus, dainty Quintianus.

This is natural, you will say, these are bosom friends of Piso's. But is it natural to walk slowly in a garden, out of all

earshot, in chilly weather? They are not out running or playing ball, working up a sweat before a bath. They talk earnestly.
Our agents cannot follow them, can only observe from a
distance.

And this seems to me important: Natalis is *not* one of these
strollers. He has not been seen in the house since the agents
were planted. I remind you, risking your rebuke, that Natalis
has a horse-nostril nose and bears watching.

Now, our known doubtfuls are not the only men who take
these walks with Piso. Two others particularly noticed in
recent days:

One of them is Plautius Lateranus. As you probably know,
he was accused by Claudius's informers eight years ago of
having committed adultery with the Empress Messalina—no
great distinction at that moment, he was a member of a brave
little army—but Claudius spared his life, simply stripped him
of his consular rank. This Himself restored in his first year
as Emperor—one of the acts of forgiveness that Seneca pushed
on Himself along with a number of speeches on clemency that
the Emperor mouthed (having the effect Seneca clearly
wanted, of advertising what a wise tutor Seneca was). Plautius
Lateranus is a sound man, a distinct possibility for Consul
next year. Two things concern us here—his eminence and his
debt to Seneca. Because of the privacy of these garden walks
we do not know why he is consulting with Piso.

And second, Subrius Flavus, a Tribune of a Praetorian
cohort, who is significant for three reasons: he is the only
military man we have seen in Piso's house since the famous
banquet; he has long been on very good terms, as you know,
with Himself; and *he* became, through Burrus when he was
alive, a friend to Seneca. Again, nothing to go on except his
presence.

All overheard conversations impeccable.

December 17

To PAENUS, Tribune of Secret Police, from TIGELLINUS

I henceforth dedicate my shit to all those who take garden rambles. Our informers are too good at their work. They have made great strollers of the Roman upper class. The patricians have become enthusiasts for the open air. This may even be why so many of them buy ostentatious villas in the country: so they can get a breath of fresh air with friends—and not be overheard.

But we must not be carried away, Paenus. Now you accuse Natalis because he is *not* doing something suspicious. Do you remember that your young informer, whose nose impressed you more than Natalis's, told us that Natalis was flirting with Piso's wife the night of Piso's banquet? It may be that Piso has caught the pair making the two-backed beast. That would stop a "friend" from taking walks in a man's garden.

And surely not the Tribune Flavus. He is a good hearty fellow, we see him often at the palace.

Don't forget that Piso has done nothing to offend. Gave a dinner at which Lucan stirred up a little storm—according to a volunteer informer whose head we found we had to split. Himself adores Piso. Piso is a charming man. Steady nerves, friend.

To RUFUS, Co-Commander, Praetorian Guard, from
    TIGELLINUS
Confidential.
Are you absolutely sure of Subrius Flavus? I have reasons for wanting to know.

To TIGELLINUS from RUFUS, Co-Commander, Praetorian
    Guard
Confidential.
Yes, I am absolutely sure of Subrius Flavus. I have reason

to be. I take him into my confidence on many matters of consequence. Of all the officers of the Guard, I think he loves Rome the most.

December 18

To RUFUS, Co-Commander, Praetorian Guard, from TIGELLINUS

Confidential.

I fully respect what you say about the Tribune Subrius Flavus, and it is not as a colleague but strictly as an officer of the Guard that I urge you to consider at least a brief interruption in your official confidences to this officer. Certain information that has come our way suggests that a period of watchful waiting might be advisable in your relationship with him.

To TIGELLINUS from RUFUS, Co-Commander, Praetorian Guard

Confidential.

At times you seem to forget that you and I are of equal rank. I cannot change my policy toward an officer on the basis of mysterious references to "certain information." Tell me what the information is, and I will consider whether "a period of watchful waiting" is in order.

To PAENUS, Tribune of Secret Police, from TIGELLINUS

Without withdrawing my previous endorsement of the Tribune Subrius Flavus, I would nevertheless wish to be informed at once if he is seen again on one of the private strolls you mentioned. At once.

December 20

To TIGELLINUS from PAENUS, Tribune of Secret Police

I am glad we kept our agent in Lucan's household. He is

under tight instructions. Now he has found this, rolled inside a scroll of fables of Phaedrus in a library box. The agent says he has been going through Lucan's library scrolls regularly, since they seemed to him such an obvious place for Lucan to hide things, and he can therefore vouch that this letter is of recent writing, certainly transmitted within the last two weeks.

Its substance, except for an interesting reference to Sleepy-Eyes, is of no particular consequence, but its salutation tells us a great deal. It and the letter finally confirm, without too clearly delineating it, the intimacy we have speculated about for so long—between Lucan and Epicharis. The fact that Lucan hid the letter may say more than the letter itself—though perhaps the reference to Polla might account for his wanting it out of sight. But then, why keep it?

"Epicharis to Lucan, greetings:

"I hated to see you so downcast. It seems to me that your life in the capital is stale. The circle you move in, Polla's ambition, all that wine and rich food. Next time you are here we must walk down toward the docks. I think you would take great strength for your poem from what your senses would tell you there in an hour, tell you about the pulsations of life, about men going on in the face of hardship, really about a possible future—the sounds and smells and sights—the spray-bleached orange color of the lazily furled sails telling of dangerous trips, the whack of the caulkers' hammers, the odor of hemp in the ropewalks and of fish in the nets up to dry, the swearing and quarrels of harbor people, the sunburned faces of coasting men, the oarsmen's sad sad chanteys, the sharp laughter of whores, the smells of smoke and wine and piss and new bread, the clatter of kegs and bronze and iron objects dropped on the pavements by the stevedores, the gossip and filthy jokes of custodians and porters and wharfmen, the grunts of carpenters and the chunking of their adzes in timbers—oh, Lucan, I adore the raw life of those sea people. Come soon. Come soon.

"I wear every day the silver brooch you gave me.

"Did you talk yet with Scaevinus?

"Can I prevail on your patience for one more errand, dear one? Mela needs some good strong leather—tanned ox-hide would be best—a single full skin. Would this be a dreadful bore?

"Repetition is what makes women shrews and naggers, but I risk this, repeating: Come soon, my heart's heart.

"Farewell."

December 21

To TIGELLINUS from PAENUS, Tribune of Secret Police
     Urgent.
The Tribune Subrius Flavus went out for a walk with Piso in the latter's garden this afternoon in nearly freezing rain.

To RUFUS, Co-Commander, Praetorian Guard, from
     TIGELLINUS
Confidential.
I cannot divulge the nature of the previously mentioned information on the Tribune Subrius Flavus. But it comes to us from a strong source and *has been repeated*. I again urge a period of discretion.

To TIGELLINUS from RUFUS, Co-Commander, Praetorian
     Guard
Confidential.
In your refusal to clarify the compromised position of an officer I trust, I perceive that you have decided on a suspension of confidences and a period of watchful waiting with respect

to another officer besides the Tribune Subrius Flavus. I mean
your so-called dear colleague, me. I do not like this phrase, "I
cannot divulge." I wonder whether I should not remind you
that the soldierly loyalty of the Praetorian Guard rests in large
measure with your "dear colleague," who is a professional
soldier, and not with you, even though you may be temporarily
closer to a certain ear. I have noticed in the past that whenever your judgment is questioned, you take the recourse of
whispering in that ear. Do so again. You can thus command
my actions but not my judgment.

December 22

To RUFUS, Co-Commander, Praetorian Guard, from
  TIGELLINUS
Confidential.

As always, my dear colleague (which you remain), you pull
me up short when I have behaved foolishly. The information
on Subrius Flavus is that he has been drawn into a homosexual
adventure that may expose him to blackmail. I would beg you
not to confront him with this information, because we are
trying, by the most delicate interventions, to see that the relationship is broken off without damage either to Flavus or to
the Guard.

To TIGELLINUS from RUFUS, Co-Commander, Praetorian
  Guard
Confidential.

This is better. All right, I will watchfully wait a while. Let
me know when the man is in the clear.

To PAENUS, Tribune of Secret Police, from TIGELLINUS
Secret.

For obvious reasons, in warning Faenus Rufus about the

Tribune Flavus, I have had to lie about the nature of our information. I told Rufus that Flavus and the Guard may be subject to blackmail because he is indiscreetly up a delicate ass. I tell you this in case Rufus should ask you about it.

To TIGELLINUS from PAENUS, Tribune of Secret Police
   Secret.

You are like a wary insect with long, sensitive feelers. Your antennae gave you signals this time that were accurate. Not an hour after your last message, Rufus approached me in casual conversation, most offhandedly at first but with a hard push as of a cattle horn before long, about what is suspected of the Tribune Flavus. Without going into any details, I reinforced your lie to him.

65 A.D.

January 7

To TIGELLINUS from PAENUS, Tribune of Secret Police

Another intercept of Cleonicus: Seneca to Lucan, and reply. You will like this, my stone-jawed friend. A little packet of swingle tow dipped in tar, the kind incendiaries use.

"Seneca to Lucan, greetings:

"It has taken me some days to digest the note you sent in answer to my last. I should by now be quite used to the way you strike at people, but I still have my breath knocked out by your blows. I wonder, with a low heart, what can be happening to our relationship. I love you still. I feel the need in you to think about the hard questions you have posed. I want to help you think about them, and I want to think about them, too. Our ways of thinking are different. I am a philosopher, I tend to organize and systematize; you are a poet, you search for the burning metaphor.

"Still, dear Lucan, I will nurse my bruises and try to respond. You now raise the question—if I may generalize from your metaphor—whether moral license paves the way to tyranny.

"Nero's lusts are diffuse; his emotions do not flow but surge; in all his erotic dealings there is the poison left over from his desire for his own mother's flesh and his loathing of her authority.

"I will write here—because I sense that you wish to think always of the effect of these matters upon the way the ruler rules—not about Nero's bizarre lusts, not about mere easements, but about relationships. There have been only three.

"I wrote a moment ago, 'the way the ruler rules.' Perhaps I should rather have written, 'the way the ruler is ruled.' You will see why.

"First there was Octavia. Nero's mother forced Nero's marriage to this poor stiff girl, so fair at the top of her face, with silky hair and a wide forehead and round dark eyes set far apart, but cursed below with a slot of a mouth and a tiny, weak, receding chin. The reason Agrippina chose her was all too obvious, even to Octavia: She was the daughter of Emperor Claudius and marriage to her would give Nero one more grip on the succession. Nero was fifteen and Octavia was thirteen when they were cemented as if by violence.

"Nero always despised her—regarded her as his mother's puppet. He treated her like a hated younger sister. First this forlorn, passive girl saw her father, then her brother poisoned so her husband could be Emperor. Then she saw her husband fall in love with a former slave girl, Acte. Then she saw him taken with even deeper passion for that ambitious vixen Poppaea.

"The people of Rome loved Octavia, even if Nero did not. She was the last direct descendant of Julius Caesar, and everyone knew of her helpless dignity. I once reproached Nero for the way he treated her, and he said, 'Beh, she ought to be content with a wife's jewelry.' He wanted all along to be rid of her, but my colleague Burrus would not allow it. 'Give her back her dowry if you divorce her,' he said. The trouble with that was: Her dowry was the Empire. Nero brought the matter up again later on, and Burrus, always a soldier—how wonderfully blunt he could be!—said, 'You asked me about that before. You heard what I said. When I say something once, don't ask me again.' No one speaks to Nero that way any more.

"Then three years ago Burrus died. Within a month Nero announced that Octavia was barren, and he divorced her and put her under military guard in the country. Twelve days later, Lucan, he married Poppaea.

"You remember the riots that followed—how the mob climbed to the Capitol, knocked over the new statues of Poppaea and broke out statues of Octavia that had been removed and set them up in the marketplace and at temples, with necklaces of flowers on them. Nero sent out the Guard with whips and drawn swords and broke the crowds. Then he bribed Anicetus, the coarse freedman who was Nero's tutor before me, to claim that he had slept with Octavia, and Anicetus offered up a heap of gross details he need never have invented. On the basis of those lies, Nero charged Octavia with adultery, treason, vice, and abortion, and banished her to Pandateria. A few weeks later soldiers stabbed her and cut off her head and brought it back to Rome for Poppaea to see. Octavia was just twenty-two when she died, poor child.

"Between Octavia and Poppaea had come Acte. Sweet Acte. She was the best person there has ever been in Nero's life, not excepting Burrus and your correspondent. Do not forget that Nero was only seventeen when he became the most powerful man on earth. He despised Octavia. He was a handsome and virile animal, and, as sometimes seems to happen, a portion of his temporal power flowed down into his private parts, transforming itself into the restless power that itches. He could have (as lately he has) commanded to his couch scores of noblewomen, whomever he wished, humiliating husbands and becoming an arsonist of jealousies. He even lusted for his mother. So when a young friend of his, Tullius Severus, a son of a freedman in the Imperial household, came to me in secret to say that his friend the Emperor had whispered to him that what he wanted to possess more than anything in his Empire was Acte, I saw that this was an opportunity not to be missed.

"I had noticed her. Who had not? She had been a slave captured in the East, a Pergamine, and was at the time a freedmaid sewing and carrying in the palace, a woman, not a girl, four years older than Nero, exactly what an inexperienced boy needed. She had a glowing olive skin and soft and yielding motions of torso, arms, and hands; she moved in a kind of dance of giving. In some ways she was like Epicharis—perhaps this explains what has puzzled you.

"I arranged for Annaeus Serenus, a dear friend of mine, to provide a cover for Nero with Acte. Serenus was the ostensible giver of gifts (Nero's), the one who whispered 'endearments' in her ear (when to meet Nero), the one who escorted her in the palace (to the edge of Nero's bed). Nero's mother quickly saw through the ruse, and her fury turned on me. I felt its full force on my face like the hot carrion-tainted breath of a mother wolf. Blown from such a beautiful face. This episode was what gave me Nero's open trust for the first time.

"Agrippina's curses, her raving about having a slave girl for a rival—'rival' was her word, and how much it said—her foul abuses acted perversely on Nero as an aphrodisiac, driving him more than ever like a satyr to Acte. This, too, Agrippina quickly understood, and she suddenly turned herself inside out, saying that her rages had been feigned, and she abruptly handed over to Nero the whole of her enormous fortune and even offered her own bed as a hiding place for his romps with Acte. This was too fast a shift of wind, and I warned Nero to watch out for foul weather. I need not have warned him, because he was her son and had drunk guile at her nipples.

"What did he do? Two master strokes. First, he stripped his mother's lover Pallas, who had been manager of the Imperial Treasury, of his money power, and thus deprived Agrippina of what was left of her influence. Second, he inspected the Imperial wardrobe and picked out a jeweled dress straight from the lushest fables of court magnificence, and he gave it to her with flourishes of liberality, as something he had chosen for her with his own hand. She perceived the insult—he was 'giving' her a tiny bauble from the everything she had surrendered to him—and she erupted into new screams.

"But Nero felt peaceful with Acte, and there followed three good years for Rome.

"Then Nero fell in love with Poppaea—was trapped by Poppaea's tricks. Acte, patient creature, retired to a hillside villa at Velitrae and prayed at a temple for Nero's love to come back. It never did.

"So then there was—and now there still is—Poppaea. Poppaea's mother was the most beautiful woman in Rome in her time; I used to tremble, actually to tremble, when I looked at her. You will have observed that Poppaea herself is handsome rather than beautiful; she has her superb amber-colored hair and that pinkish, radiant complexion. She has everything but the exquisite softness of her mother; indeed, she has survived, and Nero's mother is now dead, precisely because she proved even harder at the core than Agrippina. That kind of hardness shows in a woman's mouth. Poppaea has a soldier's mouth.

"Poppaea was originally married to a good man, Crispinus, and had a son by him. But then along came Otho, the wildest and handsomest young man in the capital, one of Nero's best friends, along with Severus. Poppaea dropped Crispinus like a stone and married Otho. Now Otho made the mistake of bragging to Nero about Poppaea's late-at-night talents. Otho would get up from a banquet saying he had to hurry home to highborn sweets being kept warm for him by highborn thighs of just the right roundness; he described Poppaea's movements on the couch a bit too vividly and at least once too often.

"Nero invited them both to a banquet and placed Poppaea at his own side, and she began at once her favorite game: tease-cock. Within a few days Nero and Poppaea were meeting alone. She drove him half mad. First she would say she adored his powerful arms and his charioteer's neck. But the moment he asked for more than words she began to praise Otho. No, she couldn't stay. She was a married woman. She preferred Otho's style and taste to Nero's. At home everything was smart, dashing, refined; here at the palace you saw banality and vulgarity, an Emperor married to a piece of wood and enslaved to a slave girl, low taste, low associations. At other times she mocked Nero with being not a man but only a son, a helpless child, Agrippina's toy. Why, she asked, had Nero been afraid to marry a real woman—a woman, for example, like herself? Because such a woman would have made him realize that not Nero but Nero's mother ruled Rome.

"You know the outcome. Otho sent out of town as governor of Lusitania. Acte off to the hills. Octavia divorced. Poppaea the Empress.

"But winning the great prize did not soften Poppaea. After the riots in support of Octavia, she made a hair-tearing scene—result, Octavia's head on a tray. She kept on taunting

Nero about being nothing but his mother's tool—result, the grotesquely handled matricide.

"Oh, this one rides very high, Lucan. You look for metaphors: She parades through the city drawn by mules shod with gold. Nero is simply one of these precious-footed beasts of burden. She drives him, she moves him with goad and lash: now repeats dark threats of astrologers, now dabbles in Oriental superstitions, now drills a leak in his treasury, now flirts with the Jewish dancer Aliturus, now provokes him to feigned indifference when you and I give him evidence of plots against him. She is shrewd, shrewd. Every day she models herself more closely on the one woman whom Nero cannot shake, even though she is dead. On Agrippina.

"Agrippina is the malign creative force from which Nero cannot free himself. Poppaea is Nero's new mother. Do you know that she bathes daily in a marble tubful of asses' milk—immerses herself over and over in the maternal fluid? Her perfect skin is redolent with the sweetness for which Nero is helplessly nostalgic. She knows what she is doing: keeping Agrippina, whom Nero thought he had murdered, alive, alive, alive.

"These have been the only women who mattered. Really only one, as you see, has mattered—and she not one of the three. If you think about these relationships, you will see that Nero's licentiousness has been peripheral. His lusts are his cries of pain. Not of joy, not of exuberance, but of pain. They are his protests. They are a form of his cruelty, and his cruelty is a perverted form of his desire to be Augustus—to be wise, just, clement, and loved; to be what I always asked him to be, a good man, a good father. Do you see that? His tyranny is not fatherly, but motherly—and modeled, alas, on the sort of mother that Agrippina was. If only an Acte had been his mother—or a woman like my Paulina, or like Mela's Epicharis.

"You will find the flashing image that sets free the truth; I must laboriously generalize. The gala at the lake, the repeated episodes of loss of control to which many Romans have abandoned themselves, the transmutation of realities of power into fantasies of sensuality—yes, Lucan, these do finally become the essence of tyranny, of both the formation and the acceptance of tyranny. A tyrant is a captive in his own flesh. Nero is not the only tyrant; many men in Rome are in his fix. Forgive me, Lucan, but I see in your Polla something of Nero's Poppaea. Is that unjust? Why are you so cruel to me?

"And so we are back to the question: Who is to blame for tyranny—the tyrant or the tyrannized? Who is to blame for your outbursts against me—you or I?

"Farewell."

"Lucan to Seneca, greetings:

"If what you write is true—I am not sure yet whether I accept it, but if it *is* true, then the matricide was actually an aborted blow for freedom, a blind effort on Nero's part to purge himself of the materials of tyranny. Tell me about it, Seca. You have told me in the past that you were right in the midst of that crime. Tell me about it. I must know where freedom lies.

"I do not mean to be cruel to you. I hate cant. Sometimes you seem to me to be merely justifying yourself when I have asked you instead, because you are a great philosopher, to teach me—and Rome—how to live better.

"But write to me as soon as you can about the crime.
"Farewell."

January 18

To TIGELLINUS from PAENUS, Tribune of Secret Police
So far I have taken the following steps:

1. All agents are being approached with fresh admonitions and instructions: discretion in searching, following, conducting direct and indirect interrogations, soliciting information, bribing, blackmailing, filching of written materials for copying, etc. You will appreciate that since we are dealing with cells of from three to five persons only, and must penetrate one after another with this new training, the entire process cannot be completed overnight.

2. Great stress is being placed on circumspection in disposals. Every man is being impressed with the fact that a dead body may not tell the whole truth but never tells a lie.

3. Strict warnings have been issued against overenthusiasm in punishments and disciplinary actions short of death. Here, you will be the first to realize, the task of inculcating subtlety is not an easy one. Rough work attracts rough men.

4. In certain current surveillances we will not change agents until the refurbishing of the service is complete; this includes surveillances of the entire list of doubtfuls in the specific case you referred to in your instructions.

5. We are attempting to instill the purest forms of loyalty and patriotism in all our men. You must realize that wherever money and sex are used as instruments of police work, love of Himself and of Rome become subsidiary considerations in the minds of the types of persons we are obliged to enlist.

6. I ask more than patience from you; I ask you to practice restraint. Forgive me for this observation: There are times when your interference in our operations is both hasty and crude. It is now clear that in spite of his indiscretion we should not have disposed of the young poet Curtius Marsus, nose-of-all-noses, so hastily. I would give anything for a man with his kind of entree into the circle of writers that presently concerns us. You will say: Nothing is so urgent as the security of the Person. I agree, but I would add: Nothing is so dangerous as a tense secret policeman.

January 19

To PAENUS, Tribune of Secret Police, from TIGELLINUS

Reflections on vigilance, toward the purification of your service:

A secret policeman naturally loves his work. The very fact of secrecy is thrilling. One is privileged to know something, no matter how small or sordid a thing it may be, that almost no one else knows. Do not overvalue patriotism; your preaching to your agents on this score will be taken for what it is— bombast. No, fear for oneself and a love of humiliating others are the shining motives of your cadres. Sex is an unstable form of pressure and should be resorted to only when there is a notorious weakness to be exploited. Perversions cut two ways; the agent is often trapped by his gift for entrapment. Love of discipline, which has a social value, must always be clearly differentiated from love of hurting, which is wanton and dangerous to the lover. Money is your best tool. Men love money more than country, wife, mistress, perversion, reputation, or, in some cases, life itself. We can always find clean money to do dirty work. But a warning: He who handles and disburses such money often develops the delusion that it belongs to him. This statement can be broadened, as follows: Power sometimes fills purses, often empties heads.

I know you will continue to be grateful for my advice and interference when they are needed.

By the way, have you found the Farentum dagger?

January 20

To TIGELLINUS from PAENUS, Tribune of Secret Police

No, we have not found the Farentum dagger. I would remind you that there are at present three hundred forty thousand adult male citizens in the urban populace. Not to mention at least that many again—women and children. Not to mention an even larger number of slaves. A garrison of twelve thousand soldiers. Diplomats, merchants, travelers. No, we have not found it. But we are looking. All seven hundred fifty-three of us are looking.

February 1

To TIGELLINUS from TULLIUS SEVERUS, Senator

You asked me to see what I could do with the Consul Vestinus about his rough tongue in the presence of the Emperor.

I have talked with Vestinus twice now, both times on easy terms at social occasions. The first time my approach took the form of teasing; his response was surprisingly modest and sober—he had taken office as Consul only two weeks before, and he was wearing this demeanor like suitable clothing of office. The second time was yesterday, when my approach, while casual, was more serious than the first time.

His reply, I am sorry to report, was worse than curt. With a gesture he called his bodyguard around him; a second gesture pointed out to me a kind of protective dance the bodyguards began around his person, like a buzzing of bees around a disturbed hive, which suggested, beneath an elegant series of motions on their part, a hostile message from their master, something like this (as I decoded it): *Watch out, false friend. You are a messenger. I do not like your message.*

And then he lowered his head, as if, as Consul, to dismiss me from an audience. It was an unpleasant performance. The hostility of this dance of the bodyguard, you see, was not really aimed at me.

February 9

To PAENUS, Tribune of Secret Police, from TIGELLINUS
Discretion.

The literary evening of which you and I disapproved is to take place next week. In order to provide even a minimum of security in this situation, whose dangers we cannot accurately estimate, we will have to resort to a measure of which I usually do not approve. We will have to enlist some of the guests as bodyguards pro tem. It will be obvious to you that the utmost discretion will be required, as the nature of the suspected danger cannot under any circumstances be revealed.

Two men come to mind as likely candidates for this delicate responsibility: Petronius, who hates Seneca and Lucan (but Seneca, by the way, has had the audacity to decline to come from Nomentum); and Bassus, who is a good strong fellow and, I gather, on speaking terms with Lucan but not much more. Vagellius is too close to Seneca. Calpurnius has been patronized by Piso. Celsus, of course, is feeble.

Do what you can. But do it carefully, Paenus. Bear in mind that when it comes to action, most writers are fools.

February 13

To TIGELLINUS from PAENUS, Tribune of Secret Police

Another intercept of Cleonicus. Notice two phrases which I have underlined near the beginning of this copy; to say nothing of the way the letter ends.

"Seneca to Lucan, greetings:

"What a peaceful day I have had! I was up long before the sun and read some letters of Epicurus—one especially to Idomeneus struck me with its clarity and good sense, saying, for example, that *one should attempt nothing except at the time when it can be attempted suitably and seasonably.* He wrote, 'Do not doze when you are meditating escape.' Later I worked outside with my bailiff and a squad of slaves. I love the country chores of winter, *the period of waiting and planning for seed time.* We turned some compost and did the cold-weather pruning. In the afternoon I wrote a felicitous letter to my dear friend Lucilius. I exercised and bathed—perhaps I can confess to you, dear Lucan, that I had Cleonicus light a fire to take the chill off the water, make it tepid. My old bones cannot stand the frigid baths I took for so many winters, in water warmed only by the sun. I dined on fruit and bran. And now I sit down to chat with you. What pleasures I have!

"But now—now my heart grows heavy for the first time all day, because I remember that you asked me to write to you about Agrippina, about her death. I will try.

"Agrippina was the most seductive, the most powerful, the angriest, the most terrifying human being—no, not person, but *energy*—I have ever known. She had white-hot charcoal burning in her bowels. She used everything she had—beauty, sex, wealth, wits—for one end only, to dominate, dominate. When Nero was four years old, a Chaldean fortune-teller said that her son would rule the world and slaughter his mother. Her wild cry in answer was, 'I don't *care* if he kills me, so long as he becomes Emperor.' Later, when she had in fact maneuvered and murdered to bring Nero to power, she developed a new desire: to rule the ruler; and she put Burrus, the fist, and me, the mind, in charge of policy, believing we would be her tools, since both of us were indebted to her, Burrus for his appointment as Commander of the Praetorian Guard, and I for my summons home from exile. Then, when she found that Burrus and I had more character than she had thought, she began a long struggle with us. We won—she died violently—not because of our greater strength but because of Nero's weakness—his subjection to Poppaea, a servitude that made him compound incest with matricide to free himself from subjection to one woman so he could be fully subject to another.

"With Agrippina, one had to be constantly aware of

this sequence: She was the sister of one Emperor, Caligula, wife of his successor, Claudius, and mother of *his* successor, Nero.

"They say she had incestuous relations with all three. I never went out of my way to verify this, but it was clear that she threw every moral restraint to the winds when she wanted anything, and I have come to believe that she may have thought of incest as an ornament and instrument of policy.

"Caligula is said to have committed incest as a matter of habit with all three of his sisters. Drusilla was his favorite; Julia, Agrippina. They say Caligula's grandmother Antonia caught him when he was seventeen writing infamy with a throbbing stylus in Drusilla's belly on a table in the library of Antonia's town house, and later he took Drusilla from her husband, no mean man, an ex-Consul, Longinus, and announced to the world that his sister was his lawful wife. Once at a banquet he had his real wife recline at his right and he rotated his three sister-wives' in the place of honor on his left. After Drusilla died, he put out Julia and Agrippina as quail for his favorites. Thus Agrippina very early came to think she had an imperial playnook between her thighs.

"Then when she had sex with Claudius as his Empress she was also committing incest, because she was his firsthand niece, as daughter of his brother Germanicus.

"As to Agrippina and Nero—worst of all, mother and son—I have seen enough to call myself a witness. Just one example: I saw her approach him, during the period when she was using every wile she knew to crush his affair with Acte, one hot afternoon, when he had been banqueting and was drunk; she was dressed in a sheer tunic through which her whole body could be seen, and they went for a ride in a curtained litter, and when they returned they were obliviously— imperially—what *hubris!*—careless who saw the stains of ejaculations on his and her clothing.

"My relationship with Agrippina and Julia had started with the fact that they were daughters of Germanicus. If there ever was a pure man, it was he. After Augustus died, the legions in Germany did not want to accept Tiberius as Emperor and begged Germanicus, their commander, to take the purple on the surge of their arms, but he honorably refused and insisted on their allegiance to Tiberius. He had a glorious, brief career, one of courage and integrity; he was handsome, a hypnotic orator, a scholar of Greek and Roman writings, author of some creditable comedies in the Greek style, a man of extraordinary kindness and modesty. He often fought hand-to-hand in the field. He died at thirty-four at Antioch, and there was suspicion of assassination, because when they gathered his ashes from the pyre they found his whole heart among the bones; it is well known that a heart steeped in poison will not burn. Germanicus, as I fear you are too young to know, was the most beloved Roman of his time, the hero of my youth, and after he died—I was eighteen—I spent much time with his family. I was in a stage of daydreaming about various careers I might have, and I often wanted to model myself on Germanicus, and I imagined combats which ended with my magnanimously sparing the lives of my beaten enemies. (Burrus, later my partner in influence, was Germanicus in small.) Of all the children, I was drawn closest to Julia, who caught in her dear hands the gentle side of her father. I always thought I could bring out in Nero large traces of his grandfather. But one of Germanicus's children, Caligula, the Little Boot who grew up the pet of the Legions in the field, became a mad animal; and another, Agrippina, a kind of sorceress. How could those two have come from the loins of that noble man?

"It was clear to Burrus and to me, from the first days of Nero's reign, that we were going to have to fight with our very lives for the Germanicus in him and against the Caligula—

Agrippina in him. Indeed, I had been fearful of his dark side for a long time before he came to power; I remember that the night after Agrippina appointed me his tutor, I dreamed that I was trying to give a lesson to an insane, dwarfed, adult Caligula. From the moment of Nero's accession, Agrippina controlled him. The password Nero gave the Guard on the first day of his rule was 'Best of Mothers.' When Nero consulted on policy at the Palatine, she stood behind a curtain in a doorway to eavesdrop on every decision. Once some Armenian ambassadors were being received. I saw Agrippina coming forward with the intention clearly written on her face of mounting the dais and presiding as co-ruler with her son, and I quickly motioned to Nero to rise from his seat and step down the hall to greet his mother. This filial act adjourned the reception—and barely cut her off from a shocking claim.

"I have already told you how I encouraged Nero's affair with Acte, and how that love did indeed shake the mother's hold on Nero. When Agrippina felt her influence slipping, she resorted to wild threats that she would switch her support to Britannicus, who would have been the rightful heir to Claudius. This only led to Nero's murder of Britannicus. Then when Poppaea began taunting Nero with being his mother's puppet, and Nero's always unstable lusts were cut from their moorings, tending at times to Acte, at times to Poppaea, and at times to others of both sexes, there came a bad period. It was during the consulship of Vipstanus and Fonteius, I well remember. Quite often after the noon meal, when Nero was apt to be drunk, in the hot weather, Agrippina would present herself in voluptuous clothes and offer herself to Nero. I wasted no time in sending Acte to him to tell him that Agrippina was boasting of her 'love affair' with her son, that all Rome was talking about it, and that the troops would not stand for an incestuous ruler.

"This brought him up short—though not, alas, to his

senses. He stripped his mother of her private guard and he began to harass her, hiring men to start lawsuits against her and toughs to keep passing by her various villas in Rome, Tusculum, and Antium at night, keeping her awake by shouting abuse and obscenities.

"But then it suddenly seemed he had a change of heart. He decided to spend the five-day festival of Minerva by the sea at Baiae, and he invited his mother to sail down from Antium to join him. I was with him when he greeted her like an adoring son; he seated her above himself at the banquet that night; he was a playful boy at first, a thoughtful ruler later. I walked down to the harbor when he saw her off—she was staying halfway across the bay at Bauli. I was vaguely aware that there was some mix-up about vessels. It was a brilliant starlit night, and the sea was calm. Nero was effusive in his farewells—like a lover repeatedly kissed her eyes and breasts. We went back to the villa and to bed.

"I was roughly awakened far along in the night and was ordered to Nero's bedroom. There I was joined by Burrus and also by Anicetus—the freedman who tutored Nero before I did. And there were two others there: a sea captain named Herculeius, and a centurion of marines, one Obaritus. Nero was pale, sweating, trembling. Out from him and from the others in gobbets and lumps a story was vomited:

"Nero, having decided to get rid of his mother, had consulted that devious packet of evils, my predecessor in tutelage, Anicetus, who suggested an insanely complicated device for the murder: a vessel that would be designed to fall apart at sea with Agrippina aboard. Anicetus argued that disasters on the water were so commonplace that this way Nero would escape all suspicion; afterward the Emperor would piously put up shrines and temples in honor of his dear dead mother.

"Nero liked the plan and ordered it carried out. Agrip-

pina agreed to join him at Baiae and sailed down from Antium to the Bauli house in her own trireme. Before the banquet she was told her ship had been damaged in a collision at
the mooring but that a beautiful vessel had been put at her
disposal to take her across the bay to join her son. She gave
Nero a fright—had she been told of the plot?—by deciding to
go to his villa by litter instead. But Nero thought he carried
off the banquet well, and she agreed to go home in the vessel.

"Nero waited up, in a crisis of nerves, to hear of the
outcome. Several hours later a freedman of Agrippina's, Agerinus, was ushered in from the gates of the villa, and he breath-
lessly said that Agrippina had sent him running to tell Nero
that the gods had been good to him and to her, that she had
been miraculously spared after an accident out on the water,
that Nero was not to worry and should not visit her, because
she needed rest. The only details Agerinus could add were
that Agrippina had swum some distance toward shore—what
a powerful life force she was!—and had then been picked up
in a skiff by fishermen who had been wakened by shouting
and had put out on the water to see what the trouble was;
she had a wound on her shoulder.

"This message panicked Nero. He could imagine Agrippina going to the Praetorian Guard or to the Senate with a
story of his treachery, or even starting a general revolt of
slaves. Within an hour Herculeius and Obaritus, who had
been aboard the vessel, and Anicetus, who had been waiting
on shore, arrived at Nero's villa and told him what they knew.
After the craft had started out, they said, Agrippina had lain
down on a couch and had begun talking with great joy about
Nero's sweet behavior toward her that night, with her favorite
attendants, Acerronia, reclining at her feet, and Crepereius,
standing near the helm.

"The ceiling over the couch, which had been weighted

with lead, suddenly collapsed. Crepereius was instantly killed, but protuberances over the couch saved Agrippina and Acerronia. The mechanisms of further collapse of the vessel failed for some reason. Herculeius quickly ordered the few crewmen who were in on the plot to rush to one side of the craft to capsize it, but those who did not know about the plan scrambled to the other side to right it. At any rate, Agrippina and Acerronia slid or were pushed into the water.

"The men heard a voice shouting, 'I am your Emperor's mother! Save me!' Those who knew of the plot at once struck at the splashing form with oars, boathooks, and punting poles. When they finally hauled a dead form aboard they saw that the one who had claimed to be Nero's mother was, after all, her attendant Acerronia, who had evidently realized that the crewmen were out to kill her mistress, and who had proved to be a courageous and loyal woman.

"Agrippina was nowhere to be seen. When the crewmen reached shore they found a huge babbling crowd of fishermen and country people on the beach, clambering over piers and moored fishing boats, and wading out into the water, excited as simple people will become. They spoke of a miracle. They told the crewmen that the Emperor's mother had been taken from the water alive by some of their friends. Her rescuers had carried her to her own villa at Lucrinus.

"Nero was by this time frantic with fear. He called Agrippina's messenger Agerinus back into his room and told him to repeat his story before witnesses, and while he was doing it Nero dropped a knife in front of Agerinus—it was so crudely done; everyone could see it—and began shouting, 'Look! Look! The assassin! My mother sent him to kill me.'

"Then he called for Burrus and for me. Nero was almost incoherent, and the others had quite lost their nerve, too, being afraid that this panicky, guilty Nero would have them all killed for their mishandling of the murder. How awful to see an Emperor of Rome reduced to such a cringing figure! I need hardly say that Burrus and I were appalled—not only by the stink of the crime but by the idiotic plan and by the botch that had been made of it.

"I believe the bungling to have been inherent in Nero's divided soul. He was driven by the struggle within himself to choose crude help of the kind a fool like Anicetus would give him. Perhaps you are right that he had some urge, mute and dim, to rid himself of what you called 'the materials of tyranny'—but in the moment of crisis he did not turn to Burrus and to me, or to the Germanicus in himself; he turned for counsel to the brute Anicetus, to the very trait in himself that he wanted to murder.

"Burrus and I stood silent a long time. What could we say? We were now witnesses. Any word would be a word of complicity in one horror or another. It came to me with terrible force that either Nero or his mother must now die violently.

"I spoke a few short words to Burrus. 'Can the Guard take over?'

"Burrus, cold as stone, said, 'I will not allow it. The Praetorians remember Germanicus, and they would never lay a finger on a child of his. Anicetus started this. Let him finish it.'

"Anicetus, afraid for his life, said he was willing, and Nero then displayed, even in his panic, a touch of his mother's bitter irony. 'This night makes me Emperor at last,' he said, 'and look, Seneca and Burrus, my wise men, look who gives me the gift—a former slave.'

"And so Anicetus, Herculeius, and Obaritus went with some marines to Agrippina's villa.

"As they broke into Agrippina's room the lone slave

girl who was with her ran out, and they heard Agrippina say, 'Do you, too, leave me now?'

"The three men closed around Agrippina's couch. She said with great calm, 'If you have come to ask how I am, tell my son that I am better. If you have come to commit a crime, you are the guilty ones. My son would not dare to harm me.'

"Herculeius hit her on the head with a club, but it was a glancing blow. Then, seeing Obaritus pull out a sword, she proved herself to be the tyrant's mother through and through. She pulled up her tunic and uncovered her naked privacy and spread her thighs and shouted, 'Stick it in there, you whore chaser. That's where Nero came from.'

"All three stabbed her near the heart.

"And so it was done. Have you ever noticed, Lucan, how a son, after a mother dies whom he has loved, will subtly change and become more and more like what she had been? This happened to Nero. The murder took place more than five years ago, and in all the time since then I have seen the Germanicus slipping away and the Agrippina taking hold in him. Every single day he has grown more brutal, more witty, more avaricious, more seductive, more suspicious, more lascivious, more conceited, more power-mad—yes, Lucan, more and more a tyrant, yet more and more at one with the temper of Rome.

"I spent years trying to get away from Agrippina alive —only to find that she lived on in her son. I have finally broken away to Nomentum; I have managed to remove myself physically from her-in-him. But how can Rome remove itself from her-in-him, from him-in-itself, from itself-in-itself? All of Rome cannot move to quiet Nomentum. This is Rome's sad fix just now: Agrippina the sorceress lives. Nero lives.

"But do you follow what I am saying? Rome cannot

deny the spirit of Caligula–Agrippina–Nero coiled in its heart of hearts. It would still be there even if Nero did not live. Germanicus, Augustus, Burrus, Cato—they are in Rome's heart, too. Which brings us back, Lucan, to your question: Whose 'fault' is tyranny? What can a writer do?

"For myself: I failed in my effort to turn a single Roman from the Agrippina side to the Germanicus side.

"I shudder. Another time, Lucan, I will write of happier matters. My lovely day is in ruins around me. See my shaky handwriting. Here in my dark room I tremble—for all of us, for dear Rome.

"Farewell."

February 15

To PAENUS, Tribune of Secret Police, from TIGELLINUS

I hasten to assure you that the literary evening went off without any of what we had feared. Not, however, without tension.

Thanks mostly to the wit of Petronius, there was much laughter early in the evening. The dinner was held in a new dining hall of the palace, one that has a fretted ceiling of ivory, whose little panels rotated, at one moment at the height of the fun, and the company was showered with flowers. Our scribblers were enchanted by this device.

After the banquet, Himself proposed some "controversies," like those which teachers of rhetoric throw at their students. It was a delicious situation, with Himself—in his best mood, imposing as his own colossal statue out on the ramp of the Golden House—taking the part of the rhetorician and treating these vain hacks like schoolboys. And everyone got into such good humor that for over an hour I could not help thinking, Paenus, that you and I had been having bad, or possibly mad, dreams.

But then, in the midst of the gaiety, Himself (who, by the way, had not failed to install on a pedestal beside his couch the figurine of the girl who wards off plots; had not failed, either, to pour her a libation, casually lying to the writers, saying that she was a private goddess of his who tended his venereal energies) suddenly proposed a controversy on the topic of an assassination of an Emperor.

I tell you, Paenus, I felt as if he had hit me a punch with his big fist in the pit of my stomach. But I was bound to remain silent and passive; or at least to limit myself to laughter, with which I covered my anxiety. Himself had at first not wanted me even to be present, but I had insisted, for reasons you can understand, and he finally agreed, on condition that I would not once open my mouth to speak, saying: Yes, it would be good to have one brutish ignoramus among the wits, just as a single gross garnet should always be set in a collar of rubies to highlight the value of the true stones. You may be sure that if my mouth was sealed I kept my eyes open.

The self-control on the part of our doubtfuls was extraordinary. It reminded me of your thin gleanings from the occasion at the Lake of the Golden House. Lucan, who was at his most electric, delivered a brilliant declamation on the topic, and the only possible sign of disturbance on his part was a flaming blush that stayed on his face the whole time he talked, though he had his ashen look before and after. But his words were gracious and grave, and I was actually afraid that Himself would soften and impulsively forgive Lucan everything and ask him back into the Circle of Friends.

What saved—or reversed—the situation was the obvious jealousy of Petronius, who insisted on following Lucan and did something at once hilarious, ugly, and frightening. With that viciously penetrating precision of his, he parodied Lucan's declamation in such a way as to render Lucan's impeccable

arguments ironic and therefore, all of a sudden, nakedly subversive. Only Petronius could have gotten away with such an
outrage. But it was a dangerous thing to have done. It released an energy in the doubtfuls.

There was in fact a moment during Petronius's declamation
when I became greatly alarmed, because it suddenly seemed
to me that the dangerous game about which we have speculated was about to be played out.

I saw Piso touch Lucan's arm. It seemed to me to be a
signal. Lucan became extremely agitated. Others of the doubtfuls glanced at each other.

We were abysmally ill-prepared to defend Himself. Petronius, whom you had, let us say, half alerted, was speaking.
Bassus, who was with us, was nodding from overeating, over-
drinking, and boredom. I half rose in my seat.

A most unexpected cascade of laughter from Himself broke
the tension—seemed to disconcert the doubtfuls, especially
Lucan, the person who seemed most prone to act; I took the
cue and laughed with Himself.

Himself kept glancing at me as if to ridicule the fears I had
expressed to him beforehand. I saw that the moment of peril
had passed. I had a queer feeling of emptiness, of having seen
a ghost. Had I been imagining things? I know no more than
I did before the evening. At least we got by it.

February 18

To TIGELLINUS from PAENUS, Tribune of Secret Police

You will be interested, I wager, in someone else's view of
the literary evening. Intercepted letter:

"Lucan to Seneca, greetings:

"Those people have gone mad. Let me tell you about
the banquet you missed. Do you remember, Seca, that in one

letter I said they are going to drive us to what we shrink from even imagining? I believe this. They have begun it. In your answer to me then you philosophized blandly about what a writer should be and do—or mostly, rather, about what he should not do. They are making us think hard about what a *man* should do.

"After the banquet was over, Piso came home with me, and we sat up till dawn, alternately talking and weeping. As you know, I have in the past thought Piso a pleasant but trivial man. But I felt very close to him during this night in which we shared our grief over what is happening to Rome. My esteem for him deepened. During the dinner I think he saved my life by one timely gesture—but I will come to that.

"What made the occasion so heartbreaking was that up until a certain point we were all immersed in the old innocent gaiety. Nero was quick and mirthful, and unaffectedly courteous. He behaved toward me as if he regretted the proscription and was on the point of lifting it. Even Petronius, who is high in favor with Nero just now, was unusually restrained at the beginning of the evening; he could not help throwing a few darts, but they were more playful than hurtful. And, as if he had been cautioned beforehand, he kept the full distance of a plow and a team of oxen from me.

"Will you stand back, dear Seca, and allow me to say that I felt left out, that I realized I had missed the radiant luxury of the palace life, that my old affection for Nero stirred like a sleeping bear in the wintry cave of my heart?

"All went well until the banquet had been cleared except for the wineglasses, which were filled again to the brim each time we took a sip. Then Nero proposed that we be a school of rhetoric, he the teacher, setting controversies to be declaimed on. This began in fun. He set us first a controversy I vaguely remembered as one of your father's, my grand-

father's. Your absence had been noted, I should tell you, at
least ten times during the evening, with regrets tinged with
pique. 'Seneca would have liked that . . . Seneca would have
said . . . Lucan, what does your uncle think about so-and-
so? . . .' Perhaps I should have pricked up my ears when we
got as our first controversy one originally set by Grandfather:

"*A husband and wife have taken an oath not to survive each other. The husband goes on a voyage and sends a
messenger to his wife with news that he has been accidentally
killed. She jumps off a cliff into the sea, but fishermen rescue
her, and she is restored to health. Her father orders her to
leave her husband. She refuses. She is disinherited.*

"During the declamations, amid the wild laughter, I
suddenly felt queasy. My revived tenderness toward Nero was
replaced by a surge of anger and fear. There leaped into my
mind a haunting image: the dwarfs, hunchbacks, and cripples
in the foot race by the lake at that gala in the gardens of the
Golden House. It suddenly seemed that all this game of wits
that we were engaged in was another such contest, perhaps
devised for Nero's entertainment by that oaf Tigellinus, who
was present but sat uncharacteristically silent all evening—
that *we* were the deformed, we the helpless ones struggling
for some undefined prize of favor or influence. Suddenly all
the intellectual sparkle and the display of skills were disgusting, depraved, groveling. Later, as I was talking with Piso at
home, it came out of me that this plunge of mine into outrage
came while one of the declaimers was touching on the
woman's rescue by fishermen, and I must have remembered
at the edge of my mind your description of Nero's mother
being rescued in vain one criminal night. How could Nero sit
there gargling wine and laughter?

"A second controversy:

"*Under the law, a man must support his parents or be*

imprisoned. A man kills one of his brothers for being adulterous and another for being tyrannical, though in both cases the father had begged for mercy. The son takes a voyage and is kidnapped by pirates, who write to the father for ransom. The father replies that he will pay double if the pirates will cut off his son's hands. The pirates' outlaw honor is offended, and they release the son. The son refuses to support his father.

"The declamations begin. All who try them except Petronius, who is intoxicated with his present pre-eminence, skirt gingerly around the matter of the brother killed for tyranny. There is on this account a certain awkwardness yet still much laughter. Perhaps others besides myself have shuddered at the thought that the man who set this topic has on his hands the blood of his stepfather, his brother, his wife, his mother. . . .

"But suddenly Nero stops the declamations. 'This is boring,' he says. He is pale and seems pleasurably agitated. 'I have thought of a better controversy. Try this one, my dear friends.'

"And then the Emperor of Rome sets this for us to weave our wits around:

"*An Emperor of Rome swears the Senate to loyalty to him and faithfulness to its laws. One of its laws decrees that murder shall be punished by death, another that desecration of an altar is likewise a capital crime. Lightning strikes the altar of the Temple of Jupiter. The augurs advise the sacrifice of a prominent person. The Emperor, who has tired of his wife, provides her for the propitiation. A Senator stabs the Emperor in the name of his oath. The Senate refuses to bring the Senator to trial.*

"Only one man belched laughter along with Himself when this topic had been proposed—Tigellinus. And it was then that I remembered that sentence in my earlier letter to you, Seca. They are driving us into a corner. They need our guilt. They are mad. I wonder why they have chosen us to be the instruments and victims of their awful need. Why we who want only to be free to create works of art for the glory of Rome? Is it because we are the only ones who can recognize horror when we see it? Is sensitivity the one unbearable threat to the powerful?

"My reaction to the proposal of this third controversy was, above all, one of great sadness. I saw that for me there would be no road, no road at all, no road ever, back to friendship with Nero and back to peace of mind. I looked at Nero and suddenly saw, beyond the wine-marinated eyes and cheeks tight with pleasure and malice, another face—the one you described in your last letter to me, Seca: the face of the Nero who had learned that his mother had been rescued by fishermen. The face of the tyrannicidal tyrant—cringing in guilt and fear. I was frightfully sorry for him, and I hated him.

"And so when it came time for my declamation I was careful to treat the topic with great respect, and I cast my response almost in the form of a plea. I felt great agitation and emotion. The good side of me, which you, dear Seca, have tried to nourish, came forward. And I thought I made Nero listen to me.

"But when I was finished Petronius, obviously impressed by the pure feeling I had put into my declamation, and out of a motive of wishing to push me into the shadows— seeing a rather easy job of it because I had been so serious— asked the 'teacher' to be heard. He proceeded, with that devilish cleverness of his, to turn everything I had said right inside out. Nero and Tigellinus topped the laughter of all the others. At one moment I felt that I was going to lunge at someone. I did not clearly know at whom—Petronius, Nero, or Tigellinus, one of the three. At Caligula, Agrippina, or

Nero, one of the three. At part of myself. At part of Rome. I felt a fool's action pouring into my limbs. It was just then that Piso, beside me, understanding more than I had thought he could understand, gently touched my arm. His tender gesture had great force—indeed, had the effect of putting chains and fetters on me.

"Nero and Tigellinus began once again to howl with laughter. I felt suddenly hollow—an empty, empty, empty man.

"Ah, Seca, I am afraid. I am afraid because I am losing touch with my craft. I am finding it very hard to write poetry. I no longer even think in terms of that question you and I have wearied so: What is a writer's responsibility?

"Farewell."

February 25

To TIGELLINUS from PAENUS, Tribune of Secret Police
Our agents in the Piso household report:

In the ten days since the literary evening, there has been a marked increase in the strolling-by-twos (Piso and a variable one other) in Piso's gardens. In these ten days Piso has moved three times: to his estate near Lake Albanus, to Baiae, back to Rome. At each place, these walks. As before, sleepy-eyed Scaevinus, dainty Quintianus. Again, not Natalis. Lucan less than before, but at least twice. No more appearances of the Praetorian Tribune Subrius Flavus. But now a string of new faces —all men of equestrian rank: Julius Augurinus, Munatius Gratus, Vulcatius Araricus, Marcius Festus, Cervarius Proculus.

The damnable thing is that these walks may be perfectly innocent. Piso is a sociable man. I heard someone remark once, "The worst thing you can say about Piso is that he has three hundred best friends." The walks may be innocent.

(You see, I am learning skepticism from you, Tigellinus; skepticism even of my own better judgment.) Or they may not be. (My own better judgment.)

Indoors, meanwhile, the observed activities and overheard conversations are as soft and mild as goosedown; principally thief-checkers and music. As you may know, Piso is a brilliant thief-checkers player; crowds gather around him whenever he plays in a public place, as at the baths. With these guests of recent days he has always played for money and has always won, but he sets modest stakes and, being generous, always gives the guests presents on their departure which far outvalue their gambling losses. He tends to bore them by singing to them from his large repertory of tragic parts, to the lyre. He has a good voice, but like most people with good voices or ideas that they consider good, he finds it hard to stop. At whatever estate he visits there is a steady stream of poor people and slaves at his gates petitioning him to represent them in the courts. He has two freedmen trained in law who weed out the nuisances and shrewdly select a very few affecting cases that he has a good chance of winning, and he takes them on, enhancing every month his reputation as a defender of the poor. His popularity with the mass of the public and with slaves has never been higher. In this sense, of course, he is potentially far more dangerous than Lucan, who is, after all, only a poet.

March 4

To TIGELLINUS from PAENUS, Tribune of Secret Police
  From Cleonicus:

  "Seneca to Lucan, greetings:

  "Your last letter, my dearest nephew, with its friendlier tone and its touching reference to my 'nourishment' of your better side, relieved my great sadness over what had seemed a fissure in the rock of our love. I yearn to see your face, to drink with my eyes from your eyes the distillation of our kinship. There might have been a chance for that, but I denied it to myself. Nero commanded me, too, to the literary occasion at the palace, which you described in your letter. I took my courage in hand and declined, pleading ill health. The fact is, dear Lucan, I have never been healthier or stronger; the air here even in winter has a certain fullness; it is sweet and moist like the meat of a perfectly ripened pear. I thrive on it, and on a life that is totally free of pressure.

"I am heartily glad, after having read your letter, that I missed this literary evening. But I do not like the sound of debility, along with desperation, that comes through to me, even at this distance, in your written voice. Be careful, Lucan. Distance yourself from anger, from that frenzy to which you are so prone.

"I do not like to hear that the Muses are teasing you. They flirt with one, Lucan, they are flighty and fickle. But you must be a steadfast suitor. Court them patiently.

"Especially am I sorry to learn that you have stopped agitating the very questions you have put so insistently to me in recent weeks. I felt that after my last letter we were coming straight back to them, and I want now again to write to you about them, hoping that you will answer me. For *I* am caught up in them now.

"A writer cannot change the world; his duty is to describe it. It may be that because a writer, like a sculptor or painter or musician, has wider-ranging and more sensitive perceptions than a man of affairs, he can describe the world in ways that open the eyes of the man of action, and therefore affect the action. This would be a happy outcome if all writers were good men, or sages. But alas, the magical gifts of art are distributed by fortune at random. The seeds are thrown by the sower's hand in an April wind. Consider a man like Petronius. Where you see horrors, Petronius sees picnics. He is an apt friend for the worst Nero I know; yet even I cannot help seeing that he glows with talent.

"Then what should a writer do who sees horrors? Of course he will write in order to heal himself, but his writing will not wipe out objective horrors. Should he not then approach power, in his life as a man outside writing, in order to try to obliterate, or at least mitigate, these horrors that remain?

"My experience suggests to me, Lucan, that power—at least as it is presently misconstrued in Rome, the power of the Agrippina side of Nero—cannot any longer be directly influenced, cannot be turned toward wisdom by counsel. Nor can it even be changed by the very means it understands best —by violent force. The story I have told you of Nero's effort to purge himself by violence of the Agrippina in himself, of the 'materials of tyranny,' has a sad lesson: His effort led only to an opposite end—Agrippina confirmed in him, and in us. You may say: A serious writer's concept of power would be different—thoughtful, benign. But power consumes its own source, and all men who approach too close to it are swallowed sooner or later by power itself and its maintenance.

"Where does that leave the writer? I was greatly moved by what you wrote about the power of art: recognition. I have come after all my years at the arm of the throne to believe that the writer should stand aside, should describe, should ponder the moral implications of what he recognizes—recognition meaning, I take it, the ability to see in others what is in oneself, and in oneself what is in others. It seems to me that the reason you were so shaken yet so strong at the literary evening was because you saw that much of what was in Nero, for better and for worse, was also in you. You must not let this recognition paralyze you. A man in power—for that is what you are, as a writer, in this sense of being able to open men's eyes to each other—a man in power cannot rest. Write, Lucan, write.

"I think I am almost a free man. I am trying to move toward wisdom. If I have a writer's power, I have no need of it—perhaps this is partly because I am getting old. I have no need of power over anyone, certainly not over my beloved wife Paulina, now my only constant friend. I am not yet a sage, but I would like to be. I have no fear of death.

"Farewell."

"Lucan to Seneca, greetings:

"Your letter, dear Seca, seemed to be designed to calm me, with its hilltop detachment and the advantage over me of assurance that old age unfairly gives you. Instead of easing me it made me irascible, jumpy, and anxious. When I come at the end of each of your letters to your brief soaring declarations about death, your little blackbirds flying into pink sunsets, I feel as if I had ants under my skin. I still live in Rome, Uncle. Your bucolic ramblings do us no good. We are in a predicament, you are in a country daydream.

"I agree with you that not all writers are good men—but that is irrelevant. Mark my words, Petronius may not be driven into the same corner with you and me, but he is just as great a threat to the tyrant as we are, perhaps greater, because he has more humor than you or I have. He sees incongruities faster than we do. A truly funny man is very dangerous to the seat of power.

"You tell me peremptorily to write. Sit down. Write. 'A man in power cannot rest.' As if my difficulty were laziness. How little, after all, you recognize.

"But write to me again. Seca, Seca, Seca.

"Farewell."

March 7

To TIGELLINUS from PAENUS, Tribune of Secret Police
Another gleaning from a scroll in one of Lucan's library boxes—a new, a pungent view from this particular correspondent. Was it Natalis who first spoke of this woman's gift for "provocations"?

"Epicharis to Lucan, greetings:
"You were so worked up before you left that I never had a chance to say what I thought. You dramatize and enlarge all things, for you are an epic poet. But I have a different view from yours of tyranny—a quieter but more awful view— more as of mildew than of earthquake. I am closer to faceless people, those without names, than you. The effects of tyranny, my dearest one, are to be seen not so much in executions, privations, surveillances, matricide and fratricide, ruined reputations, unjust trials, exile, and murder, shocking events of the capital; no, tyranny has finally achieved its foul purpose when among the many, scattered at large, there are acquiescence, apathy, complacency, bland acceptance of outrage, pride in vulgar triumphs, blurring of the meaning of words, confusion in moral standards—in short, a blight of the communal character. It is when people who are thought of as good solid citizens, those who make up the backbone of the populace, become touched by this blight and do not realize it, become not only the infected but the infectors—this is when tyranny has won the day. The 'good' citizens then say: *What a beautiful day! What a fine year this has been! Are you going to the amphitheater this afternoon?*

"You would do well to listen with a more attentive ear to your uncle.
"In haste. Farewell."

March 15

To TIGELLINUS from PAENUS, Tribune of Secret Police
  Urgent urgent urgent.
  Here it is. I waken you in the night with good reason. An intercept of Cleonicus. Here it is, Tigellinus.

"Seneca to Lucan, greetings:

"I write to you again sooner than I had thought to do.

"It is the hour of beginnings, for the day and for me. The sun will soon rise. A peculiar terraced fog, hugging the ground, rises step by step up the levels of the vineyard across the valley. I have never before seen such a weird geometric mist. Augury? In full view of it, and by lamplight in my still-dark room, I commence, with trembling hand, a fateful letter to you, my dearest nephew.

"On this most important morning of a life that has not been lacking in importances, I turn to you, Lucan. I have talked all night with Paulina. Now I must talk with you—a writer, a kinsman, a friend, a critic, a dear part of myself.

"Everything has changed. The world of action, of shove and shout and cut and take, has penetrated this philosopher's refuge. Yet I feel safe here at Nomentum. While what I am to describe to you comes to fruition, I shall play the part of a serene old man, far removed from influence, weary indeed of a surfeit of it, an old countryman who seems mainly interested in the system devised on these umber hills by my neighbor Columella and by the freedman Sthenus for the abundant cultivation of grapes, and in the capital they will say that Seneca is at one of his villas writing tragedies, pruning vines, taking cold baths in all weathers at the age of sixty-two, and sending homiletic epistles to his friend Lucilius Junior, who, poor fellow, is already all too amply instructed by his wordy friend.

"I was wakened in the night by the hand of Paulina—how shrewd of them to use her, to know that though I trust my brothers and my nephew and my friends and my freedmen and my slaves with my life, because I value life but do not fear death, this generous creature is the only one besides yourself to whom I entrust *secrets*—to be told in a whisper of her warm breath that a clandestine visitor was waiting to talk to me in the potting shed of the topiary nursery; I must go there in silence without slaves and without light, she said.

"I felt the way along the walls of my room to its door, made my way through the atrium by a dim sight of the pool, groped from column to column of the peristyle, and went out at the back of the house. The night was chilly; no stars could be seen; the moon, I recalled, had waned far past the third quarter and must have been low in the sky. I could just make out the white paths. My feet were bare. I walked with the slow way-feeling shuffle the honor guards use at the tomb of Augustus, and I kept to the dew-wet myrtle and ivy off the paths to avoid a crunching noise on my beloved Pentelican gravel. I know every turning of the garden maze, and soon I was in the ornamental nursery and was approaching the potting shed when I saw a specter come from it toward me.

"It materialized and touched me for recognition, a calloused hand on my jowls, rough fingers shaping my nose, a palm—vanity crackled in me alongside a sense of danger—checking the bald isthmus at the top of my head. A harsh whisper: 'Are you alone?' I whispered in retort: 'Identify yourself at once.' My eyes were adjusted to the dark, but I could not see features. The shape whispered a name. A distinguished name, Lucan. 'How am I to know that you are————?' A rough hand took my hand and placed my fingers on a certain tactile identification which satisfied me. Some day I will tell you more.

"And so we two important men stood there among the peacocks, bears, rabbits, doves, and dolphins of box and yew and privet and holm oak and holly, and we exchanged exceedingly dangerous words.

"This visitor told me straight out that certain civilian and military men intended to assassinate Nero and invite me to become Emperor.

"Did I feel an instantaneous thrust of elation? I felt, first of all, a chill in my limbs, the wind on my wet bare ankles and insteps. Certain animals hide themselves from discovery by confusing the marks of their footprints around their lairs; I think my mind was doing similar work to prevent discovery of where it lived with respect to this sudden intruder on its peace: the thought that Lucius Annaeus Seneca might become Emperor at Rome.

"Where were all the easy, wise sayings of the Stoic? 'What a great man! He has learned to despise all things.' My mind scrambled among trivia. Had this visitor come here alone? How had word been given to Paulina? And suddenly this absurd thought: Could this be a practical joke? No, no, such a visitor as this did not fumble among leaf-bearing animals in a topiary garden in the shank of a cold night in order that a few might join in laughing at an honorable old man. But what if—and this was all too possible, and no joke—what if this visitor had come to test me? What if he was on an errand for Nero himself? What if malice was what gave this night wind such a cutting edge?

"I could not, in view of these thoughts, respond in any telling way. My visitor generously whispered that he knew what I must be thinking, that I must consider, as a measure of his trust in me, how he was putting himself at my mercy. He wanted no sign from me; he knew all too well, he whispered, that within a tyrant's reach men could not open their

hearts to each other in a sudden rush. He would simply inform me; I should ponder what he told me. There would be
a time for answers.

"My visitor then told me that the plot is already on a
developed footing. He said he could not—until the time would
come for my reply—tell me the names of the principal conspirators, but he did say that I would be astonished and
pleased by some of those names. He mentioned one. He said
that several of the civilians who have conspired favor as Nero's
successor the man he named, but the military conspirators,
he said, are behind me. Need I point out to you, my dear
nephew, that after the assassination of Caligula it was the
Praetorian Guard that found the old laughing-stock Claudius,
at that moment a most surprising candidate for the succession,
cringing behind a curtain, his hands shaking, his big head
lolling with started eyes on his weak neck, and hauled him out
and made him Emperor, and not a bad one he proved to be?
And that after the assassination in turn of Claudius it was
the Praetorian Prefect Burrus who brought out at the palace
gates not the heir Britannicus but the dead Emperor's stepson
Nero, and at a command from Burrus the duty guard saluted
the boy—he was only seventeen—and placed him on a litter
and took him to their camp at the city walls, where Nero
promised the troops a donative, and they (not the Senate,
not the people) acclaimed him Emperor? If the military
chooses Seneca after the death of Nero, Seneca will be Emperor. . . . If Seneca decides he wants to be Emperor.

"Then I was alone. How did this visitor know his way
in my gardens? I shivered and turned toward the house. I
remember thinking, beside the path where it turns at the bed
of camellias: It is understandable that some men would support the other candidate, because he is an elegant man, he
gives sumptuous banquets, he is truly generous, he has taste

in literature, he knows exactly what Senator, what writer, what orator, what actor, what charioteer is 'acceptable' at any given moment, and he stands for many of the old Roman virtues as opposed to the Greek affectations, as many view them, of Nero. But I could not help thinking that Seneca would be better for Rome. This was not vanity, Lucan, not immodesty; I am far beyond such foibles. It was a question of experience. For seven years Burrus and I *were*, in all but name, jointly Emperor. I am the better man for the task. And yet . . .

"I have been up all night, as I say, talking with Paulina. I asked her at once how she had been warned. She told me that a peasant woman, her head covered, had come to the servants' quarters yesterday with a basket of pheasant eggs and asked to see the mistress of the house, and when Paulina presented herself the woman, coughing like a consumptive, said in thick dialect that she had seen a fox's earth in a glade through which she had come, not far from our villa, and that she wanted to show the mistress where it was so the predator could be destroyed. Paulina offhandedly told the woman to inform our freedman Florus, who takes care of such things. The woman thereupon stopped coughing and quickly lifted the cloth at her face, and Paulina, after a moment's astonishment at such honeyed skin on a farm woman's face, recognized her as someone in disguise—Epicharis, whom of course you know. I am so fortunate in Paulina that I do not need the luxury of envying my brother Mela this fine creature, whose fascination to me is that she seems both womanly-yielding and bronze-strong. I have often wondered how you felt about a woman who had taken your mother's place in your father's heart. Paulina, on recognizing her, quickly said that she would like to see the fox's covert, and the two walked out in the woods where no one could possibly overhear, and even there Epicharis impressed Paulina with the danger of

her errand by keeping her voice at a murmur. At exactly the
seventh hour of the night, she said, Paulina should waken me
and tell me to go to the potting shed—and so forth, exactly as
I have told you Paulina did later instruct me. No more would
Epicharis say, no matter how Paulina teased her for even the
smallest satisfaction—not a word more. Quite likely she knew
no more. She did give Paulina the pheasant eggs; and she gave
her, though Paulina did not decipher it until nearly dawn, the
metaphor of the fox, the predator that must be destroyed.

"If Epicharis, then Mela? If Mela, then you, Lucan?"
If my brother is in it, I said to Paulina, then doubtless his
son Lucan would also be in it. Or might be. This speculation
gave me strange feelings—palpitations, in fact, which I confessed to Paulina and now confess to you. I have here an un-
easy puzzle of love and trust. If you are in it, and if my name
had come up as a candidate for Emperor, should not you have
been the one to come to me and tell me? Would not this
have been the natural way? Does your not having come mean
that you are for the other man? This is all too possible. I
know that that other man is a close friend of yours. You have
often disagreed with me. My mind flew back over the correspondence we have had in recent weeks. You have put to
me urgently the question: What are the limits of a writer's
duties—to himself, to his art, to his fellow men, to posterity?
You are a poet. As a poet, in the successive books of the
Pharsalia, I have seen you gradually coming to the point: The
predator must be destroyed. But could you, did you dare, be
other than a poet? This you seemed to be asking me. Poetry
cannot be an agent; poetry must soar above agency. But if a
poet's vision is of a need for an act, then may not the poet
become the agent?

"I have taken the view with you—as recently as ten
days ago—that a writer should not step too close to temporal
power. You seemed to reproach me for holding this view; you

lost your temper with me, you cut me, hit me. Were you testing me? Did my answers turn you to the other man?

"One refrain in your letters haunts me. Over and over you have said: They are going to drive us to do what we do not wish to do.

"Of course I never thought, as I wrote to you, of such a preposterous idea as being Emperor. I thought in terms of a writer's being close to power, as I have been, not of a writer's *having* it.

"I thought in terms of moral influence, not in terms of murder.

"What am I to say to you now? Why have you not come to me?

"You see how I take you into my confidence—put my life in your hands. Why have you not trusted me?

"I do not hesitate to put my life in your hands because I love you and because I feel calm in the face of mere physical danger. Fear for my body I do not feel. Whatever I decide, death will come when it comes. Think, Lucan, a man's power, or lack of it, or closeness to it, or aloofness from it, does not give him power, or deprive him of power, over his own life. Fully as many men have been killed by angry slaves as by angry monarchs. Since the day I was born I have been walking toward death. My pace is still steady.

"No, Lucan, the fearful dangers are moral dangers. What am I to think of the violent death of Nero, whom I have loved in the past, whom I now hate? What am I to think of the rights and wrongs of tyrannicide? Is the murder of a murderer not a crime? What *now* are the responsibilities of a writer? Is recognition enough? What am I to think of what power can do to any man, be he writer or not? Am I so vain as to think I would be immune to the temptations of absolute power?

"Do *you* wish to be Emperor?

"Ah, Lucan, the questions we have been asking each other are now enlarged a thousandfold. Entirely changed.

"I must think. I must think. I must think.

"Write to me. First write to me a note by my trusted Cleonicus assuring me that having read this letter once over, you have then destroyed it. Your life, about which I care, as well as mine, about which I do not, depend on your doing so.

"Farewell. Write to me."

THREE

March 16

To PAENUS, Tribune of Secret Police, from TIGELLINUS
First of all, Paenus: Keep your head. Follow my example.
At times like these I purposely slow everything down. I think
more deliberately, I speak measured sentences, I even walk at
a more leisurely pace than usual. You can watch me. In my
youth I was forced to live for a while as a thief, and occasionally I had to keep out of the hands of policemen. I found
that a very good tactic was to show myself fleetingly here and
there before informers, or to leave unmistakable traces of my
presence at widely separated places. Once the police began
hurrying and scurrying—dashing to investigate one report after
another—I knew I was safe.

We cannot pounce. We must first be very sure of our
ground.

We must find out who the night visitor to the author of
this letter was. "A calloused hand." "Rough fingers." But "a
distinguished name." And the assurance that the military
adherents favor the author of the letter, not his rival. All this
points to a soldier. If a distinguished name, a soldier of high
rank. I need not stress that this suggestion that military men,

perhaps members of the Praetorian Guard, are involved in this business comes as a great shock. We thought we were simply dealing with a circle of arrogant, vain, effeminate, erratic, corruptible writers and their weak-willed hangers-on.

Am I right in thinking that your penetration of the Guard with agents is weak in all ranks? We have not time to repair that deficiency. *Do not send fools blundering into the Guard.* For the moment I will take responsibility for the delicate task of opening up information on the military side.

I am not yet telling Himself about the letter we have intercepted. Himself loses all judgment when it comes to the author of that letter. I shall protect the Person for now in whatever ways I can without disturbing him.

Keep cool.

Orders:

Free your best and *subtlest* men from other concerns to concentrate on this pile of stinking night soil.

Send me your file on the author of the letter.

Commence surveillance of Mela and Epicharis.

Commence close surveillance of Piso. The unnamed rival in the letter fits a description of him.

Commence surveillance of Natalis.

To RUFUS, Co-Commander, Praetorian Guard, from TIGELLINUS

Secret. Urgent.

I must talk with you on a most urgent and most secret matter. Meet me punctually on the fourth hour in the gardens of the Golden House, near the statue of Apollo on the path to the lake.

To TIGELLINUS from PAENUS, Tribune of Secret Police

You are consistent, as always, in your inconsistency. You

tell me to slow down, and you send me scrambling in all directions.

It will be a pleasure to commence—or, if I may use the word, recommence—surveillance of Natalis. Your other orders also noted for action.

To PAENUS, Tribune of Secret Police, from TIGELLINUS
Rest your wit. Get busy.

March 17

To TIGELLINUS from RUFUS, Co-Commander, Praetorian Guard

Secret. Urgent.

I have given myself twenty-four hours before commenting on your performance in the gardens yesterday. I needed twenty-four hours. In the first place, you seemed to me incoherent. In the second place, you lost yet again, and worse than ever, all sense of military propriety. I repeat what I have said before: You and I are of equal rank.

What makes you think you can use the Emperor's name to order me to conduct a purge of the Guard; then cancel it, excusing the inexcusable order on the ground that an augury had made it seem desirable; and now reinstate it, mumbling that you cannot reveal what makes it necessary this time, and that you don't want the Emperor upset by the details of such trivial matters as this? Trivial? The ruin-by-slaughter of his protective force? Carousing has weakened your brain, Tigellinus.

I have had enough of your "cannot reveal." I will give you twenty-four hours to make good on your reasons for this "command"; if I have not heard or seen the reasons by the fifth hour tomorrow I shall go to the Emperor. I am sworn to protect his Person.

To RUFUS, Co-Commander, Praetorian Guard, from
    TIGELLINUS
Secret. Urgent.

I will not be given an ultimatum by you. I suggest that
you carry out forthwith the careful investigation I proposed.
If you do not feel able to do this, rest assured that I will very
soon have a colleague of equal rank other than yourself.

I repeat: We are in an emergent situation. Act promptly if
you are loyal to Himself.

To TIGELLINUS from RUFUS, Co-Commander, Praetorian
    Guard
Secret. Urgent.

So we are to brawl, are we? I am a soldier, Tigellinus, and
you are a horse dealer. Something has made you lose your
nerve. I have not lost mine.

To RUFUS, Co-Commander, Praetorian Guard, from
    TIGELLINUS
Secret. Urgent.

In the files of the Secret Police reposes a clear proof, supported by the testimony of persons still living, that you were,
on nine separate and distinct occasions, the backstairs servant
and servicer of the pleasures of the sister of Caligula, wife of
Claudius, mother of Nero. A member of the Guard does not
violate an Imperial Person. I can have you snuffed out in half
a day.

March 18

To RUFUS, Co-Commander, Praetorian Guard, from
    TIGELLINUS
No answer to my last, soldier?

To RUFUS, Co-Commander, Praetorian Guard, from
    TIGELLINUS
Please give me daily reports on the investigation of the
Guard. I know that you will proceed with the utmost regard
for secrecy and subtlety in your inquiries.

Confidential
THE SENECA FILE

〖 Lucius Annaeus Seneca

〖 *For recognition:* Stature so short as to seem stunted, head
unusually large, bare-bald except at sides and back, narrow
shoulders, low paunch, stiff thin legs like hoe handles. The
awkwardness of this squat figure is offset by a round face of
imposing radiance, intelligence, and serenity; right eyebrow
much higher than left, consequent expression of perpetual
surprise, thought by inferior persons to be an expression of
disdain; limpid, responsive dark brown eyes; long straight
nose; narrow but full, sensitive, and sensuous mouth; small
wen on lower left chin.

〖 *Weaknesses:* Vanity, inconsistency, asthma, prolixity, si-
multaneous love of poverty and luxury.

〖 Born in Cordoba in the 24th year of the reign of Augustus.
Presently sixty-two years old. Father: Marcus Annaeus Seneca,
the rhetor, whose loathing of everything Greek might perhaps
be noted in view of Himself's Graecophilia. Mother: Helvia,
irreproachable matron. Elder brother: M. Annaeus Novatus,
adopted by his father's friend Junius Gallio, became Consul
and, thirteen years ago, Proconsul in Achaea. Younger brother:
M. Annaeus Mela, who, unlike his Senatorial brothers, re-

mains satisfied with equestrian rank; married a woman from
Cordoba, fathered the poet Lucan.

⟮ As a boy, weak in the lungs. Taken to Alexandria for his
health under care of an aunt.

⟮ Lifelong conflict, perhaps a consequence of this early delicacy, between impulsive asceticism and love of comfort. Under the influence of his teacher Sotion, took up the doctrines
of Pythagoras, who, being a believer in reincarnation and the
transmigration of souls, argued against meat-eating on the
ground that one might be committing murder or even parri-
cide when slaying and devouring an animal. Seneca later gave
up vegetarianism, either because, as some say, he was afraid of
being considered a Jew, or because, as others say, his father,
fearful for his health, insisted on a normal diet. Seneca began
as a young man to affect poverty; to sleep on a hard couch;
to take unheated baths; to refrain from using ointments and
unguents; to avoid hot-air baths; to refuse wine; to abstain
from oysters, mushrooms, and whatever might be considered
condiments rather than nourishment. To much of this rigor
Seneca was trained by his later teacher, Attalus the Stoic.

⟮ The Stoic teachings, however, opened the way to luxury as
well. Seneca has often written that whether a man has or does
not have material things is a matter of indifference. Though
the cold baths, the hard couch, the abstention from wine
continue, there is all too much evidence that Seneca has not
remained indifferent to his worldly condition. See the denun-
ciations of Suilius, below.

⟮ Seneca served adequately as Questor under Tiberius, in the
twentieth year of that Emperor's rule. Served as Consul
Suffectus, third year Nero.

⟨ During Caligula's reign, he distinguished himself, and almost got himself killed, on account of his dazzling skill in oratory, in pleading cases at law. At one trial Caligula spoke before the Senate in his torrential and raucous voice, pouring out invective, and when Seneca followed with a cool and ornamental response, full of balanced clauses and sudden epigrammatic explosions and mellifluous excursions into history and mythology, and the Senate lost its collective head in its applause for his eloquence, Caligula became insanely enraged and wanted to have Seneca executed at once; but a concubine persuaded the Emperor that Seneca would soon die of his asthma anyway, and he was spared—Caligula satisfying himself with the contemptuous remark that Seneca's speeches were "sand without lime." (The asthmatic Seneca has outlived Caligula, so far, by nearly a quarter of a century.)

⟨ In this connection, the moralistic philosopher once remarked that longevity at an Emperor's court depends on one's ability to be grateful for injuries.

⟨ The best catalogue of Seneca's weaknesses and vulnerabilities came with the denunciation of him by Publius Suilius, seven years ago.

Background: Suilius had been a notoriously venal informer under Claudius. Seneca, at the pinnacle of his influence with Himself (this takes place in the fourth year of his reign), decides to crush Suilius, who has destroyed so many good men; invokes, to punish him, the Cincian law against taking money for pleading causes. But Suilius is by this time a very old man with a nasty temper, and is still helplessly gluttonous for victims. In his own defense he impeaches Seneca as follows:

First, Seneca is vengeful. His motive for attacking Suilius is his desire to destroy all the friends of the previous Emperor,

Claudius, under whose reign Seneca endured a well-deserved exile of eight years.

Second, he is an impudent adulterer. The reason for Seneca's exile: He had violated the sister of Caligula and Agrippina, Julia Livilla.

Third, he is a hypocrite. He spent his years of exile in Corsica, which he called, in his "Consolation" to his mother, "terrible, uncouth, wild, horrible." In all Seneca's writings on the Stoic acceptance of hardship, one finds a humming tension that comes from his not meaning a word of what he says. "The wise man"—from the same letter to his mother, a private communication published to the world out of vanity, as is every sentence he writes—"The wise man cannot be set back by any blows of fortune. The rougher the ground under his feet, the worse his food, the more squalid his hut, so much the easier can he turn his thoughts inward or lose himself in gazing at the stars. . . ." This (snorts Suilius) from the man whose country houses today rival those of the Emperor!

Fourth, he is a groveling flatterer. From Corsica he wrote another "Consolation," to the rich freedman Polybius, who was Claudius's literary secretary, on the occasion of the death of a brother of Polybius. In the great vault of human literary endeavor there has never been flattery so abject, so maladroit, so transparent—Seneca will say *anything* in the hope of being pardoned and being allowed to come home. He writes that Polybius, author of pedestrian prose translations of Homer into Latin and of Virgil into Greek, is fully their match—all he needs to be remembered like them is to write a life of Claudius. Seneca so far loses his head as to compliment Claudius even on his wonderful memory—Claudius, who, the day after he had his wife executed, asked why she was late for dinner.

Fifth, he is laughably insincere. Witness the funeral oration

on Claudius that he wrote for Nero. All Rome laughed at that
scandalous cynicism.

Sixth, he is corrupt. Has it been by practicing the virtues
of a "sage" and pronouncing philosophic epigrams that Seneca has, during four years as the Emperor's adviser, piled up
three hundred million sesterces?

Seventh, he is an embezzler. What happens to the wills of
rich men who die in Rome without heirs?

Eighth, he practices usury. It is well known that Seneca
drains the provinces by lending money at extortionate rates
of interest.

Ninth, his vanity is at the heart of his inconsistency. The
advocate of a frugal life who writes of the simple beauty of a
two-day journey on a rough cart carrying the barest necessities
—this is the same man who owns five hundred matching dining tables of cedar from Gaul inlaid with ivory from the
Syrtes. The philosopher who writes so trenchantly against
luxury insists on chipped white marble from the quarries of
the Acropolis itself for the garden paths of his four villas.

*(As is well known, Seneca persuaded Himself that any man
could build palaces out of blocks of envy, and for his "slander"
Suilius was banished to the Balearics. The charges against
Seneca stand unanswered on the record.)*

❪ Five years ago, we also know, the Britons under Queen
Boadicea massacred seventy thousand Romans and allies at
Camulodunum, London, and Verulamium. Among the gravest
causes of the uprising was Seneca's speculation. He had had
forty million sesterces out at usury in Britain (Stoic "indifference"), and hearing through his privileged position of the
unrest on the island, he had called his capital and exacted
every grain of his interest, causing immense hardship among
influential Britons.

(Seneca is also blamed by many for the murder of the ex-Consul and Prefect Pedanius by one of his own slaves four years ago. Many people say that the widely published sentimental views of Seneca on slavery were what gave the murderer the sense of moral justification and the plain courage to carry a torch into his master's bedroom and stab him on his couch. This was a frightfully dangerous case; as punishment of the murder, which had been so threatening to every slave owner in Rome, all four hundred of Pedanius's slaves were put to death, men, women, and children, and mobs with rocks and firebrands turned out in the city to protest this harshness, and to carry out the sentence Himself had to line with soldiers the entire route by which the victims were dragged to execution. A recently published sample of this notorious sentimentality of Seneca's on the subject of slavery:

" 'They are slaves,' you say. No, they are men. 'They are slaves.' No, they are comrades. 'They are slaves.' No, humble friends. 'They are slaves.' No—fellow slaves, if one reflects that all are subject to the same fortune. This is why I smile at those who think it is a disgrace for a man to dine with his slave. . . . The man you call a slave came from the same seed as you, grows up under the same sun, breathes, lives, and dies like you. We Romans are excessively haughty, cruel, and insulting to our slaves. This is the core of my advice: Treat those you have at your mercy exactly as you would wish to be treated by those who have you at their mercy. Perhaps some day you will be a slave."

(Seneca has for many years shamelessly published subversive views.

Examples:

He chides Brutus, because killing a tyrant did not kill tyranny.

His Stoic hero is Cato. "Cato died with liberty, and liberty died with him."

"Hell," he writes, "is far from being the place of terror it is fabled to be, for in that free state there are no fresh tyrants." This appears in his "Consolation to Marcia," which Seneca wrote to her because her father, Cremutius Cordus, had in Tiberius's time been driven to suicide, and his books had been burnt, because he had praised tyrannicides.

Seneca has openly written that he himself could be a tyran-nicide—e.g., in "On Benefits," writing "hypothetically" of an Emperor to whom he is indebted and who becomes tyran-nical: "If I despair altogether of his amendment, I shall at one blow discharge my debt to him and confer a benefit on mankind, for to such a nature death is a cure, and to speed his departure the only kindness I can do him."

(Appended to this file are Seneca's letters in recent corre-spondence with Lucan, which you have already seen.

To PAENUS, Tribune of Secret Police, from TIGELLINUS
I have read the Seneca file, and I am thoroughly dissatisfied with it. It is a bungle. A perfect expression of the clomping around in military boots studded with hobnails that your sup-posedly secret police have been doing, when they should have been moving on silent sandals. That this file has been hastily and sloppily thrown together is not by any means the real com-plaint. The error of the file is that it speaks only of foibles, fol-lies, and weaknesses in Seneca. If he was such a wrong-headed, fallible culprit as this file pictures him to be, how could he have been for so long the second most powerful man in Rome?

No, Paenus, when you are trying to decide how to come to battle with a great enemy, you have to know his strengths.

You have to know what powers must be dealt with, what endurance he can command under pressure, what reserves he can bring to the battle.

You have left out all the large measure of Seneca—and very large it is. His hold on Himself's heart has a sound basis. You have forgotten to note that Seneca became his tutor when he was a boy eleven years old; that, forbidden by Agrippina to teach her son philosophy, Seneca concentrated on the elements of upright character—on modesty, courtesy, simplicity, sobriety, endurance, willingness to work hard, avoidance of flattery and of excessive passion. Let us not quibble about whether Seneca is himself a paragon of these qualities. You do not note that *these lessons took root*.

Your file leaves out the great Quinquennium all Rome speaks of—the first five years of Himself's rule, when Seneca and Burrus steered the way, a time unequaled in our history for peace, wealth, wisdom at home and abroad.

Do you think it is easy for *me* to remind you of these things? People constantly tell me that I am a horse dealer, Paenus. I had to follow in the footsteps of a man whom Himself regarded as a great and very kind philosopher. I hate Seneca; partly I hate him because I see his worth.

If you listen even now to Himself, Seneca was a good and true friend. I remind you (oh, yes, I have a file of my own on Seneca) that somewhere he quotes Hecato: "I can show you a potion, compounded without drugs, herbs, or any witches' incantations: 'If you would be loved, love.'" In his own heavy way, Seneca loved Himself.

Seneca had what I consider a malign softening influence on Himself. He tried to teach Himself to hate bloodshed, and to the extent he succeeded in this he also succeeded in confusing Himself on the scores of valor, law-keeping, vigilance. Himself for a very long time kept his distance from the combats of the

arena, gladiatorial shows, the sight of slaughter—but also from
the sight of courage. One consequence of all this was Himself's predilection for singing, acting, reading poems in public;
he needed to test his gifts, but the only contests Seneca permitted him were in the Greek style, without bloodshed. *Many
people give Seneca great credit for this*—a fact which your
report totally ignores.

In those first years Seneca taught Himself another lesson
you and I despise—of mercy. Your file leaves out *these* words
Seneca put in the mouth of the most powerful man on earth
in those early days: "The humblest blood is precious to me;
my sword is in its sheath; if a suppliant has nothing else to
plead except that he is a man, yet as a man I will favor him.
My severity I hide; my clemency is in the open and ready for
use. I have rescued the laws from neglect, and I observe them
as if I too were accountable." You do not have to like this,
but give Seneca credit!—the public does, *and Himself does.*
Oh, you have given me a feeble file.

After Burrus died three years ago, ambitious men—I was
one of them, Paenus, and probably you were, too—revived all
the old Suilius slurs about Seneca's wealth and . . . and all
that your miserable file recooks, and Seneca went to Himself
and said: You do not benefit from the advice of a discredited
man; let me retire, let me give you all my wealth, which I owe
to you anyway, let me give you all my estates, let me retire to
a small country house. You and I can see through the hypocrisy in this, Paenus, but many thought it was the sincere act
of a great man, of a philosopher.

And his greatest strength you have also left out of your file
of dirty crumbs. He is not afraid of anything. He is not afraid
of Himself, or you, or me, or death. Many people make fun
of what he has written about the way a man should be willing
to die. But I know this man. Here he means what he says.

This is, I think, in fact, our principal hope. If we come to a showdown, I am not sure that Seneca would fight. He regards death as the one sure liberty, the only escape from tyranny. I think he might prefer that liberty to a fight for power, because, being honest although vain, he would wonder whether he, any more than the student he loved, would be able in the end to avoid being influenced *by men like you and me*, Paenus, to avoid becoming a tyrant himself.

As for his views on tyrannicide: Even an ignorant clod like yourself should know that these mouthings have been the clichés of the schools of rhetoric and philosophy since the time of Cicero and Cato. They mean nothing. They are just words that schoolboys memorize.

After reading this file of yours I have concluded that our greatest danger at this moment comes from the feeblemindedness of the protectors of the Person. I wish I could have your throat cut. But who would I put in your place? Secret policemen see everything as if it were under water or beyond a column of smoke. The whole flock of you are worse than useless. You are dangerous.

March 19

To TIGELLINUS from RUFUS, Co-Commander, Praetorian Guard

Report on first day of check of Guard: No substantive findings.

To TIGELLINUS from PAENUS, Tribune of Secret Police

You have a marked talent for disheartening your subordinates. Since the last Cleonicus intercept I have been working all hours, as you can imagine. I feel most heavily the responsibility reposed in me. I do the best I can. Yet the officer to whom I report has nothing to say to me except that he should have my throat cut. I trust he will remember that if he feels that we are in a tight position, it is because I and my service, though we are sensible of our imperfection, have brought a great deal to light.

To PAENUS, Tribune of Secret Police, from TIGELLINUS
"Sensible of our imperfection." You have been reading too many letters written by Seneca. Stop whining and get busy.

March 20

To TIGELLINUS from PAENUS, Tribune of Secret Police
First product of surveillance of Mela's household: this letter, found in a jewel box of Epicharis's, copied, returned. Note with care the examples Lucan cites from his own work.

"Lucan to Epicharis, greetings:
"What am I to do? I cannot get ahead. This has never happened to me before. I sit at my desk and nothing comes but anger, dullness, and a stupid appetite for daydreams that will not take form. I have done everything I could think of to waken my muses, feast them, and even get them drunk if I could. I have reread and reread the parts of Livy that up to now have given me the yarn for my beautiful weaving; I have read Virgil, to remind myself of the standards I must better; I have read here and there in *Metamorphoses*, which has always in the past had the effect of making me want to pour out my genius, has always sent me running to my tablets. Now I cannot focus on the books. I am stuck. Caesar is stuck in Egypt. I have not more than two hundred lines to go to finish Book X. I know where I want to go. I want to carry the great work through to the death of Cato, and indeed I have already experienced again and again, with hot tears in my eyes, the flooding emotion that will be contained by the care-

fully built dikes of that last book. If I can ever reach it. I
range back, reading and thinking about my earlier passages.
I marvel at the conciseness I could achieve:

> "*Delay wounds the well-prepared.* . . .

> "*A people in want knows not fear.* . . .

> "*Popular crime goes unavenged.* . . .

> "*Thinking nothing done when anything remained to
>   do.* . . .

and how I could characterize the different prides and jealousies of Caesar and Pompey in a single lightning stroke:

> "*Caesar could bear no man in front of him,*
> *Pompey none by his side.* . . .

and my soaring passages: the crossing of the Rubicon, the
deaths at Massilia, Vulteius on the raft, Pompey's farewell to
Cornelia on sending her to Lesbos, the complaints of the
mutineers against Caesar, the storm on the Adriatic, Pompey's
dream of Rome, his murder, Cato's speech in the desert, the
serpents. . . .

"It is a massive and brilliant work, and I stand by the
lines in the last book before this one, when I address Caesar
and tell him he will live as long as Homer's heroes because of
Lucan's poem. Lucan will not die, my dear. Lucan will live
forever.

"But my poem is like a swift ship that has run aground
on a sand shoal. It seems that the helmsman must wait for
the full-moon tides to lift free the keel. Why, why, why are
they so long coming?

"*He* has done this to me. He has silenced me—at least

as a poet, and for the time being—better than he thought he could. Do you know something? In the very moment of detesting him, I am lonely for his company. I realized this, with a pang, at the literary evening I told you about. He has fascinated me, and I would be a liar if I denied that I took pleasure from being a most privileged insider, one who could with impunity tease and even (then!) abuse the most powerful man; he *enjoyed* my sharp tongue, because he was stuffed to the point of nausea with the flattery everyone else dealt him. In the end, though, he could not stand my genius, which put his paltry talent in the shade. But now, sitting at my desk unable to write a line of poetry, I am face to face, after all, with his magnetic and destructive power.

"I cannot even write a casual sylvan poem. If I could, it would be about the tiny gold chain you wear on your ankle. Construct the poem in your mind, if you will. You know what is held by that delicate golden fetter until I am able to see you again and touch that chain again with my trembling fingertips.

"Advise me. I cannot write to Seneca; I thank heaven I can still manage to write to you. You are so wise and alive and strong. Advise me.

"Farewell."

To TIGELLINUS from RUFUS, Co-Commander, Praetorian Guard
Second day of investigation: No findings.

March 21

To TIGELLINUS from RUFUS, Co-Commander, Praetorian Guard
Third day of investigation: No findings.

March 22

*To TIGELLINUS from RUFUS, Co-Commander, Praetorian
     Guard*
Fourth day of investigation: No findings.

March 23

*To TIGELLINUS from RUFUS, Co-Commander, Praetorian
     Guard*
Fifth day of investigation: No findings.

*To RUFUS, Co-Commander, Praetorian Guard, from
     TIGELLINUS*
Let us stop this game of street cats. Report to me when you
have found something to report. Find it.

To PAENUS, Tribune of Secret Police, from TIGELLINUS
You should know that I discussed the entire Piso–Lucan–
Seneca affair with Himself again yesterday (omitting, however, the most recent intercept, for reasons I have previously
mentioned to you). I gave him my frank opinion—that the
time has come to break this nasty business over our knee.
But Himself insists on restraint, on waiting. Someone, he still
says, will lose his nerve and come out with it. I pressed him
hard; he is obdurately stubborn about this threat. His reasons
must be made of stone. Somewhere in them is his lingering
awe of his old teacher and adviser. Somewhere also a revival—
perhaps at the literary evening—of his former affection for
Lucan malignantly mixed up with envy of Lucan's poetic gifts.
Somewhere also a perverse desire for a thrill, even a dangerous
one. He is bored, Paenus. His great palace is built. The new
ideas involved in the reconstruction of the city are now old
ideas to him. He is bloated like an overfeasted man with
ordinary entertainments. We must find new objects for his
huge, vital attention.

It occurred to me that we must make special efforts to enliven the circus games next month in honor of Ceres, to find a few horses with truly great hearts. We will have him watch these proud ones training beforehand—give them to the Green team. I know a line of superb bay runners derived from a strain raised on the Plain of Alashkert, captured by Corbulo. I will work on finding some of them. I mention this to you because, while the games promise Himself some diversion, they also (he becomes so engrossed) expose him to close approach. We will therefore have to discuss special security precautions later.

March 25

To TIGELLINUS from PAENUS, Tribune of Secret Police

Close surveillance of Piso brings us nothing new for the moment. He has been staying in the city in recent days. A dull dinner party which included—among those we must now consider doubtfuls because of before-noted garden strolls—Scaevinus, Quintianus, Munatius, and Vulcatius; but not others. Conversation proper. Emotional timbre on the soft side; little drinking, only Sleepy-Eyes Scaevinus drunk—it would have been more noteworthy if he had not been.

Our two agents do feel, however, that Piso's demeanor lately has been abnormal in its quietness, its subdued quality. He maintains at all times his accustomed propriety, but they feel it is under harness somehow. The skin of his face has become sallow and flaccid, and there are gray patches under his eyes of a peculiar triangular shape, reaching far down into his cheeks. He is at his thief-checkers board day and night.

To PAENUS, Tribune of Secret Police, from TIGELLINUS

Now you feed me the desperate information that a man has bags under his eyes from playing too much checkers.

To TIGELLINUS from PAENUS, Tribune of Secret Police
Cut my throat. That would be more pleasing to me than
this continuous chopping at my shoulders. I am doing the best
I can with limited resources.

To PAENUS, Tribune of Secret Police, from TIGELLINUS
"Limited resources." Does this phrase suggest a request for
more money for your elite corps of deaf-mutes and blind men?
You are not only incompetent. You are mad.

March 26

To TIGELLINUS from PAENUS, Tribune of Secret Police
Surveillance of Mela's household brings us this letter, copied
before the original was dispatched.

"Epicharis to Lucan, greetings:
"Two days ago I went for a stroll along the cart track
you and I followed on that divine afternoon. There had been
a tramontane wind for several days, which at first had swept
the sky clean with its raw, cold breath, but now it had turned
sweet and mild, and with the sun like your warm hand on my
shoulder, I felt the optimism and yearnings of springtime turning over in me. I ached for your company. Lizards were out
on the rocks sunning themselves. A thousand sparrows darted
among the live-oaks and shouted your name. Sap was dripping
from broken twigs, and buds were fat and yellow.
"Do you remember the hill beyond the farm where we
saw the seven black lambs? As I walked, following the cart
ruts around its shoulder, I saw in the corner of my eye, up at
the crest, a figure, a creature of some kind. Looking more
closely I made out a person lying supine on the bald, stony
crown of the hill. The form did not move. I left the track
and struck out through the brush, climbing. There may have

been a path, but I could not find one. I tore my clothes and scratched my feet.

"At last I broke out onto the barren upper reaches of the hill. Dry boulders—tufts of nettle and spikey grass—a place that even goats had avoided. There on the hard ground a man lay flat on his back, looking stonily at the empty sky above him. I bent over him and put my hand on his forehead, which burned like a sun-baked rock. At my touch the man started feebly to cough. A terrible anger began to flame in me, as I realized who this was—a slave, Lucan, sick in the lungs, abandoned by a master to whom he had become a burden.

"I flew down the hill weeping and ran all the way home, and I asked Mela to let me have four strong men and a litter, and we went and got the man and brought him here. I have been nursing him day and night. I feed him tiny sips of hot gruel and bathe his face with damp cloths. Just today he has begun to be able to speak. He spent two nights in that north wind. He is young, younger than you, and very ill. I don't know whether he will live. He is too frightened yet to tell me the name of his master.

"Ah, Lucan, I know that you will find your way back to your poem. How urgent it is! This kind of heartlessness, in which Rome wallows, wounds me, wounds you. I am only able to reach out to one person at a time, but you can speak to many through your powerful poem. Speak, *speak*, dear heart!

"Farewell."

Comment from our agent:
Our brief penetration of the Mela household tends to make us feel that Mela's role, if any, in whatever is being concocted, is a wholly passive one. He has chosen, first as wife and now as mistress, women who take charge of him. He condones, or

at least does nothing to limit, the activities of Epicharis, even though he must surely see that they are deeply disturbing to the proprietors and householders of a wide region.

These activities of hers are incessant, but they seem to us to be scattered, impulsive, and deficient of any coherent political meaning or effect. She is a meddlesome sympathizer. I confess that we have not yet worked our way deeply enough into the Mela establishment to be able to rule out the possibility of clandestine meetings or rendezvous, and we do not know what messages Lucan may or may not have been carrying back and forth from the capital. But all we have seen, really, is a woman who goes to the market every day overflowing with agonizing concern. She is physically so lovely that it is all too easy for her to take reward for her gestures in the adoration of others' eyes—or, in the case of males, in signs of acute but strictly forbidden desire.

We speak of gestures; this is all her activities consist of— bits of pantomime. Glimpses of gentility (for she *seems* to be a rich lady) leveling itself with common folk. She relieves an old woman of her market basket and carries it for her. She bends over a beggar's leg and washes an open ulcer with lint soaked in oil of eucalyptus. She squats on the harbor mole in peasant fashion and helps an old man to clean his bucketful of fish. As we have seen, she rescues a sick slave set out to exposure and tries to nurse him back to health—to be a slave to Mela?

It is true that the edge of anger and the "gift of provocation" (mentioned in our instructions) are always in evidence. She talks and talks. But we have not yet uncovered any specific or patterned incitements on her part. She makes these ignorant people feel dissatisfied, but so far as we can tell she does not organize their resentments in any way. Hence we feel that her activities could go on for a decade and still not produce significant rebellion.

The slaves in the Mela household are not in agreement about her relationship with Lucan. Some say they have seen signs of physical transactions between the two, but when these persons are pressed, it turns out that none has seen embraces, nobody has surprised the pair in hiding, there are none of the usual accounts of disarrayed clothing or semen on bed-sheets. The rest of the slaves affirm that Epicharis is faithful to Mela and that she treats Lucan as a nursemaid would treat a child. Difficult to evaluate these contradictions. It must be said that the "best" slaves in the household are fierce partisans of Epicharis. This has made our penetration difficult. From our point of view her gestures seem trivial and shallow; these "best" slaves obviously see them otherwise.

The least that can be said is that Epicharis has a talent for attracting love and gratitude.

March 27

To TIGELLINUS from PAENUS, Tribune of Secret Police
This comes by way of Cleonicus:

"Seneca to Lucan, greetings:
"Why have you not written to me?
"Since the visit I described in my last, I have been having anxious days. You can imagine that I expected a prompt second visit of some kind, further discussions, an ear for an answer from me. But no one came. I lived the life of a lonely farmer-philosopher. I waited and waited. Nothing from the man who visited me. Nothing from you.

"I had come to the view that I could not refuse this nomination, and I prepared my mind as well as I could for power or for death. Still no visitor, no message even.

"I have taken great pleasure recently from my topiary garden. I will not bore you with that. You reproach me with

being in a country daydream, but I am much in the city in my
thoughts, at your side, so to speak.

"Day and night I think back over our correspondence
of recent weeks. One keeps wondering whether he has been
able to say what he really meant. You make an interesting
distinction in your last letter between the writer and the man
he is. Perhaps I would have to admit the possibility of such a
duality—that as a writer one is simply an instrument, a stylus
as distinguished from the hand that moves it. And perhaps
the hand has other work to do besides manipulating the stylus.

"Your vehemence puts me in doubt. I have always
wanted your love, Lucan. You puzzle me. The very intensity
of your reproaches seems to reach out to me, as if in a cry for
help and love; but your words keep me at arm's length. I
keep wondering whether I have said something in the past or
in these letters which either hurt you or went so roughly
against the grain of your thinking that you felt cut off from
my love.

"I remain your Seca. Write to me and reassure me. I
must hear.

"Farewell."

To PAENUS, *Tribune of Secret Police, from* TIGELLINUS

In his wisdom Himself chose yesterday to expose his Person
in a walk with Poppaea through the Forum to the Capitol. I
argued against it, with what effect you can imagine. I had a
squad of the Guard accompany him, keeping a decent distance
so as not to make too great a show of unusual precautions. All
went well, I am thankful to say—except for one incident.

In front of the Basilica Julia, about fifty paces from the
Arch of Tiberius, the Consul Vestinus appeared, having come
down the hill from the Capitol. He had with him his offen-
sively exquisite personal bodyguard. As the Consul made

obeisance to Himself, this group of mincing armed dancers, approaching well within the confines staked out by the Praetorians walking with Himself, formed a semicircle around Vestinus and joined him in bowing.

Because Vestinus knew of Himself's displeasure with the private guard, and because these young armed men approached dangerously close to the Person, this act, couched in gestures of humble submission, was most offensive.

Himself was enraged but said nothing—grandly accepted the insulting homage.

Now, Paenus, your task: Find out if Vestinus is involved *in the business*.

March 28

To TIGELLINUS from PAENUS, Tribune of Secret Police
Since you harp so much on my incompetence, it gives me satisfaction to report to you that Natalis, whose surveillance you resisted so long, was followed yesterday on a trip, which he had announced to his household as having as its destination Allia. Where did he go? To Nomentum, where he spent four hours walking in the vineyards with Seneca.

March 29

To TIGELLINUS from PAENUS, Tribune of Secret Police
The agent in Mela's house sends us this:

"Lucan to Epicharis, greetings:

"You bid me go back to my poem, as if it were a meal and I had simply lost my appetite and should sit down and force something down my gullet. It is not as simple as that.

"I go walking in the back streets of Rome, hoping that I may find my way through the twisting alleys back to myself, back to the poet in me. Today I was walking in a little street

of carpenters' shops not far from the Tiber and near the warehouses below the island. The sun was high, and light poured
down into the narrow gorge of this alleyway redolent with
odors of sawdust, of the curls of planing, of glue, varnish, and
sweat. Suddenly there was a tiny, dark, vaulted arcade off the
street, and through at its far end was an open courtyard, full
to the brim with sunshine that seemed liquid. The arcade was
bracketed by two mirror-makers' shops, and both walls of the
arcade were lined with scores and scores of mirrors, rectangular
ones of polished stone from the one shop, smaller round ones
of brilliant metals from the other. The luminosity from the
street and from the courtyard sparkled magically in these
mirrors, and I was drawn irresistibly into the cavern, whose
proper medium was darkness, now punctuated but not quite
dissipated by the glistening of the mirrors.

"At the center of each side was an especially large
stone mirror, and when I stepped between these two, which
were directly opposite each other but were not exactly parallel,
I suddenly saw my figure repeated endlessly in mutual reflections. I drew back at once, for I was deeply moved by the idea
of the two empty mirrors reflecting in infinite layers of contemplation the void that stood between them. I tried to peek
around the edge of one to get a look at this endless reverbera-
tion of still and pure space, but at once my head appeared—
my heads, scores and scores of them retreating into invisibil-
ity; and I drew back again.

"I think of the place between those mirrors as a
metaphor for my poem. Whenever I move into it, these days,
I see the many images of myself, and I am not pleased; I
draw back. I want the poem to be a magical dialogue of reflections, with pure Rome between the mirrors, Rome as it truly
was (is), with all its pain, wonder, and glory, its contradiction
of love of liberty and love of tyranny, its need for Caesar and

for Cato, its vitality and squalor and pride and bustle. But I feel that I distort this Rome when I intrude on it. I have reached the point where I cannot bear to peek around the frame.

"Perhaps the trouble is that all of Rome is in me—not just the love of liberty, as I used to think, but the love of tyranny, too; and looking in the mirrors is displeasing because though I may be a creator I am still only a man. All this stems from an absurd fastidiousness in me. I know that I cannot stay out of my poem—that my poem must perforce be the essence, not of Rome, but of Lucan. Still, the facing mirrors repel me.

"I am at peace these days only when I am with you. Here in Rome I want to shout, quarrel, shock people. I must break away and come to you. I will. I will.

"Farewell."

March 31

To TIGELLINUS from PAENUS, Tribune of Secret Police
From Cleonicus: Old man Seneca is befuddled by the pressure he feels himself to be under. Thinks he is being mysterious about certain things, but from this letter we can now be *sure* that his rival is Piso.

"Seneca to Lucan, greetings:
"How thankful I am, my nephew, for three people in this world I can trust with the heart of my heart. Paulina. You. My dear Cleonicus. When you think that one of these is a woman and another is a former slave of mine, it becomes clear that human transactions need not all be matters of self-interest, of hard dealings by hard men, of the strong using the weak. You three love me. I love you. It is as simple as that.

"At last I have had a visit from the city—but an unsatisfactory one, Lucan. Antonius Natalis. You know him.

"I have known this fellow for many years, and I have not, to be honest, had a high opinion of him. Our acquaintance has been casual, one based on the fact that he was an intimate, and I a social friend, of a man you know very well. I don't care for men who do nothing with themselves. Natalis's grandfather made a fortune in the grain trade and bought several large country estates, on the rents of which Natalis's father and now Natalis have lived well enough. This one is a fop—dresses himself with a woman's care and spews the deadliest gossip. He has not trained himself for any usefulness whatsoever; knows neither rhetoric nor even any commercial skills. I suppose you know that he has made a hobby or pastime of studying Greek literature, but in conversations I have found this side of him to be shallow and affected. I know that you speak highly of him; I have heard you make a judgment that he 'has sympathies,' or, as I think you put it, 'has correct and true sympathies'—meaning, I presume, that he agrees with you on the things about which you are so emotional.

"Natalis, on entering my house, seemed for a time quite unable to tell me why he had called on me, but when the room was for a moment free of slaves he asked me in a whisper to walk outdoors with him where we could not be overheard. We strolled among the vines. Still for a time he was most awkward. Finally he blurted out that he had come as a messenger of goodwill from our mutual friend.

"Why, Natalis asked, did I shun this man's company? Why had I cut myself off from him? This person and I had once been good friends, says Natalis—should not good friendship be nourished by frequentation?

"Mind you, this Natalis said not a word about all that business my previous visitor had mentioned, not a word about this certain man *being the other choice*. It was all in terms of 'friendship'—a message from a friend with hurt feelings.

"This messenger was obviously not the one to whom I should give any positive answer on my own behalf. I did not like it. I excused myself to Natalis, saying that I have been in poor health; I need rest; this is why I have retired to the seclusion of Nomentum; I cannot see even old friends at this time.

"In short, I refused to talk to *the other man*. I could only guess that his motive for this invitation was to try to persuade me to accede to him, to swing my supporters to him. Of course I have no intention of doing this, and in the state of uncertainty in which I find myself I do not dare to speak to anyone.

"Why have you not written to me, or come to me? I am puzzled by your silence.

"Farewell."

April 2

To PAENUS, Tribune of Secret Police, from TIGELLINUS
   Secret. Secret.

I have read and thought carefully about Seneca's last two communications to Lucan, and I have taken note of the Natalis visit.

Have Seneca poisoned. Work with extreme care. I have not discussed this with the authorities, who might not approve. Extreme care, do you understand me? This must appear to be the result of a sickness. Do not consult Locusta as to what to use; find other advice. She might go to the authorities, for whom she has so often officiated. But do not use any method other than a subtle poison.

Extreme care, Paenus. Your life and mine, and perhaps another's, depend on this mission.

April 5

To TIGELLINUS from PAENUS, Tribune of Secret Police
Urgent.

The informer Valerius has come to us just now with the following information.

This took place about an hour ago, at the public toilet at the baths of the Field of Mars. Lucan entered and seated himself. The toilet was crowded. From under him, in a few moments, came the sound of a fart for which, Valerius says, Lucan must have been saving up for days; a noise from a legend, Valerius says, which echoed without end in the marble-walled toilet.

At once the others who were defecating in that large room heard Lucan intone in a theatrical voice, mimicking the public delivery of none other than Himself:

> *"You might have thought it thundered under*
> *the earth . . ."*

Every literate man who was shitting there recognized this as a famous line written and read by Himself at the Neronia, and everyone fled from the toilet in terror. They had to arrange their clothes as they ran. Several stumbled and were trampled.

April 7

To TIGELLINUS from ALBINOFULVUS, Chief Magister,
Imperial Stables

In response to your oral commands of last week I have been on a tour of all the stables within three days' journey of Rome. I am glad to say I have found two superb fours, neither of which have raced here, one from the Alashkert line you suggested, the other from a longer-shanked, heavier-haunched strain of grays from farther south, from the region of the middle Tigris River. The latter are derived from desert herders' horses, bred to run hard in soft footing, immensely strong.

I was wondering whether the worshipped Person might not be pleased to take an exercise turn in a chariot behind one of these fours. Confidentially, if he would, I could render them safe by exercising them hard for three days straight beforehand. Even under these circumstances the worshipped Person would, I am sure, derive great pleasure from the hot, nervous energy of these fine beasts.

The horses will in any case be at the peak of condition for the Circus of Ceres.

I await instructions.

April 10
To TIGELLINUS from PAENUS, Tribune of Secret Police
You mocked a previous item on checkers, but read this and think about it.

While playing yesterday with Sleepy-Eyes, Piso advanced three petty thieves to the far row and thus converted them into bandits—counters free to move, as you must know, in all directions. Scaevinus had managed to convert one. Piso then conducted a pursuit of Scaevinus's single bandit with his three. He began to refer to Sleepy-Eyes' bandit as "the terrible one." When he finally managed to corner it against one side of the board, where his three blocked all escape and destroyed Piso's counter, he jumped up and danced around the room—a most unusual celebration for one who almost never loses at thief-checkers. Scaevinus fell off his chair laughing. We are told that Piso was not drunk; Scaevinus, as usual, was.

April 11
To TIGELLINUS from PAENUS, Tribune of Secret Police
From our agent in Mela's household this letter, which contains disturbing phrases:

"Epicharis to Lucan, greetings:

"You asked before you left how long I could remain serene. What does 'how long' mean? Perhaps I ask less of life than you do. What for me is a moment is for you a month. Please understand me, dear heart: I am not asking you to ask less of life. Your great beauty is your urgency. I kept thinking when we were talking about the future that your eyes were pools of Vulcan's heat, and that in that heat irresistible instruments could be forged. I am no less dissatisfied than you are, but my method is to work in modest ways. If I can heal a single wound or relieve one tired frame, I feel mended, refreshed. You dream feverishly of . . . of what? . . . of a typhoon . . . of getting back to your poem.

"You will. Soon. I feel sure of it.

"I never think of you without awe for your gifts, among which is the gift of enlarging all that you touch.

"When you left, I got out your books, and I put them around in the places you like best when you are here—one on the chair in the atrium, where you like to look out at the sea; one on your couch in the dining room; one on the extra table your father set up for you in the library—so I could pretend that you were still here. Your father does not mind; he smiles at my folly without knowing how much it means. I caress the books; I pick them up and read, as if looking into your eyes.

"You seemed refreshed when you left. You will be back at work soon again. Avoid quarrels with Polla; they drain you. Think of me, smile, be at peace.

"Farewell."

To ALBINOFULVUS, Chief Magister, Imperial Stables,
    from TIGELLINUS
Himself has taken most warmly to your suggestion of the

other day about the exercise-ride. We will set it for the day after tomorrow, if the weather is fine, at the eighth hour.

I have been thinking about trying to build Himself's pleasure in this Circus of Ceres, and I want your help. We will do this partly by our conversation with Himself day after tomorrow. But I have a further thought. To heighten the dramatic tension of the Circus itself, it would be a good plan to control, to some extent, the outcome of the races. I realize, considering the traditional inviolacy of the teams' integrity, that this is a delicate matter.

The point would be to have the Green team fall far behind at first, then, as the races followed, gradually catch up and at last take the day in the final race. This could be achieved in part by simply using your weaker horses in the early races and these two new fours only toward the end. But we must *ensure* the outcome.

Let me know what you think. I will arrange to talk privately with you while Himself is driving day after tomorrow.

April 14

To TIGELLINUS from PAENUS, Tribune of Secret Police
Cleonicus intercept, which I send you with great regret and in great distress. This kind of thing always happens when we work under pressure both of time and of the contempt of superiors.

> "Seneca to Lucan, greetings:
> "We have reached bad days, Lucan.
> "Yesterday came to me my faithful Cleonicus to say that a certain slave in my kitchen had been making preparations to poison me but had lost his nerve at the last moment and had gone in tears and terror to Cleonicus to confess. I asked to see the slave, and he was brought to me. He was a

fresh-cheeked boy of about eighteen. I did not recognize him, though Cleonicus says he has been a slave of ours for six years. How sad this made me, Lucan—that among my servants and dependents there could be someone who is a total stranger to me. I suppose this is inevitable. There are seven hundred souls on my various estates, and to have known them all as I would like to have known them would have been a life's work; I could not have been a philosopher and certainly not a porter of influential burdens at court.

"This boy was in a terrible fright. At first I thought he was afraid that I would have him destroyed in some barbaric way. But no, he was not afraid of me. Worse, he had no feelings whatsoever about me, either of guilt or compassion or love or respect or fear. I was a stranger who happened to be his master. He was only afraid of the persons who had promised him not only his freedom but *fifty thousand sesterces* of hard Roman money to put me out of the way. How could a poor, uneducated slave resist such offers as those? Now he feared for his life.

"In his babbling it came out that he had lost his nerve because he had become convinced that the substance he had been given to use would not in fact kill me, he would make some mistake, he would be found out. This was enough to persuade me that the boy had at base a pure and candid heart: An innocent-hearted man, no matter how tempted, falters at the threshold of a terrible crime. Of course he was too terror-stricken to tell me who his tempters were. Another man would have tortured him to find out—but such a man, Lucan, would have done so because he was afraid to die, and I am not. Instead of torturing this poor, rattled, peach-cheeked dependent, I made plans to protect him—and myself —from . . . Natalis? Natalis's and our mutual friend? My previous visitor, not being satisfied with my response, or having been an agent of others who were testing me and did not like what I had or had not said? More powerful persons, who have been informed of my visitor and his proposal by others, perhaps by some of the soldiers who were supposed to favor me?

"This incident has not abashed me, Lucan. No, it has, rather, toughened the muscle of my resolve. I must do what I can to make outrages of this sort unnecessary. I will not be poisoned, at any rate. I am living now exclusively on fresh fruits. I drink water straight from a cool stream. The young slave is in a safe place. And I wait. It is not easy, but have I ever asked for an easy life, Lucan?

"My wait would be much less difficult if you would write to me. At least let me know by Cleonicus's return that you have destroyed this letter.

"Farewell."

April 16

To TIGELLINUS from VALERIUS FLAVUS, Senator

You may have heard that a scurrilous poem by Lucan is circulating throughout the city by word of mouth. He has lampooned all the most important persons. His old teacher Cornutus forced him to change almost everything, so the poem became a generalized satire, but *many people* are repeating both versions, first the innocuous one, then the unexpurgated, and there is laughter in the city over this. I need not do more than compare a few phrases in the publishable text with their counterparts in the original. This line, for example, having been tempered by Cornutus, is inoffensive enough:

Who has not an ass's ears?

But from Lucan's hand had come this line, and we know what it means:

King Midas has an ass's ears.

This corrected line slanders no one in particular:

The ambitious man sniffs the courtier's fish.

But the original, Tigellinus, accuses you of lowering yourself to a most humiliating *fellatio* in order to keep your influence:

The seller of mules eats Imperial fish.

This line comments in a general way on the power many rich women enjoy today in Rome:

Women play their husbands' lyres.

But its original, Tigellinus, means that a certain important man is no more powerful in the presence of a wife than he was in the lifetime of a mother:

Juno plays with Jupiter's bolts.

Sacrilege apart, this last line also has in it a subtle suggestion that this important man's private parts are now reserved as the toys exclusively of one woman, that wife; there is *also* in it a subtle reference to a recent allusion to thunder in public toilets that is now famous all over Rome.

To VALERIUS FLAVUS, Senator, from TIGELLINUS
You are a mischievous informer. Keep your loathsome reports coming. Someday I want to learn why you hate Lucan so.

To TIGELLINUS from PAENUS, Tribune of Secret Police
We cannot establish any link between the Consul Vestinus and the Piso group. Apart from his having kept his private bodyguard, he has been scrupulously correct.

April 17

To PAENUS, Tribune of Secret Police, from TIGELLINUS
Secret.

The Seneca letter. When this is over we will have an accounting with you and your service. Cancel the order concerning Seneca. He will ruin his digestion on raw fruits, stream water, and expectation of poison. This diet may kill him; it will surely hurt him more than your butchers could.

I hesitate to consult further with you, but I have no choice. The time has come when we must try to bring pressure to bear on one of the Piso–Lucan circle to inform on the whole pack. Which man or men would you suggest? I probably will not take your advice, but I might as well have it to guide me as to what not to do.

April 18

To TIGELLINUS from PAENUS, Tribune of Secret Police

As to pressure: I think Quintianus. He is proud of being a pederast and so probably cannot be blackmailed, but his way of life leaves him peculiarly open to attacks by jealous persons, threats of beating, and ridicule. Ever since Himself lampooned him, reports have been trickling in of an ambiguous attitude on his part—a desire, on the one hand, for redress, which may have led him into this circle in the first place, but also a powerful attraction to Himself and a wish to be loved again by him. I quote from your own communication to me of last September 21, referring to this man: "We can easily get to him in due course by way of his failing." I have very little laughter left in me, Tigellinus, but, you see, here is a way for me to make a recommendation that you will follow: agree with you. Otherwise I might be so foolish as to suggest Natalis.

To ALBINOFULVUS, Chief Magister, Imperial Stables, from TIGELLINUS

Himself directs me to thank you for a pleasurable afternoon. The horses, he said, were like sea waves in a southwest storm —beautiful, swift, white-maned on gray backs, irresistible, and dangerous.

Confidential: I liked very much your plan for controlling the outcome at the Circus of Ceres. You are right: The people surrounding the Red Team are thoroughly corrupt, and we can leave it to them (checking, of course, from time to time) to work on the other teams. Put the scheme into effect.

April 20

To TIGELLINUS from PAENUS, Tribune of Secret Police

A new filch from the Mela household; this again was found in Epicharis's jewel box, and is obviously of recent date. I am alarmed by the ambiguous "Soon, soon." I advise an immediate alert of all agents. I await your instructions.

"Lucan to Epicharis, greetings:

"I have written something! My hand moved, the stylus made marks! A foolish satire, to clear my head of rage. I was wildly happy, and I took it to the old horned one [Cornutus], and he shook his head and said I would displease somebody. So he went over the poem with me, and we changed all the references to somebody and his wife, and there is nothing much left but a dried fig of a poem, but I do not care. All that matters to me is that my hand moved, the words were there!

"One day soon I will step boldly again into the space between the double mirrors.

"Soon. Soon.

"Farewell."

To PAENUS, Tribune of Secret Police, from TIGELLINUS
Urgent.
No alert. Himself *still* says: Wait.

To TIGELLINUS from PAENUS, Tribune of Secret Police
Cleonicus intercept: an uncharacteristically short letter
from Seneca.

"Seneca to Lucan, greetings:
"You used to praise my serenity. Why are you testing
it so? Why have you abandoned me? Write.
"Farewell."

April 21
To TIGELLINUS from VALERIUS FLAVUS, Senator
In recent days Lucan has, I believe, gone mad. Now he is
making the wildest of threats. *I heard him with my own ears*
promise a certain man, whom I can name, that he would
deliver a head with the neck of a bull and the hair of a girl—
he can only have meant one head in Rome, Tigellinus—to
this friend one day soon on a trencher, garnished for roasting,
with an apple in the mouth and parsley over the ears and a
coronet of bay leaves.
I do not hate Lucan. I am fascinated by him. If he has in
truth gone mad, it must be the toxin of conceit that has done
him in. As you doubtless have observed, writers are peculiarly
susceptible to this poison, but I have never seen one, not even
Petronius (who is purged by humor) or Seneca (who is saved
by his greatness, and in whom conceit appears as a grotesque
modesty), that is so egregiously in love with himself as Lucan.
His wife Polla has been one of his chief poisoners. Here is the
only thing that keeps Lucan from being a great writer: He
loves himself so much that he has no love left over for
mankind.

FOUR

April 24

To PAENUS, Tribune of Secret Police, from TIGELLINUS
Himself was right all along—he *knew* that *someone* would crack.

Come at once to the small reception room next to the throne hall. Important interrogation in the Presence of Himself. You will keep the record as usual; bring a stenographer.

To RUFUS, Co-Commander, Praetorian Guard, from
    TIGELLINUS
Come at once to the small reception room next to the throne hall. Important interrogation in the Presence of Himself. The witness is offering information, but you had better bring the giant Cassius, on the remote chance that force may be needed.

INTERROGATION:
Volusius Proculus

In the Presence of the Emperor. Attending: Tigellinus, Rufus, Paenus, Cassius; Felix, Stenographer.

TIGELLINUS asked HIMSELF if he wished to have TIG. do the questioning, and the order was given to proceed. TIG. asked DEPONENT his name. Reply: VOLUSIUS PROCULUS.

TIG. asked identification.

PROCULUS deposed that he is Captain in the Fleet at *Misenum*; seventeen-year veteran.

TIG. asked PROCULUS what he wished to state.

PROCULUS at this time appeared extremely nervous, assured HIMSELF that his only desire was to protect his Person, stated that as a fighting sailor, on the deck of a ship, he had no fear, but he had not imagined he would be brought before the Person of the EMPEROR.

HIMSELF urged PROCULUS to calm himself, saying: We are merciful.

WITNESS expressed profuse thanks, said he had never thought to enter . . . (*intending to continue*).

TIG. cut PROCULUS off with admonition to come to the point and not waste the EMPEROR's time.

PROCULUS apologized once more, then said: You see, it was the woman EPICHARIS, she suggested to me . . . (*intending to continue*).

HIMSELF interrupted, asking who this woman was. TIG. replied that extensive information had been assembled on this woman and directed PAENUS to summarize it. PAENUS reported that the woman is mistress of ANNAEUS MELA, who in turn was identified as brother of SENECA and father of LUCAN; that she is the bastard daughter of Sen. APICIUS MARCELLUS by UNIDEN-TIFIED slave woman captured in the East; that she is notorious in the district around *Misenum* for her agitation on behalf of slaves and the poor; that unknown to MELA she has been exchanging what appear to be love letters with LUCAN.

HIMSELF, seeming annoyed by parts of this information, directed DEPONENT to continue.

PROCULUS: She tried to enlist me in a conspiracy to . . . I am afraid to say it.

TIG. admonished DEPONENT to speak out, threatening the persuasion of the giant CASSIUS if the DEPONENT hesitated further.

PROCULUS: No, no. Why do you threaten me, Commander? I have come of my own will. . . . A conspiracy to . . . to murder NERO CAESAR. She tried to get me to join and enlist others from the Navy. She said there would be many chances to do the thing at sea as warm weather came on because the great CAESAR loves to sail out of *Puteoli* and *Misenum*.

TIG. asked where this had taken place and how DEPONENT had happened to talk plots with this woman.

PROCULUS: We all know her.

TIG.: Carnally? What are you trying to suggest?

PROCULUS: No, nothing like that. She is strange. She is a strange, fierce woman. She is often in the marketplace. We saw her one day helping to carry a slave, one of her own, in her own litter.

TIG. asked what the WOMAN had said about a conspiracy.

PROCULUS: That important men were in it; it would surely succeed.

TIG. asked what important men, and at this point DEPONENT began to behave in an evasive manner, blurting out among other things that the WOMAN had said many foul things about NERO CAESAR. . . .

TIG. asked if the name LUCAN had been mentioned.

PROCULUS said he had heard that name somewhere, but he did not think the WOMAN had mentioned it.

Had SENECA been one of the "important men"?

PROCULUS said he had heard SENECA speak once at the *Rostra,* but . . . he could not remember.

PISO?

He could not remember.

TIG. directed CASSIUS to refresh DEPONENT's memory, but at this point HIMSELF intervened, ordering TIG. to restrain CASSIUS and asking DEPONENT straightaway: What foul things about me?

With elaborate obeisances DEPONENT said he had come to help NERO CAESAR, to warn him; that he was telling everything he knew; that EPICHARIS had mentioned no names.

HIMSELF observed that this was because she knew she was talking to a fool, and reminded DEPONENT that he had asked him a question. DEPONENT confessed that he was confused, that he had not expected to be brought into the Presence, that he only wanted to do his duty. He then angered HIMSELF by asking what question HIMSELF had asked.

HIMSELF repeated: What foul things about me?

PROCULUS: About your mother.

HIMSELF: Yes?

PROCULUS: And that NERO CAESAR had taken all the power away from the Senate, but that these important men were going to make NERO CAESAR pay for having done that.

HIMSELF: What about my mother?

PROCULUS: That she . . . that she is dead.

HIMSELF now rose, and all who were seated rose with him. HIMSELF said with heat that the interrogation was a waste of time, directed TIG. to arrest EPICHARIS, said he could not decide whether to reward DEPONENT or have him flogged, and commanded TIG. to hold PROCULUS for a confrontation with the WOMAN.

The interrogation was adjourned.

PAENUS AFRANIUS (Recorder)

April 25

INTERROGATION:
Epicharis

In the Presence of the Emperor. Attending: Tigellinus, Rufus, Paenus, Cassius; Proculus in confrontation; Felix, Stenographer.

TIGELLINUS directed the Captain PROCULUS to repeat the charges he had brought the day before against the woman EPICHARIS.

PROCULUS: Well, she came up to me right there by the stand where the fennel and eggplant and mushrooms were being sold, and she began by asking me if I was a brave seaman . . . (*intending to continue*).

TIG. directed PROCULUS not to give a full recital but to state the substance of the charge.

PROCULUS now spoke straight to HIMSELF, protesting that he was a loyal officer; that he had been seventeen years in the ships; that NERO CAESAR could see what the WOMAN looked like; that it was natural that a man would be drawn into conversation . . . (*intending to continue*).

HIMSELF ordered PROCULUS to come to the accusation.

PROCULUS: That she tried to enlist me in a plot to assassinate great CAESAR.

TIG., turning to EPICHARIS, asked her what she said to this.

EPICHARIS: That the man lies.

Here HIMSELF intervened: You deny the charge?

The WOMAN said very warmly: Where are his witnesses? He speaks of a market stand. Where are the vendors or other sailors to support his lies?

TIG.: You deny having talked with this man?

EPICHARIS: No.

TIG.: You have talked with him?

EPICHARIS: He comes here not to save NERO but to save himself.

TIG.: What does that mean?

Now PROCULUS began to babble: She came up to me, I distinctly remember, by the fennel and eggplant. She began by complaining about the prices, she said that poor people could eat only feed corn and hog fat, then she . . . (*intending to continue*).

TIG. sharply cut PROCULUS off and asked EPICHARIS what she had meant—*save himself rather than* NERO CAESAR?

EPICHARIS: He talks as if I had been a stranger accosting him in the market like some prostitute. He knows very well we had spoken to each other in passing numerous times. We first met one day when there was an accident, a vendor's stand was knocked over by a centurion's horse, there was an argument, the vendor was wronged and I took his part, this officer was a witness. Often since then we had spoken a few words to each other. This last time, three days ago, he had been drinking, he asked me to walk away from the market with him, he was wild and angry. He said that I was a person who tried to see that justice was done. He said he had been wronged, he wanted my help. He said that six years ago he was the helmsman of the vessel that was used for the EMPEROR's matricide, he was almost killed when the vessel's roof fell, and he said that his assistance to NERO CAESAR in a very great crime should have brought from NERO CAESAR a very great promotion. Instead he had been ignored. He had not even been advanced since then in the regular line of seniority. Not a single coin had crossed his palm. . . .

HIMSELF again intervened, asking PROCULUS with great annoyance if this was true, if he had indeed made these complaints to a virtual stranger?

Once more, profuse obeisances and protestations from PROCULUS, who again mentioned the long period of his service and added the fact that he had suffered shipwreck off Africa. He was intending to continue in this vein when HIMSELF asked his question a second time. With scant control PROCULUS now continued to use a hasty tongue to tell how the WOMAN had tried to enlist him in a conspiracy, how he had risked his life in the past for NERO CAESAR, that he had come this time to save NERO CAESAR's life, and so on . . . (*intending to continue*).

The EMPEROR, pronouncedly choleric, now rose, and all who were seated rose with him. HIMSELF declared in a loud voice that he had had enough; that the EMPEROR of *Rome* was not accustomed to ask a question *three times*. He ordered CASSIUS to take the SEA CAPTAIN outside and to teach him how to testify in the Imperial Presence, to give a lesson that would not soon be forgotten. CASSIUS removed PROCULUS, who to the moment of exit continued to sing frantic praises of his own past services to NERO CAESAR. HIMSELF then turned to TIG. and objected that these proceedings had become a scandal, that witnesses were allowed to rant, that what came forth, in sum, were accusations not against the accused but against the State. There was complete confusion. Why had TIG. not prepared the witnesses beforehand? Everything should have been stripped down to six sentences. He had never had his temper so tried.

TIG. now reminded HIMSELF that it was HIMSELF who had ordered these raw hearings. TIG. averred that he had offered to squeeze the truth out of these vermin without bothering HIMSELF but that HIMSELF had expressed interest . . . (*intending to continue*).

HIMSELF stated with asperity that he had a great deal on his mind; that the Circus of the festival of Ceres was only three

days away; that gibbering, cringing men were a great annoyance to him. He could not waste any more time thus. He
directed TIG. to let the SAILOR go, to give him five hundred
sesterces after CASSIUS had taught him how to answer questions, then to let him go. He commanded TIG. to hold the
woman EPICHARIS. HIMSELF told TIG. that he was not satisfied.
He repeated that he was not satisfied *with any of this*.

TIG. requested HIMSELF's permission to ask the WOMAN
some further questions. HIMSELF said he was of the decided
opinion that TIG. had better do just that, and left the room.

TIG. now told EPICHARIS that information had come to the
palace to the effect that she was intimate with her master's
son LUCAN.

EPICHARIS, speaking again with warmth and firmness of
nerve: Master? No man is my master. If you mean ANNAEUS
MELA, he is my lover and my friend.

TIG. corrected himself with ironic precision, now using the
phrase, *your lover's son*. Information had come that she was
in love with her lover's son.

EPICHARIS, passing over TIG.'s sarcasm: LUCAN? I am fond of
him, poor boy. He is starved for a mother's care. His own
mother rails at him. He is like a little boy. I am amazed by
the greatness of his poetry, I see him as a pathetic boy who
comes with big eyes and wants to walk on the grounds with
me. NERO was very cruel to proscribe his work.

TIG. observed that the DEPONENT was not in a favorable position at this moment to pass judgment on the EMPEROR of
Rome.

EPICHARIS: I cannot help it. It was very cruel. LUCAN is a
better poet than he is, and he is jealous—everyone knows that.

Now TIG. tartly ordered EPICHARIS to hold her tongue, ad-
vising her that she would have reason to regret speaking foolishly. He then asked: How often does LUCAN visit MELA?

EPICHARIS: Seldom. The father and son are awkward with each other. MELA has often told me how much he loves LUCAN and how hard it is for him to talk with the boy. There are long silences, and LUCAN loses his temper.

TIG. asked when LUCAN had last come to see MELA.

EPICHARIS: Let me think. Oh, it has been some time.

TIG. now began to press EPICHARIS on this point, saying he would like to know exactly how much time. But the WOMAN continued evasive, or forgetful. Several questions and answers were exchanged, but neither persuasion nor threat could move EPICHARIS away from the assertion that she could not remember. TIG. therefore shifted ground and asked when she had last visited her master's brother.

EPICHARIS: You are fully as boorish and malign as everyone says you are. Perhaps you did not hear me say that no one is my master.

TIG. insisted that she knew very well what he was saying; that he referred to SENECA. He wished to know when she had last visited SENECA.

EPICHARIS: MELA never goes to see SENECA. MELA is a sensitive, gentle, and retiring person. Both of his brothers are pushing men, ambitious men. MELA has no use for any of that. He stays away from all that, and . . . (*intending to continue*).

TIG. now explained with exaggerated patience that he had not asked her when her master had gone to see SENECA, but rather when she had gone.

EPICHARIS stood silent.

TIG. directed her to respond.

EPICHARIS: I will not speak to you if you persist in calling MELA my master.

TIG. reminded the WOMAN that he had ways of persuading her to speak to him, whatever he might choose to say. This, he said, should be taken as a warning. Again he asked when she had visited SENECA, and promptly suggested that it had been on the fourteenth of March. Was this not so?

EPICHARIS: I go where MELA goes.

TIG. suggested that it had been in the disguise of a farm woman selling pheasant eggs. Was this not so?

EPICHARIS: I have told you that MELA does not go to see his brother.

TIG. said that detailed information had reached the palace ... (*intending to continue*).

EPICHARIS, with much spirit: Which cannot be proved because it is false. And let me tell you another thing. Your EMPEROR has behaved despicably toward SENECA. I am not myself fond of SENECA. His manner is too portentous, everything is inflated in him, the smallest gesture is burdened with a cartload of significance, when he strikes an attitude it is as if he were modeling for a sculptor who was carving his statue for posterity in stone. He has not a grain of the unaffected Stoical purity of MELA. Still and all, NERO has cast SENECA aside in the most heartless way—under your brutish influence. TIGELLINUS, you busy yourself with what you call information, but you have no real information at all. You have no idea what the ordinary Roman thinks of you and of your EMPEROR. Every Roman knows that SENECA has been treated badly.

Now TIG. turned what she had said around and suggested that she had made it clear that SENECA felt he had reason for resentment.

EPICHARIS: SENECA never utters a resentful word. He is sad about what is happening to his former pupil—but resentful? He is a philosopher, TIGELLINUS. I suppose you would not know the meaning of that word.

TIG. rose from his seat and sternly said that he observed EPICHARIS was not disposed to answer his questions in a straightforward way, and he directed PAENUS to put EPICHARIS in chains, speculating that perhaps the weight of the chains would take some of the vainglory out of her. He gave her notice that she would be questioned again, after she had had a few days to carry the chains and refresh her memory.

The interrogation was adjourned.

PAENUS AFRANIUS (Recorder)

To ALBINOFULVUS, Chief Magister, Imperial Stables, from TIGELLINUS

I hope you will be able to give me assurances that all is under firm control with respect to the races at the Circus of Ceres. Himself is looking forward to the occasion with tender anticipation.

To PAENUS, Tribune of Secret Police, from TIGELLINUS

I have discussed with Himself our unsatisfactory results with Epicharis, and he has authorized torture but insists on waiting two days, until after the festival of Ceres, to see whether mere confinement will not break her. I pointed out to Himself that the arrest of Epicharis will have given the alarm to all the others, if there are indeed others, and could have the effect either of precipitating a rash act on their part or of allowing them to cover their tracks and hamper our efforts to expose them. But confidentially, Paenus, Himself was badly upset by Epicharis—by her cool and brazen reference to the matricide; by her close association with Seneca and Lucan; by her being so stubborn; and perhaps also by her very good looks. It frightens him when people are not frightened of him. Have you noticed that he carries his little ivory girl-goddess to these interrogations?

Paenus, we are going to be tested at the Circus during the

races. We will have to keep a wall of courage and sharp steel around Himself. As you know, he detests visible protection. Outline a plan to me of a protection that is both obvious and subtle.

To TIGELLINUS from PAENUS, Tribune of Secret Police
Now you ask another of your preposterous riddles: for protection that will be invisible to Himself yet fearfully seen by his enemies. Next you will ask me for a blindfold that will improve a man's eyesight. I have, however, one thought. Arm some women. Have you noticed how strong some of Poppaea's freedwomen and slaves are? They are quick, too, and dextrous. Let them carry hidden weapons. Poppaea will enjoy the intrigue of arming her coterie and will surely wish to carry a dagger herself. It gives Himself pleasure to have women swarming around him. This must be regulated with care, however, as Himself will be wanting to discuss wagers and to rerun the races in conversation with men. You and I must be armed; the principal freedmen; Rufus, of course. With the help of the women we can have a thorny hedge around him.

To PAENUS, Tribune of Secret Police, from TIGELLINUS
At last you have had a good idea, and in the face of my sounder reason, which tells me that coming from you the idea must have a flaw hidden in it, I allow myself to congratulate you. I have already discussed the vigil of the Amazons with Poppaea, and, as you foretold, she is entering into the thing with a ferocious pleasure. Himself will be safe. My only concern is: Will we ever be able to disarm these women?

To TIGELLINUS from ALBINOFULVUS, Chief Magister,
    Imperial Stables
All is ready.

To begin with, the new fours, both the Alashkert chestnuts and the Tigris grays, are in superb form. They would win in any case. They will each run twice; thus four races are certain. But we have further assured, by "conversation," a dramatic day. We will get the stunts out of the way in the morning— besides seven regular races, there will be two races of three-horse chariots, one of pairs, and one each of sixes and eights. I loathe those races of more than fours; so many beautiful horses are injured in them. The twelve races in the afternoon, all of fours, will be serious affairs.

By midday the Green team will be badly behind. The Green will win the first afternoon race, so that the greatest gambler of all will not go into the afternoon in bad humor. . . . But I will not tell you the sequence, Tigellinus, lest we be treated to the shameful spectacle of the Co-Commander of the Praetorian Guard, certain of outcomes, betting against the Emperor's chariots in certain races.

For the desultory periods between races I have found some exceptional entertainments: a pair of Assyrian acrobats who leap back and forth, somersaulting in the air, between two galloping horses; a squad of Spaniards who mimic warfare convincingly on horseback; a fine bay jumper that soars over a chariot harnessed to a four; and the usual pennant-snatchers, dancers on bareback, and clowns. After the sixth afternoon race there will be a shower of oranges, sweets, and ginger, intermixed with tickets of chance for a villa at Antium and with several hundred filled purses.

We had almost no trouble gaining the cooperation of the Whites, the Blues, and the Reds in assuring final victory to the Greens. (We *will* see trainers and charioteers betting large sums against themselves—ample consolation, in most cases, for the double shame of losing and doing it corruptly.) The only team we had some trouble with was the Blues, mostly because of the vanity of a promising young driver of theirs, Priscus, who at the age of nineteen has won two hundred forty-three races and at first did not fancy the idea of wasting an afternoon; he already has so much money that he considers himself above mere bribery. But the management of that faction, as you know, have hearts of tufa. They persuaded Priscus that he should bear in mind the hazards of his profession—reminded him that drivers are apt to die rich but very young. He understood what they were saying.

Wait, Tigellinus, till you see our grays at the start of the last race, which will decide the day. Handsome Classicus will be our driver in his green tunic, helmeted, the traces tied around his waist, while in front of him will be that noble four, pawing the track, powerful as ocean waves, as our poet-Emperor said—tails knotted high, manes interlaced with pearls, breastplates covered with amulets of their winnings on tracks on other soils, collars bearing the iridescent green ribbons of the Imperial team. I have never in all my years at the stables seen such magnificent horseflesh. It will be a fine end to a fine day.

April 26

To TIGELLINUS from EPAPHRODITUS, Freedman of the Palace

Urgent.

Excuse my disturbing you at this hour and on a festive day.

One of the keepers of the gate of the Servilian gardens came to me a half hour ago saying that since before dawn a man had been beating at the portal with a staff and that no amount of shouting that the doors were shut to strangers would satisfy him. I ordered him admitted, and they brought him to me. His wife is with him. He is a certain Senator's freedman— I will mention no names here. I have taken a dagger from him, which he says he did not mean to use, another person meant to use it. He has things to say that Himself must hear.

INTERROGATION:
Milichus

In the Presence of the Emperor. Attending: Tigellinus, Paenus, Epaphroditus; wife of Milichus; Felix, Stenographer.

The EMPEROR warned the DEPONENT that he must say what he had to say quickly, because the Imperial cortege was about to leave for the Circus.

TIGELLINUS directed DEPONENT to tell his story.

In a misguided rush the DEPONENT said that he and his wife had been discussing certain events of the previous day and night in his patron's house; that the wife had insisted that he come directly to NERO CAESAR, that he and his wife were conscious of their duty; that the gatekeeper . . . (*intending to continue*).

TIG. ordered DEPONENT to put things in straight order, and to begin by identifying himself.

DEPONENT: I am called Milichus. My patron is FLAVIUS SCAEVINUS. I was given my cap of freedom . . . (*intending to continue*).

At this point TIG. reminded HIMSELF that the above-mentioned SCAEVINUS was a Senator; that he was a close friend to PISO; that SENECA had doubtless presented SCAEVINUS to HIMSELF, as SCAEVINUS had often backed SENECA in his projects; that HIMSELF would be most readily put in mind of SCAEVINUS by the exaggerated expression of boredom and dissolute exhaustion he constantly wore; and that he had been present and vocal at the much-discussed PISO banquet of the previous September. HIMSELF nodded to indicate that he had the right person in mind.

TIG. ordered DEPONENT to speak.

MILICHUS: He gave me my cap of freedom eight years ago. I have been his chief housekeeper. For several weeks he has not been himself, everything has been upside down in our house. Run here! Run there! He threw an iron comb at me the other day, it could have put my eye out. My wife and I have talked often about his flying off this way and that, lately. I thought it was his liver. It did not seem to be women. My wife said he had come to the stage of his life when he was forced to see that he was a trivial man who would be forgotten the moment he died, even by his own family—the dangerous age when a man of moderate ability comes to the conclusion that life is meaningless.

HIMSELF urged the FREEDMAN to move along to whatever it was he wanted to tell.

With excuses for his awkwardness, MILICHUS continued: Yesterday my patron was gone out of the house from the fourth to the ninth hour. When he came back in, he was in a very strange condition. As always he had drunk wine at the midday meal. He did not now behave in the usual dimmed and zigzag way, though. He was both agitated and depressed, I could tell he was depressed, but he covered his sober thoughts with nervous, cheerful chatter. And he began a series of actions that suggested an imminent collision with his Fate. First he had me get out his will and before witnesses he made some changes in it and sealed it with wax; his hands trembled so that he had me melt and drop the wax and press his ring into it. Then he gave me the dagger—that man has it—to sharpen. He said a dagger must be used. Disuse had dulled this one. Its sitting in a sheath had dulled it, he said.

TIG. asked EPAPHRODITUS if he had the dagger. EPAPHRODITUS protested that TIG. should know he would not bring a dagger into the Presence. TIG. asked where it was. EPAPHRODI-

TUS said he had with due propriety left it in care of the Centurion of the Guard at the Servilian gate. TIG. asked if EPAPHRODITUS could describe it. EPAPHRODITUS attempted a description. Short blade, wood handle. He could not say exactly. Well, it was a dagger. He had been more interested in what the INFORMER had to say. TIG. ordered that the dagger be sent for, and EPAPHRODITUS went to the door and instructed a Guardsman there to fetch it.

TIG. ordered MILICHUS to go on.

MILICHUS: He told me to oil a stone and bring the dagger to a sparkling point. That was what he said. Sparkling. But I had no sooner started working on it than he summoned me and completely changed the order for his dinner, ordered a big banquet—very queer, very morbid—for himself alone, himself and his wife. Look, it was past the tenth hour, almost the eleventh. We had to run out to more than one market, I can tell you, for a goose, fresh asparagus, oysters from the Lucrine rocks, shallots, a mullet, white truffles, some larks, a certain grade of tripe—all his favorite dishes, as I knew. And a fever in the kitchens, as you can imagine, to get all these delicacies ready in time for his dinner. And while as usual he drank too much with this banquet, he did not seem drunk in the usual way. His cheeks were pale, his eyes as keen as he wanted me to make the dagger. He would seem to be in deep thought, then he would chatter and titter as if flirting with his wife (an absurd idea, I promise you on the blood of my heart), and he began calling all his household people, one by one, and he gave seven caps to slaves—that is a large number to set free at once in a household of his size, you know—and he gave money to some, the spaces between his fingers had never been so wide open, honestly. Then he walked up and down, and he called me in and told me to collect some clean tow and lint and some ligatures and straps for tourniquets—all the materials for the stopping of wounds. And was the dagger bright? I told him I hadn't had a minute's time. . . . We talked, my wife and I; this bizarre behavior of his was based on something. And we put together things we had heard, remarks, oblique exchanges with certain men about future conditions. Some mysterious references that had seemed to be code words. Arched eyebrows, you know? And it came to us in the middle of the night that you would be in danger at the Circus today, great CAESAR. And we saw that we had a duty to come to you before dawn.

Here TIG. rose and, clearly suspecting the usual dream of incredible enrichment through rewards for informing, began a testing of the DEPONENT's veracity and motives. Putting his hands on the FREEDMAN's chest and pushing, he asked why MILICHUS was trying to discredit SCAEVINUS. Had he no loyalty to a patron? Did he forget that SCAEVINUS had set him free?

MILICHUS, not having anticipated heavy shoves of the sort TIG. was adeptly giving him, at first staggered and stammered and made a poor show of his honesty. His WIFE ingeniously said that she and her husband were trying to save SCAEVINUS from harm, they were preventing . . . (*intending to continue*).

But TIG. silenced her, saying that he was questioning her husband. And with new cuffs and pushes he accused MILICHUS of trying to take revenge on SCAEVINUS for having thrown objects at him, such as the iron comb he had mentioned.

MILICHUS, glancing at his wife, obviously hoping for new resources of imagination from her, could only think to agree with what she had last said, that the couple had a motive of wishing to spare and rescue their patron.

TIG. now asked the FREEDMAN if he knew the penalty for unduly disturbing the EMPEROR of *Rome*, especially on a festival morning when he was impatient to go to the Circus.

MILICHUS, becoming terrified, fell to his knees in the direction of HIMSELF while his WIFE coolly suggested that the

EMPEROR summon SCAEVINUS and satisfy HIMSELF of the honesty of a poor but loyal man.

TIG.'s previous mention of the Circus caused HIMSELF calmly to say—more concerned, it seemed, for the promised entertainments of the day than for his very life—that it was time to leave.

At this juncture the Centurion SULPICIUS ASPER came at the door, carrying the weapon. TIG. asked for it, and as he examined it, the EMPEROR rose, and all who were seated rose, and HIMSELF now said impatiently: It was time to go.

TIG. was saying: Yes, this was it, this was the one. Many men had been looking for this dagger.

But HIMSELF, already leaving the room, gave scant attention to TIG., and speaking casually over his shoulder, ordered: 1) SCAEVINUS to be arrested, 2) MILICHUS and by all means his WIFE to be held for confrontation, 3) the interrogation to be held on the next day. Then he left, *adjourning the interrogation.* But as an afterthought, putting his head back in the door, he added: 4) EPICHARIS to be tortured, also on the next day.

PAENUS AFRANIUS (Recorder)

To ALBINOFULVUS, Chief Magister, Imperial Stables, from TIGELLINUS

From HIMSELF, a message to all personnel of the Green Faction, to you in particular, but also to the drivers, trainers, veterinarians, stablemen, grooms, stable guards, dressers, waterers, saddlers, tailors, members of the claque:

This has been an exemplary day in the history of Rome, for courage, determination, skill, and long practice prevailed over great adversaries and discouragements. Accept the gratitude of the Emperor of Rome.

For the breastplate of every horse that ran today for the

Green, even though it may not have won, a silver plaque, engraved: CERES THE PROVIDER, *Year XI of Nero*. And in addition, for the breastplates of the Alashkert chestnuts and the Tigris grays, these added words: A GREAT HEART.

Confidential:

I had no idea you were such an artist of intrigue. Perhaps you have been long enough among horses. Perhaps you should come to the palace, where races are not always won by fast legs. You will be rewarded. For the moment, my thanks and admiration.

To ABASCANTUS, Imperial Treasury, from TIGELLINUS

Gifts of honor, twenty thousand sesterces each, to all drivers of the Green faction who competed on this day. Fifty thousand sesterces to Albinofulvus, Chief Magister of the Green Faction.

To VEIANUS NIGER, Tribune of the Praetorian Guard, from TIGELLINUS

Consult with Paenus and, upon establishment of appropriate guilt of its owner, seize an estate in the Campania and give it to Albinofulvus, Chief Magister of the Green Faction. Inscription at the gates: *Honor to Rome.*

To PAENUS, Tribune of Secret Police, from TIGELLINUS

I sit alone at the writing table in my office, in the flickering light of a single lamp, and I wonder what kind of dream it is in which we live. Whose dream? Today it was surely Nero's dream. When he chose to drop the handkerchief himself for the start of the last race and stood there, the trumpeters at the ready beside him, the Tyrian toga of the presiding official over his scarlet tunic, his brow crowned with the wreath of golden leaves, holding up in one hand the baton with its eagle poised for flight, in the other the white signal cloth into whose delicate fabric the whole day's outcome was interwoven, while the din of two hundred thousand shouting voices filled the bowl of the Circus to overflowing, he wore an expression—did you see his face, Paenus?—which was so naïve, so careless, so free of pain and power that I, terrified, as you must have been, by the exposure to assault up there on the tribune where our Amazons could not surround him, actually wept for his innocence. I am a hard man. You know that all too well, Paenus. I do not think I have come to the point of tears in a decade. I am so puzzled by the fickleness of danger. You and I were tense all day—and nothing remotely threatening happened. It seems to me that, by and large, men want to accept authority. They need it, they cheer with open throats for its strong arms and medals. Was I weeping because the challenge to authority we had expected hadn't materialized? I think that vigilance, to which I am very much attracted, is making a woman of me.

But we cannot relax, Paenus. I assume that Scaevinus has been brought in. I am very tired tonight: I will entrust the torture of Epicharis to you and Cassius. It should be done tonight—after midnight because Himself ordered it done tomorrow—or early in the morning; in any case, before the interrogation of Scaevinus. We want names. Report the results to me as soon as you are finished, no matter what the outcome or the hour.

I am not as rough a man as you think. I know your worth. You are a good policeman, Paenus.

To TIGELLINUS from PAENUS, Tribune of Secret Police
Scaevinus is in chains.

We will do Epicharis tonight. Cassius makes good use of darkness.

Thank you for your words, at long last, of . . . what shall
I say? Consolation for past error? I have not thought ill of
you. A man with such an honest nose as yours (large but
straight along the bridge, and bosky in the nostrils) cannot be
all "rough," as you put it.

April 27

To TIGELLINUS from PAENUS, Tribune of Secret Police
Forgive the dark hour. You commanded a prompt report.

We are finished with Epicharis. She would not utter a
word. She is now unconscious and so weakened by pain that
she would not be able to speak even if she were willing. That
is a strong (and, forgive me, beautiful) woman. Cassius, as
usual, was as imperturbable as one of his machines, but I
myself, rather than Epicharis, was almost broken by this
ordeal, Tigellinus. You said you were moved to tears by the
innocence of Himself's face at the Circus today. What made
you think that I was not very tired, too, tonight? Perhaps it
was my weariness, perhaps the relief I shared with you that the
Circus went off well, perhaps my surprise at your five short
words of praise that made me vulnerable tonight. But I think
it was something else: the sight of a tranquil face. Not innocent but tranquil, even in extremity. I have never watched
a woman giving birth to a baby, but I can imagine that the
pains of parturition may produce some such results as I witnessed tonight—with the difference, of course, that here the
joy was in withholding rather than expelling. Contortions, yes,
gallons of sweat, strong signs of the pain, involuntary out-
cries; yet always on the face a deep contentment, a pride, a
sense of what it really means to be a woman. She was obviously sustained by love for Mela, fortunate man; perhaps by
love for Lucan. But there was something more, which struck
at the very core of my sense of profession. Am I really a good

policeman? Thank you for your congratulations. I am very tired.

We know no more than we knew before. When we first took Epicharis in the room, and she saw the machines, she looked me straight in the face and said that she would never as long as she lived speak another word to me. I knew by her look that she meant what she said. But of course we had to go through with it. She kept her promise. She made no coherent sounds.

To PAENUS, Tribune of Secret Police, from TIGELLINUS
I have your report on Epicharis. We will let her live with her pain overnight and torture her again tomorrow. You will not be present. You have in you the makings of a traitor. You lust after a woman on the machines. For shame!

To TIGELLINUS from PAENUS, Tribune of Secret Police
I knew you would have to punish me for the crime of having been praised by you. I think I like stupid Cassius's company better than yours. There is no sentimentality in him. He tortures out of a sense of duty.

INTERROGATION:
Flavius Scaevinus

In the Presence of the Emperor. Attending: Tigellinus, Rufus, Paenus, Cassius; Milichus and wife in confrontation; Felix, Stenographer.

Directly SCAEVINUS was brought into the room TIGELLINUS stood and drew the dagger from within his clothing and threw it on the round marble table behind which SCAEVINUS had been posted, and said: Where did you get that weapon?

(PAENUS meanwhile stood and interposed himself between HIMSELF and SCAEVINUS, because the bold gesture of TIG., intended to shock and frighten the ACCUSED, might have given a desperate and determined man precisely the opportunity he had long sought.)

SCAEVINUS, however, appeared as usual to be languid, bored, barely interested in what was happening around and to him.

SCAEVINUS: Oh, that. A very old dagger. It has been in my family for generations. For reasons that were never explained to me, it was venerated by my ancestors; it had some religious weight for them. It was therefore always kept in a wooden lockbox in my bedchamber. I see MILICHUS here. When he and his wife disappeared yesterday morning I searched the house to see what he had stolen, as I assumed plunder to have been his motive in leaving. He had never been any good. I found this knife gone. It was the only thing he took—so I was forced to change my assumption. He apparently wanted to take revenge on someone, but I am glad to see you have arrested him.

TIG.: No, SCAEVINUS, MILICHUS's motive was something else. I should think you might have guessed that, having spent the night in chains.

And TIG. told MILICHUS to repeat what he had said the day before.

MILICHUS now repeated his accusations, but in the presence of his patron, and perhaps remembering TIG.'s threatening test of his veracity the previous day, his tone of voice was markedly different: hesitant, stumbling, wheedling. His wife, standing beside him, jarred him with her elbow now and again, interpolated vivid particulars, and only succeeded by her forwardness in further weakening her husband's narrative.

SCAEVINUS seemed to wake up somewhat during this performance, and when MILICHUS subsided, the PATRON launched, as if he were the accuser rather than the accused, into a resolute assault on his FREEDMAN. After calling him an ingrate and a depraved foot-licking informer who hoped to milk the Imperial treasury with his lies, he turned to his own defense in a relaxed and rather convincing way.

SCAEVINUS said: He had often reviewed his will, given gifts, and freed slaves on impulse, without reference to sacred days or special occasions. On this particular day, he had been accosted in the street by a creditor, who pressed him for payment. This annoying encounter having reminded him of his many debts, he had begun to doubt the worth of his will, especially as to its codicils of bequests to slaves, and this had moved him to give more freely than usual. Yes, he had eaten well that night; he was well known for his table; he had long expected to be rebuked by the censors; life was dull—there was not much, for him, besides the palate, the palestra, and the penis. All that about things to stanch blood—the FREEDMAN had invented all of it, as he had the whole texture of his tale, in hope of a reward for informing; he must have had daydreams of being a great SUILIUS or VALERIUS.

These references to notoriously rich informers made HIMSELF, in good humor because of the successes in the Circus the day before, begin to laugh. In fact, SCAEVINUS was making a strong impression on the EMPEROR, who seemed inclined to side with an aggrieved Senator against a treacherous ex-slave; so that efforts TIG. now made to press SCAEVINUS about the dagger came to very little.

TIG.: Will you deny that this dagger had until recently been enshrined in the Temple of Fortune at Farentum?

On the face of SCAEVINUS there was a response of what seemed to be genuine surprise—an unaccustomed animation, two eyebrows up, wide eyes. One remembered the account of SCAEVINUS's long sessions with his barber before the triple mirror in the mornings, his rehearsals of expressions and attitudes, his life of vanity and feigning; yet this response was so swift and complete as to be rather convincing.

SCAEVINUS: It was? Well, it is quite possible that MILICHUS took the dagger from my room some time ago. This search yesterday was the first time I had opened the lockbox for . . . for years. MILICHUS, did you . . . (*intending to continue*).

Now HIMSELF mildly intervened and, adopting his usual attitude of tolerant and slightly amused skepticism whenever danger to his Person was being discussed, observed that the interrogation did not seem to be getting anywhere.

Whereupon the WIFE of MILICHUS, desperate to save her husband from the ignominy of an Imperial rebuke, at last scored a point.

WIFE of MILICHUS, to her husband: Tell them about NATALIS. That he was with NATALIS all that day.

MILICHUS then eagerly corroborated that SCAEVINUS and NATALIS had conferred for several hours on the day in question.

This evidently meant little to HIMSELF, who was stirring to rise and cut short the session, but TIG. (who had only recently taken a keen interest in NATALIS) at once commanded the urgent arrest of NATALIS and asked permission of HIMSELF to carry on further investigations without bothering HIMSELF until definite charges could be developed, and the EMPEROR with a gesture signaled something between indifference and acquiescence.

PAENUS AFRANIUS (Recorder)

To PAENUS, Tribune of Secret Police, from TIGELLINUS
In these next hours I am going to have to spend some careful time with Rufus planning dispositions of the Guard in

case we need to show our strength; and after that I must see to the second session with Epicharis.

When Natalis is brought in, I want you to question him and Scaevinus separately, asking each what the subject of their conversation yesterday was. If they both tell the same story, without having had a chance to confer, then the composure and spirit Scaevinus showed in his interrogation will have been borne out. I cannot say exactly where that would leave us. But if they disagree . . .

Report to me as soon as possible.

Have Epicharis taken to the room with the machines and have Cassius stand by.

To TIGELLINUS from PAENUS, Tribune of Secret Police
Urgent.

They do not agree.

Natalis came in roaring. He demanded now to be taken to the Emperor, now to be confronted by a proper tribunal, now to be heard by the Consuls. His bravado was somewhat deflated by my putting to him the single question: What did you discuss day before yesterday with Scaevinus?

I then lied, warning him that Scaevinus had already admitted they had had a long talk, and saying it would be best for everyone if there was agreement on all points between the two.

Natalis entered on a list of topics they had talked about. Feigning a strain on his powers of recall, one saw instead a clear tax on his gifts of invention. He mentioned: Some problems of rent collection on estates he owns to the north of Rome; a literary discussion (interesting that he should have brought this up) on the degree of Seneca's independence, in his tragedies, of his models in Aeschylus, Sophocles, and Euripides; and then a pause. I waited in silence. After a careful search of the ceiling, Natalis added: Some gossip about Statilia Messalina, wife of the Consul Vestinus; plans for a dinner party; a project for the addition of a room to his house for readings, with a dais, armchairs for guests of high rank and benches for others, and curtains for those, such as his wife, who might wish to hear without being seen. And more such.

I cut Natalis off, dismissed him under guard, and summoned Scaevinus.

When I put the question about their talk to Scaevinus, he asked with a convincing air of indifference what Natalis had said. You can imagine that I had a good laugh at that. I told him it was not going to be so easy.

Quite casually then, and with greater facility and fluency than Natalis had exhibited, Scaevinus said the main thing they had talked about was his indebtedness, the general precariousness of his means, and various schemes to recoup them. He mentioned various other topics, not a single one of which coincided with those that Natalis had listed.

I recalled the two men, one after the other, and confronted them with the variance in their accounts. They remained strikingly cool—Natalis especially having recovered composure—and each swore that the other was lying. I could not shake anything out of them, with nothing but oral menaces at my command.

What next? Torture? I believe Natalis is very afraid of it.

To PAENUS, Tribune of Secret Police, from TIGELLINUS
No, let Scaevinus and Natalis stew a while. I have persuaded Himself that it is time to arrest Lucan and Piso and question them. Bring them in.

I will be ready to go to Epicharis in a few minutes. Is everything ready?

To TIGELLINUS from PAENUS, Tribune of Secret Police
Urgent.

Epicharis is dead.

Following your instructions after the Scaevinus interrogation, I ordered her moved to the room with the machines. Because her limbs had all been pulled out of joint last night, she was of course unable to stand, and two men carried her in a wooden chair; an officer of the Guard was with them. The bearers put the chair down by the door of the torture room and, secure in the certainty that she could not rise to escape, the three stood somewhat apart waiting for the Tribune of the Guard to come to unlock the door of the room. During this time, without the slightest awareness on the part of the three that anything was happening, Epicharis somehow —the pain must have been great—managed to remove her breastband, to fasten it in a kind of noose around her neck, and to loop it over the arched back of the chair. Then, with great fortitude, using a combination of the weight of her body and what little strength Cassius had left in her last night to tug at the noose, she cut off her breath, ensuring that she would speak no single word under duress at *your* hands to harm Mela, Lucan, Seneca, or their friends. You had so intimidated me by your last message last night that I was keeping my distance—not that I can be sure that my vigilant presence would have made any difference.

After your message just now asking if all was ready, I went to check—and found her body.

Call me a traitor or whatever you wish, I am convinced that Epicharis was stronger than Cassius, stronger than I. She has now shown herself stronger than you, too.

To TIGELLINUS from PAENUS, Tribune of Secret Police
Urgent.

We have Lucan.

Piso was not at his house.

Stormy behavior of Lucan, violently protesting his arrest. Angry accusations that you, Tigellinus, are indulging a long-standing jealousy in persecuting him—a jealousy founded on your total want of education and sensibility, and upon your knowledge that even Himself's proscription of Lucan was a perverse product of Himself's recognition of Lucan's genius. A tirade. It continues at full shout in the next room as I dictate this.

Cassius and the stenographer are here. We are ready to interrogate.

To PAENUS, *Tribune of Secret Police, from TIGELLINUS*
   Urgent.

Himself insists, against my advice, upon questioning Lucan in person. Himself wanted to talk with him alone, but Poppaea and I have persuaded him after much argument that both of us should be present.

Send Lucan to Himself's bedroom at once.

To PAENUS, *Tribune of Secret Police, from TIGELLINUS*
   Dictated in haste.

The great blustering poet is abjectly broken, admits a plot, and has given names. What a pathetic performance!

Himself commands the arrest (using for the purpose joint squads of newly recruited soldiers and trusted agents) of:

> Tullius Severus
> Afranius Quintianus
> Glitius Gallus
> Annius Pollo
> Plautius Lateranus

Lucan confirms complicity of Piso, Scaevinus, and Natalis.

Himself orders Lucan to be allowed to return to his house, where he is to remain until further notice. See to it that he reaches his house, that he is left free within it, but that all gates are closely watched. If he tries to escape he is to be executed on the spot.

I am to make a record of the Lucan interrogation. I will dictate it as soon as I can.

Any word of Piso?

To RUFUS, Co-Commander, Praetorian Guard, from TIGELLINUS

Urgent.

Himself commands the arrest, on information of sedition, of the Praetorian Tribune Subrius Flavus. This is the man, Rufus, whom you said you trusted more than any other officer of the Guard. Lucan names him as complicit in a conspiracy against the Person.

Himself also commands the arrest, on the same information, of the Praetorian Centurion Sulpicius Asper—the man who was entrusted to bring Scaevinus's dagger into the Presence not three hours ago.

Himself orders that you use for these arrests, and that you put at the disposal of Paenus for necessary arrests of civilians, only raw recruits, men who have joined the Guard within the last two weeks; he cannot know which veterans, if any, to trust at this moment.

To PAENUS, Tribune of Secret Police, from TIGELLINUS

Urgent.

Himself greatly agitated by the Lucan revelations. Dispatch all the agents you can quickly assemble who have special training in hand-to-hand combat to the Imperial chambers for emergency protection of the Person.

Trust you have sent out teams for the arrests. We must move fast. We need more names. This is the moment when, if they have any spirit, those who remain at large can act.

Courage. If you could have seen the groveling performance of our poet, the self-proclaimed genius, the insufferable egoist —he went like a bubble!

To RUFUS, Co-Commander, Praetorian Guard, from TIGELLINUS

Urgent.

Himself commands a maximum show of force in the city. Station the Guard at the city gates and at all approaches to the palace, according to our agreed plan, modified however as follows:

Largest contingents, horse and foot, in the Forum and at the Capitol. Patrols along the banks of the river. Mix in German soldiers, from the Legions encamped to the east of the city, with each complement of the Praetorian Guard. Himself feels that being foreigners, and therefore disinterested, the Germans are to be trusted more than Romans in a Guard tainted by officers like Subrius and Asper.

As part of the show of force, prisoners should be dealt with roughly. They should be put in chains; some should be dragged. But leave enough life in them to confess and give names. Tell Paenus this.

To TIGELLINUS from RUFUS, Co-Commander, Praetorian Guard

Urgent.

Piso is showing himself at the Rostra of the Forum. A large crowd is gathering.

221

To *RUFUS, Co-Commander, Praetorian Guard, from*
TIGELLINUS

Himself commands that a troop of soldiers be dispatched
to find Piso, whether at the Forum, or at the Praetorian
Camp, where he may well go to try to win the support of the
Guard, or at his house, or wherever he may be, and to pronounce the sentence of death.

The Emperor orders that you use for this purpose a mixed
troop of raw recruits and Germans, as previously stipulated.

To *TIGELLINUS from RUFUS, Co-Commander, Praetorian*
Guard

A prompt and ironic arrest has been made, as commanded,
of the Tribune Subrius Flavus. Why ironic? It was he who
brought us, a few minutes ago, the news of the Piso challenge.

To *PAENUS, Tribune of Secret Police, from TIGELLINUS*

Here are my minutes of the interrogation of Lucan. I shall
dictate them straight off while we are waiting for new arrestees to be brought in, and will charge you with putting
them in the proper form for the record when you have time.

Himself commanded the four agents who had brought
Lucan to the bedchamber to leave the room, and I took them
out and posted them beyond the second pair of doors.

The interview began awkwardly. Himself and Lucan com-
menced to bicker, like former lovers who could not understand
why they had had a falling out.

Lucan asked what all this meant. What was Himself doing
to him?

The Emperor asked Lucan why he hated him so much.

Lucan said it was the other way around. He was the injured
one. Himself had put a gag in his mouth.

Himself began to recall Lucan's most extravagant eulogies —the "Praise of Nero" which Lucan had read at the Neronia; the lines in the first book of the *Pharsalia*, including:

Rome is my subject, and you are my muse!

Lucan accused Himself of turning against him, saying with insulting arrogance: You had the power and I had the genius.

Himself became extremely angry at this, and said that that might be, but Lucan was greedy to want them both.

Now Poppaea spoke aside to Himself, suggesting that perhaps it would be best if she and I were to carry the questioning forward. She asked me if I was not well prepared to question Lucan, and I said I was well and long prepared. At first Himself was petulantly scornful of Poppaea's suggestion, but she said that picking at scabs could only bring out blood and pus, and she stroked Himself's arm, and while Himself hesitated I took the initiative and asked a question which caused such effective confusion in Lucan that Himself made no further objection, evidently deciding to let the interrogation drift to the Empress and to me, at least for a time.

My question: What is a writer's responsibility, Lucan?

Lucan, faltering, asked what I meant. What was I trying to say?

I then asked if Lucan thought Seneca would be a good person to consult on the issue: What is a writer's responsibility?

Lucan, greatly surprised and enraged, took refuge now in an outburst of obscenity directed at me.

I then said that if I were Seneca, I would give this advice: Think about this sentence, my nephew, written by Epicurus: *Ungoverned anger begets madness. . . .* What would Lucan say to that advice?

By now it was clear that Lucan understood the thrust of my questions: He was warned that I had had access to his private correspondence. He was exposed and stood confused.

At this point Poppaea broke in with a series of questions. Not for the record, Paenus—we should have had this remarkable woman in our apparatus all along. She was devastating. Her first questions were based on pure speculation, or actually on lies. She did not wait for a ready answer to each question, which in any case Lucan was not now in a condition, or at least was not disposed, to give.

Was Lucan aware, Poppaea asked, that his wife Polla, who pretended to be so solicitous of his welfare and reputation, was a whore? Would he like a list of the men she had slept with in the last six weeks? Did Lucan realize that when he fell out of favor at court Polla had decided he was no longer the right steed for her ambitions?

Lucan shouted that she was lying—making things up to beat him with; but his manner showed that he half believed Poppaea. It almost seemed that he wanted to believe her.

I then said that Lucan had been a priest of the College of Augurs for three years—that he had mocked his priestly duty on the single occasion when he had undertaken an auspice; that he had scorned the documents of office. Was that made up to beat him with? Did he think that a man of genius was above civilian duty? Did he think it was the responsibility of a writer to scorn the fortune and welfare of his fellow men?

At this Lucan turned to Himself and in a tone that fell weakly between pride and supplication asked why he was treated in this way.

Poppaea, now showing, or feigning, great anger, quickly asked what ever had made Lucan think he could get away with a second public reading of a poem which in a contest had defeated a poem written by his friend the Emperor of Rome.

LUCAN, in a kind of agony: My friend? My friend?

HIMSELF: I *was* your friend.

Seeing Himself touched and softened by Lucan's discomfiture, I quickly remarked that Lucan had written in one of his letters to his uncle: *Who said that my* Pharsalia *is about the past? Not I. . . .* What then *was* his *Pharsalia* about?

This time I waited—all three of us waited—for an answer. Lucan looked so comically upset that I could not desist saying that Seneca had written to him: *The responsibility of a writer is to avoid frenzy.*

Now Lucan said with suddenly renewed spirit: My poem is about Rome's need for another Cato.

Himself did not like that remark. One could see within both these men a turbulent rush back and forth of conflicting emotions. Though Himself and Lucan were at this moment simultaneously very angry, the Empress and I sensed that the anger in Himself could not be depended on. It might give way after another exchange to another moment of more kindly melting and remorse. Lucan was clearly rattled now, but he was far from ready to make either concession or confession.

At this time Poppaea demonstrated two things—that she can shoot an arrow with terrible aim into the vital spot even of a leaping deer; and that she, if not Himself, had carefully read such of our reports as I had from time to time made available to highest eyes.

She said contemptuously that Lucan looked not so much frenzied as like a hunchback at the start of a race who was afraid of being outrun by a dwarf.

This brought a sharp and unexpected crack of laughter from Himself. Lucan grew pale.

POPPAEA: You do not like that, do you, Lucan?

The parade of little shocks and surprises seemed to be bringing Lucan to the edge of the kind of anger in which the most self-destructive indiscretions are seated. I therefore added one more. I asked what Lucan had meant when he had written to Seneca: *I do not wish to be free and dead, I wish to be free and alive.*

Poppaea asked, without giving Lucan time to answer me, what he had meant when he had written: *King Midas has an ass's ears.* One actually heard a rather ugly grunt from Himself at that question. She added at once the further question, what he had meant when he had written: *Juno plays with Jupiter's bolts.*

It was necessary to follow quickly with another blow, and risking Himself's anger at me I hastily asked Lucan what he had meant when he had promised to deliver to a friend a severed head with the neck of a bull and the hair of a girl.

Now came Poppaea's master stroke. She turned to me.

POPPAEA: Send for Epicharis. Bring Epicharis in.

Your message to me about Epicharis's death had reached me just as I had been about to go to torture her. I had hurried then to the entrance to the machine room to see her body with my own eyes, and on my return to the Presence I had described to Himself and the Empress exactly what these eyes had seen: The chair bearing the dead woman's body, with the noose of her breastband still at her neck, her clothing disordered, her bosom exposed, her limbs awry and joints swollen and purple, and, perceptible on closer inspection, the small contusions and burns and incisions of Cassius's skill; her face, however, still set in that calm that had carried you, Paenus, the night before, to the rim of subversion.

What a diabolical idea of Poppaea's! One could read from Lucan's expression that he expected to see a living Epicharis, that he took strength from this anticipation, being confident of her stubborn spirit. Of course he had known of her arrest. Could one see as well a glimmer of a lover's hope? What would happen to his confidence and hope when he saw the wrecked shell I had seen? I turned to go to the door. But—

HIMSELF: I will not allow it. No, Tigellinus.

I turned back. Once more one saw that an uncontrollable thaw of feelings had set in. Poppaea began to remonstrate.

HIMSELF: No, Poppaea, I will not permit anything of the sort. (*To Lucan, very gently:*) Epicharis is dead.

LUCAN, horrified: *Dead?*

Lucan evidently had seen Himself's compassion and had been convinced by it of the truth of the death.

Poppaea and I realized that we must follow up firmly, because Himself was also shocked by Poppaea's idea and was overflowing with a perverse and unreasoning sympathy for Lucan.

TIGELLINUS: She died under torture.

POPPAEA: She told us everything. She was very cowardly, Lucan—that surprises you, doesn't it? She gave us names.

I remembered Lucan's superstitious terror of the unlucky number seventeen, and I said Epicharis had given us seventeen names.

Once again Himself afforded us a surprise: It was clear that in spite of his sudden outpouring of pity for Lucan he understood exactly what point we had reached. He did not deny our lies. Instead—

HIMSELF: Lucan, why did you join a plot against me?

Lucan suddenly burst into tears.

LUCAN: I . . . My mother made me.

POPPAEA: Your *what?*

HIMSELF: Your *mother?*

LUCAN: Oh, yes, she is in it. She forced me to join. Atilla. My mother. (And other similar protestations, at length, interspersed with sobs.)

HIMSELF (with a candor which, in its offhandedness yet its chill delivery, put me quite off balance—and clearly did the Empress, too): Come, now, Lucan, not your mother. You're just saying that in the hope that a man who killed his mother will admire a man who is willing to destroy *his*. Isn't that so?

LUCAN: No, no! She forced me to join. (And more such, but with less sobbing.)

TIGELLINUS: Who were the other conspirators besides your mother?

LUCAN (so far beyond honor as to grovel in his dishonor): I do not like to betray my friends.

HIMSELF: Not your friends, only your own mother, is that it?

At this Lucan plunged with a kind of horrible joy prostrate into that filth of his bad faith, and he recited quickly these names: *Caius Piso, Antonius Natalis, Flavius Scaevinus, Afranius Quintianus, Tullius Severus, Glitius Gallus.*

Then Poppaea asked a question whose answer I was most curious to hear: Which man had Lucan favored for the succession—Seneca or Piso?

LUCAN: Piso.

By answering thus Lucan confirmed the complicity and focal positions of both.

TIGELLINUS: What military men have been involved?

LUCAN: I only know of the Tribune *Subrius Flavus* and the Centurion *Sulpicius Asper*, but I believe there are others. Piso would know.

And so it suddenly appeared that Lucan in his craven condition was offering to be helpful, was offering to be the bosom friend he had formerly been, as if treason, rejection, resentment, abuse, satires, the echoes of a stinking fart—all were nothing. Himself, with his magnificent instinct for self-preservation, now saw that by acting as if the treachery had been someone else's, not Lucan's at all, and as if Lucan were still in fact a dear friend and protector—by pretending so, he could learn some more of what he now needed to know. He spoke to Lucan in a gentle, casual voice.

HIMSELF: How was the murder to have been accomplished?

They had had much discussion on this point, Lucan said, now in full possession of his double perfidy—to Himself and to his fellow conspirators. In the early weeks, several conspirators had urged Piso to invite Himself to Baiae, for all knew what delight the Emperor had taken in Piso's intimate gardens there, how several times in recent years he had visited Piso and had divested Himself entirely at Piso's house of all the forms of office, including his guards, and had indulged in bath and banquet as if he were simply a citizen and friend of the host. But Piso, according to Lucan, would not have it done this way; he would not tolerate the opprobrium of hospitality turned to the uses of murder, and he said his household deities could not be bloodied. Piso had urged instead that it be done in the Golden House, which had been built on the plunder and deprivation of the citizenry; or, better yet, in a public place, as an act of public benefaction. In the end they had decided to do it—take note, Paenus!—on the day of the Circus games in honor of Ceres. This was how they had planned to do it: The Consul-elect Plautius Lateranus was going to put before Himself a personal entreaty, and in the course of his plea he was going to drop down, in a perfectly acceptable gesture of supplication, and clasp Himself's knees. Being a powerfully built man of iron nerve, he was then to tighten his grip, topple Himself over backwards, and hold him down while others came forward to dispatch him. Scaevinus had claimed the honor of being the first to stab Himself.

TIGELLINUS: With a dagger he had stolen from the Temple of Fortune in Farentum.

LUCAN: Yes.

So much for Scaevinus's calm denials.

I now urged Himself to put an end to the interrogation so we could hurry to the arrests that must be made.

HIMSELF, to LUCAN: Because you were once my friend, and because you have given me valuable information, you may return freely to your house. But you are not to speak to anyone on the way, and you are to stay there, receiving no visitors. If you try to leave your house, you will be killed at once. Tigellinus, see to this.

Thus the interrogation was adjourned.

*

By my own hand—T.

Still no arrestees. I must share with you some quick impressions.

I wish I could cry out in joy: At last we have them! At last it is out in the open! Instead, I am full of new concerns.

First, the extent of the conspiracy. You may have noticed the haste with which I broke off the interrogation of Lucan. I do not like to admit fear, as you know, but his having given, for example, the name of *Severus* badly frightened me. Severus has seemed one of the most trustworthy of Himself's friends. You remember that when I was worried about the effrontery of the Consul Vestinus, with his elegant private guard which so offended Himself, it was to Severus that I turned *as an intermediary*. How many others who have direct access to Himself's heart and chambers are in the plot? We need names. How many nasty surprises will there be?

Second, the present state of mind of Himself. You have seen that in spite of the vacillation in his feelings toward Lucan, he reacted shrewdly and coolly to the very serious revelations Lucan finally offered. But afterwards it was a different matter. In utmost confidence, *Himself cannot at this moment be depended on for wise decisions*. He refuses to arrest Seneca. When I began to argue with him about this, he flew into a dangerous temper. He has offered two sacrifices to his girl-goddess since the session with Lucan.

Third, my greatest alarm has to do with what we had learned from Seneca's letters—that military men are involved. We have had Subrius Flavus under vague suspicion, but the name of young Sulpicius Asper was a shock to me. I have been the very one to bring him quick promotions. Lucan says he himself was for Piso, but we know that Seneca is, or was, the choice of the military. Is there a split in the conspiracy? We must be alert to exploit it if there is. Is there a second and more serious stage yet to be revealed? In the dispositions, after the alarm, Rufus has been most cooperative. It can be no secret to you that my relationship with him has not been without tension. His good soldierly qualities, fortunately, have come out under pressure. But we cannot trust all the soldiers, and we do not know which we can. This is why I ordered you to send agents to supplement the Praetorian bodyguard in protecting the Person.

Fourth, Himself, the Empress, and I were all agreed that we should simply ignore for now Lucan's monstrous accusation against his mother, Atilla. It was blurted out in such a peculiar way just when he broke. It was as if all the spite in Lucan's cowardly nature had suddenly been focused on . . . on whom, really? On his own despicable self? On Epicharis, who had betrayed him by dying? On his *mother*?

Fifth, despite the misgivings I am now sharing with you, rest assured that I am strong and confident. Don't forget that we are dealing with mere thinkers.

*

Orders:
As the arrestees come in, we must act quickly to get more names. We must divide up the task of interrogation. Himself will not be capable of abstaining. I am glad of the revealed talents of Poppaea. She and I will join him in questioning

Lateranus, Severus, the Tribune *Flavus,* the Centurion *Asper.* Send us the giant Cassius.

You and Rufus should proceed at once to reexamine *Scae-vinus* and *Natalis,* using the information you now have to break their lying. Question also, when they are brought in, *Quintianus, Gallus.* You had better have some strong soldiers with you. Report new names to me as soon as they are given.

*

All of our energy now goes into detection, prevention, protection. It gives us strength to have these explicit tasks. But beyond the breaking of this plot, Paenus, I see a dark abyss— the time when we look with Himself to the question whether we have not done our job too well, whether we have not isolated him not only from danger but also from reality; the time, Paenus, when we think in larger terms than we ever have about the meaning of the word "security."

FIVE

To TIGELLINUS from PAENUS, Tribune of Secret Police
A runner has come to inform us that Piso has been captured at his own house. He put up no resistance and is pre-
paring himself for death.

To TIGELLINUS from PAENUS, Tribune of Secret Police
Rufus and I have questioned Natalis and Scaevinus separately. Both are broken—but that is not quite the word for it.
With extraordinary coolness, like dogs shaking their bodies
as they come out of water, they have shed their lies and have
confirmed Lucan's revelations. They wag their tails when
praised.

They give these new names: *Cervarius Proculus, Julius
Augurinus, Marcius Festus, Munatius Gratus, Vulcatius
Araricus*—all of equestrian rank.

They profess to know no military names.

These men are so sanguine in their treachery toward their
co-conspirators, so complacent and corruptible, that I would
strongly recommend your bringing them into the Presence to
confront all arrestees as Himself and you question them.

And note especially, in view of Himself's reluctance to

move against Seneca: Natalis talks freely about his visit to
Seneca. He acted, he says, as Piso's go-between with Seneca.
Says there is no question that Seneca is a conspirator. *Himself
must hear this testimony firsthand.*

To *PAENUS, Tribune of Secret Police, from TIGELLINUS*
Yes, send us Natalis and Scaevinus.
Arrest the named conspirators.

To *TIGELLINUS from PAENUS, Tribune of Secret Police*
For highest eyes.

This excellent report comes from our agent Ampius Clem-
ens, one of the arresting officers at Piso's house. Ampius got
this information both directly from Piso, who is showing the
same craven spirit as Lucan, and from the men around Piso
in his house—men whom Ampius has not failed to arrest:
Claudius Capito, Obutronius Vergilio, and *Tetius Simplex.*

Here is the report:

"Piso has written a new will which begins in these terms:
*Moved by the benign soul and radiant gifts of Nero Caesar,
who like effulgent Aurora brings new joy daily to all the windows of Rome . . .* And more like that. You can see how
abject the leader of the conspiracy is at this time. No, beyond
abject. He is in the act of letting his blood out of his veins;
his presumptuous life may at this very moment have come to
an end. Long life to Nero Caesar!

"I will quickly sketch the movements of Piso this morning.

"It seems that the conspirators, getting wind of the arrest
of Epicharis four days ago, decided to hurry things on and do
their crime at the Circus yesterday. But when they learned of
the betrayal of Scaevinus by Milichus, and of the arrests of
Scaevinus and Natalis, they decided against the attempt at
the Circus. This morning several of the civilian conspirators

urged Piso to come out in the open as a candidate for the emperorship; to go to the Praetorian camp and harangue the soldiers or to the Forum and speak to the citizens, or both. If he did this, they argued, his supporters would rally around him, many others with grudges and with a desire for freedom would join, and a brave mob spirit could be roused. Nero was not prepared for anything like this, they said. He was a singer of female parts, and his Tigellinus had a loud voice but was in fact a cowardly horse merchant, and the whole pack of them at the court were smothered by female flesh and would be thrown into hysteria by unexpected danger. Besides, Piso could no longer hope for secrecy. He would soon have to face, in any case, chains or torture or death. How much better to die, if he must, they argued, making an outcry against tyranny.

"Piso—this is the measure of the man—*half* agreed. Half-heartedly he showed himself at the Rostra. There was a great commotion, great interest, a large crowd quickly gathered. But Piso could not bring himself to cry out, *Death to Nero!* He simply showed himself there for a few minutes, while rumors flew around him. Then he weakly went home and tried to barricade the doors of his house.

"When the doors were broken down and he was confronted, he sat down forthwith, in doglike resignation, and began the new will which I have already mentioned. I will send it on as soon as we have confirmed Piso's death and taken care of the body. A document crawling with flattery of Himself—clearly written in the hope that his wife Atria Galla will be spared at least a part of his wealth. An ignoble and loathsome end. To think that Rome might have suffered under that infamous weak man! Long live Nero Caesar!"

Consider, Tigellinus, how Lucan and Piso have crawled. Do you suppose all these lovers of literature are cut from the same cheap and flimsy piece of cloth?

To PAENUS, Tribune of Secret Police, from TIGELLINUS
We have completed successful questioning of Lateranus
and Severus.

Arrest: *Julius Agrippa, Julius Altinus, Musonius Rufus,
Verginius Flavus, Cluvidienus Quietus, Blitius Catulinis,
Petronius Priscus.*

To PAENUS, Tribune of Secret Police, from TIGELLINUS
Urgent.

Himself has heard the testimony of Natalis on Seneca.
(You were right about Natalis and Scaevinus, particularly the
former. Invaluable.) We have had a difficult scene. We dismissed all from the room. I told Himself of the letter Seneca
wrote Lucan about the night visitor. At first Himself would
not believe me. I went myself to my locked files and fetched
the copy of the letter. When he read it he vented a rage not
at Seneca but at *me*—for not having told him about it sooner.
Poppaea pointed out to him that there was no good in railing
against Tigellinus at a moment when he should be sentencing
Seneca to death.

What followed was terrible, Paenus. It was as if Himself
were an accused person, Poppaea a hostile and threatening
questioner. He seemed to be in physical pain. Seneca stands
for a side of him that is very tender—and so, of course, does
Lucan, in a different and perhaps even more intense way. It
is the side of unrealized possibilities, of broken-down ambitions that sometimes apparently loom at Himself like alley
thieves in the night. For Seneca was right: Nero wanted in
earlier years to be as wise, as clement, as temperate, as judi-
cious, as honorable as Augustus. He also wanted, among other
things, to be the equal of Ovid and Virgil, to say nothing of
mere Lucan. Now some ugly thoughts poured out, snatched
from the base of his tongue by those alley thieves. He accused
Poppaea of wanting to be a man, and of having been jealous

of an old man—Seneca. He shouted that I had led him into grossness and pleasure hunts. Poppaea bluntly told him not to blame me for his lusts and for his peacock vanity, and reminded him that we should be talking about Seneca's sedition, not his own mischief. So it went back and forth—Himself trying again and again to shift the talk away from the sentence of death that Poppaea fiercely urged.

Himself refused to agree to the extreme penalty, but he did consent—pay careful attention—to send a messenger to Seneca, who would say to him:

"Natalis visited you on behalf of the conspirator Piso. Natalis says he asked you why you did not want to see Piso, and he says that you replied that frequent meetings with Piso would serve the purposes of neither yourself nor Piso, but that your life did depend upon Piso's safety. Is this an accurate description of your exchange? If so, why did you reply as you did?"

Find out where Seneca is. Get Rufus to nominate an officer he especially trusts. Go *yourself with this officer* and repeat the above to Seneca in the officer's presence. Bring us his answer. You are strictly forbidden to ask Seneca any other questions.

April 28

To TIGELLINUS from PAENUS, Tribune of Secret Police

We have finally found Seneca. He had been spending some days in Campania, and on the way back to Nomentum he had stopped over at the country house of a friend of his named Marcellinus, four miles out the Via Appia.

Rufus has appointed Gavius Silvanus, Tribune of a Praetorian cohort, to go with me. We will take a troop of soldiers and some mounted couriers. It will be dark before we get there.

To TIGELLINUS from PAENUS, Tribune of Secret Police

In view of the delicacy of this mission, I am sending Silvanus himself, together with a regular courier, with this message.

We arrived at Marcellinus's house, surrounded it with soldiers, and entered. Seneca was at dinner with his wife Pompeia Paulina, Marcellinus, and the latter's wife. This Marcellinus is a witty, easygoing fellow, considerably younger than Seneca, a close friend, I gather, of Lucilius Junior, the young man to whom Seneca writes his insufferable moral epistles. The dinner was evidently simple, the small company carefree; I heard unrestrained laughter from within as we were admitted.

Tigellinus, I entered here a quite different world from that of the craven Lucan and Piso. Seneca got up from his couch as a freedman announced our names, and he asked Marcellinus to receive us as honored guests.

My bearing was formal. I said I had a message of inquiry from Nero Caesar.

Yes, but a couch must be prepared. Wine, both in libation to the household deities and in welcome to Silvanus and me as men. It goes without saying that Seneca knows what has been happening in recent days; we could hear the coughing and chatter of the soldiers around the house. Yet there was not the slightest sign of tension, or even concern, in his manner.

Finally we were settled and Seneca turned an open face to me.

I repeated, word for word from your directive, the accusations of Natalis, and I asked for Seneca's response.

Yes, he said, Natalis had come to him, more or less as a messenger from Piso, as he understood it. Natalis had chided him, in Piso's name, for avoiding Piso. Seneca said that he had told Natalis that he was avoiding everyone; he had not been feeling well and had been declining all invitations, including even one from the Emperor, to a literary evening at the Golden House. Here I wish to report Seneca's exact words, because they are heavy with significance and they are subject to variable interpretation.

SENECA, as to Natalis: *I have no motive for placing the interest of a private citizen, even one as distinguished as Piso, ahead of my own well-being. I know that Piso is the sort of man who attracts a following, who draws flattery—but I do not have a talent for flattery.*

Here Seneca, looking me directly in the eye, broke off his report of his words to Natalis and added: *No one knows this better than Nero, who has had over the years more tongue-lashing than boot-licking from me.*

He left it at that. That was all the "explanation" or response he wished to give. He was suddenly tart and testy. I felt that I was in the presence of an immensely powerful and independent soul.

This matter is too important to be settled without most careful consideration. I hope that you, Tigellinus, and even Himself will forgive me for a word of interpretive comment, based upon nothing more substantial than the tone of this encounter—the look in Seneca's eye, let us say.

I would speculate as follows: that Seneca was approached by a conspirator, as his letter to Lucan so vividly described; that for some reason no further contact with Seneca was made; that he is hurt and angry, and at the same time profoundly relieved. I could be quite wrong in this intuition. Perhaps Seneca is a skilled actor. If he has deceived me, there is great danger. But I do not think he has. I realize that in the context of these days I stake my very life on this "do not think."

I await here, in a room apart from Seneca, Himself's command.

To PAENUS, Tribune of Secret Police, from TIGELLINUS
The Tribune Silvanus gave us your message. Himself read it several times over. He seemed much affected by your comments at the end, but at the same time he showed flashes of anger. The revelations of the past days have been pounding at him, and he is sore. Poppaea was relentless. She kept holding before him the effrontery of Seneca's "tongue-lashing." Himself finally flew into a rage—I could not say exactly *at what or at whom*. He asked Silvanus if Seneca was on the point of letting the blood out of his veins. Silvanus said he was sure that Seneca was not considering suicide; he had showed no signs of fear, no acknowledgment of guilt, not even any sadness. At this Himself, still at the peak of his aimless fury, commanded Silvanus to go back and announce the death sentence.

I cannot say to you that I am sorry.

Verify the death, and give us an exact account of it.

To TIGELLINUS from PAENUS, Tribune of Secret Police
By mounted courier.

Seneca has requested permission of me, but I do not feel that I should be the one to grant or deny it, to have near him at his death his nephew Lucan.

I realize that sending this message postpones the carrying out of Himself's command until very late hours, but I believe, I hope correctly, that Himself would want to make this decision.

To PAENUS, Tribune of Secret Police, from TIGELLINUS
By mounted courier.

Permission *not* granted. Lucan is a confessed conspirator

against the Emperor's life and is under house arrest. Himself allows Seneca the consolation of the presence of his physician and friend Statius Annaeus. We have sent for him, and he will be brought directly there.

To TIGELLINUS from PAENUS, Tribune of Secret Police
By mounted courier.
Seneca's wife Paulina, saying she does not wish to survive her husband, has opened her veins as he opened his—before the arrival of the surgeon. Does Himself want this?

To PAENUS, Tribune of Secret Police, from TIGELLINUS
By mounted courier.
No. Bind up Paulina's wounds. Do not let her die.

To TIGELLINUS from PAENUS, Tribune of Secret Police
By mounted courier.
Seneca is dead. Paulina lives. Full report in the morning.

April 29
To TIGELLINUS from PAENUS, Tribune of Secret Police
I have been up all night writing this report. I am weary to the marrow. A dim gray hint of morning in the rectangle of my window cannot pale the hypnogogic phantoms that dance in the dark corners of my room, mocking me for the stupid account I have written. They are noblewomen, these dancers, pale as woodsmoke, perhaps a chorus of Paulinas and Epicharises. They sway and dip. They point their fingers at my desk. Closing my eyes does no good; they surge into larger and more menacing dream figures. You were cruel to me after the torture of Epicharis; very well, be cruel again. Once more I have been shaken. What sort of career have I? Who *are* we,

Tigellinus? Seneca was in fact dangerous. But not, I think, for the reason we fancied. Read these poor shards of the truth of what happened last evening, and judge for yourself. I must risk sleep and the company of these women, the personages of my threadbare conscience.

The Execution of Seneca

The Tribune Silvanus returned to Marcellinus's house in the fourth night hour, and he informed me of the verdict. Though he had had it from the lips of Himself, he was unwilling to deliver it to Seneca, so it fell to me to announce the sentence. I asked Silvanus to provide a guard of six tall soldiers, and he did.

Seneca and the small company were still on couches in the dining room, and their conversation, as before, was animated, punctuated by exclamations and sallies of laughter. They fell silent, however, on my approach and that of the guard of six.

I thought it best, again, to be formal.

PAENUS: Nero Caesar has commanded me to announce to you, Lucius Annaeus Seneca, the sentence of death.

SENECA, calmly: I am not surprised.

At once a clamor of wailing and lamentations went up from Paulina and the host and hostess. A slave of Marcellinus's, who had been pouring wine, ran from the room, and soon appeared, one by one, the train of Seneca's freedmen (our famous Cleonicus, weeping like a rain cloud, among the first), secretaries, bearers, and other slaves who had accompanied their patron and master on his trip into the countryside. There was universal crying, moaning, breast-beating.

Seneca raised his arms and made arresting motions.

SENECA: My friends! My friends! Please be generous enough to let me speak to this policeman.

This perfectly accurate designation was spoken without sarcasm or even weight, but it served to reduce me in everyone's eyes, including, I am sorry to say, my own, to a rather shameful condition of inadequacy. It was as if the wine-wet mouth in that benign, rubicund face had said that such an important message should have been delivered to such an important man by a high-ranking military person, indeed by a Co-Commander of the Praetorian Guard if not by the Supreme Commander, the Emperor Himself. Seneca was the only calm one in the room. His gestures were stately, larger than lifesize. I was reminded of Epicharis's having said that his every pose was struck as if he were modeling for a sculptor chipping at marble.

SENECA, mildly, to me: It would console my last hours to have with me my dear nephew Lucan. May I send for him?

At once I realized that this was not a decision that a *policeman* could make, and I replied to Seneca that I would dispatch a messenger to Nero Caesar to ask for the Imperial pleasure. I left the room, I wrote and sent off the message, and—knowing that I could not remain apart from a man under a capital sentence—I returned to the banquet room.

Seneca was now speaking words of consolation to his wife, friends, and dependents. Where, he asked, with an indulgent smile, were all the philosophic words of good sense he had been imparting to them all these years? Certainly they should not be surprised by this verdict, any more than he was, for they all knew about Nero's cruelty. Nero had done away with an uncle, a brother, a mother, a wife; there was not much left but to get rid of a man who had been teacher, guardian, and friend all in one. Gradually, as Seneca talked, the lamentations were stilled.

SENECA: There could not be a better time for me to depart than this. There would have been little left for me save the dregs in the cask—where the amount is small and the quality vile. I am at the most delightful moment of life, when it is on the downward slope but has not yet reached the abrupt decline. I am ready. I have always said that we die a little every day of our lives; this is only an arrival. You have been patient and tender, Paulina, about my asthma; some physicians call its shortness of breath "practicing how to die." I am rehearsed and ready.

He talked on in this way, in his soothing, level, pedagogical voice. There was a certain pomposity in all this, but even the portentousness and heaviness were luminous, in a way, because this was so essentially *Seneca*'s pomposity, it had such integrity. He was being completely himself. I found that I had in my chest a warm and humid congestion, a painful small globe of mourning. (Yes, Tigellinus, I know; you will make me pay for that line—but I remind you of your response to the Seneca file I sent you.)

SENECA: Suppose I were given a magical choice—that of living my life over again. How would I have lived? What would I have changed?

Now Seneca gave a sudden, brief, involuntary start, a shudder of surprise, as if something important had just come to him. He beckoned to a person in the retinue at the side of the room; it was one of his secretaries. He bade the man keep a record of what he was saying. So even in these moments Seneca was aware of the publishability of words! And he began now to choose his expressions with greater care than before.

SENECA: We Stoics find that pleasure is a vice. The trouble with pleasure is that it is fickle, wayward, and often spurious. One says he takes pleasure in a friend's being elected Consul, or getting married, or having a child; but these happenings are not really joys but often are only the beginnings of sorrow. Joy is a permanent and stable raising of the spirit—of a spirit that trusts in its own goodness and truth. I have had such joys, and I think of them now. Solitude. I have known the pure joy of being alone in contemplation. I have gazed for hours from the walks in my garden at the rim of the Alban hills, and at the Sabines capped with snow. Friendship. I have felt a joy in thinking of those I care about, even when I have been separated from them; and in their company I have known the equal giving and taking of the best that is in us. Love. Paulina—you have entered into my being, I have seen in you not only the woman I desired but always the sort of woman one truly desires.

At this, tears came into Paulina's eyes, and Seneca quickly moved on, to spare her feelings.

SENECA: I have loved Lucilius Junior, even at a distance— a friend like a son; in recent years I have written him a letter every day. And well-being. In spite of my malady I have had joy in my body, in cool baths, in simple foods and exercise— how you used to laugh, Paulina, when I did "the clothes-cleaner's jump," imitating the launderer treading clothes in a great vat to get them clean! My body has never dominated me. He will have many masters who makes his body his master. I have had lasting joy from mine, because through it I have been in touch with the warmest and most sensitive aspects of life.

Seeming to have forgotten his own question about how he would reorder a new life, if he could have one, Seneca turned now to his host, Marcellinus.

SENECA: You are young, Marcellinus. I see in you a man who is struggling. You are marvelously witty, you can make mourners smile. When I begin to bore you with my ever-lasting moralizing, you trot out and make sausage meat of this philosopher who was caught in adultery, and that one who stole chickens from a neighbor, and the other who dressed in rags and took huge fees at court. You have great force of character, but you may be skidding toward depravity—I see that you are strongly drawn toward money-making. There is no harm in that in itself, because it is the sign of an unstable mind not to be able to endure riches. But I trust you will remember what Epicurus said: "The acquisition of riches has been for many men not an end but only a change of troubles." And if the fruit of this truth is that you decide some day to give up your riches, I hope you will avoid the perverted forms of self-display so many young men fall into who renounce their patrimonies—repellent attire, unkempt hair, slovenly beard, open scorn of silver dishes, a couch on the bare earth. Our Stoic motto is, you know, "Live according to Nature." Philosophy calls for plain living but not for penance. You can live plainly enough with what you have, without giving it up at all. But in your tendency to scan the future with a feverish eye, Marcellinus, always planning, planning, you make me think of another saying of Epicurus: "The fool, with all his other faults, has also this—he is always getting ready to live." We all live too much in the future. Some things torment us before they should; others torment us more than they should; some torment us when they ought not to torment us at all. We are in the habit of anticipating, or exaggerating, or imagining sorrow.

Here Seneca paused, deep in thought. One of his slaves stepped forward and handed him a damp cloth, with which Seneca wiped his face and his sweaty bald head; he thanked the weeping slave with a loving look.

SENECA: I have made mistakes. By the standards of the Emperor's court, Marcellinus, I am a failure. I can tell. Lately no one has come to ask my advice, least of all the man who needs it most, poor Nero. Successful men are blockaded by troops of people who call themselves friends, but those who have failed have more than enough solitude to become philosophers; they can only see the backs of those same people fleeing from the very thing that will some day test their own worth. Most of my mistakes came during my time with Nero; I won't recite them. I was—I suppose I still am—vain, and I don't like to parade my faults and errors. I have made some great and mysterious mistake with dear Lucan; there is a gulf between us. But if I put my joys and my mistakes in the balance, Paulina, I am satisfied. I would certainly accept the offer of living my life again, but, Paulina, I would live it over again in exactly the same way. I would change nothing. You see, if I identified all my past mistakes and avoided them in a new life, I would be obliged to make other mistakes in their place. One cannot even try to be wise who has not made a fool of himself, lost friends, compromised, had the shame of telling lies—as we all do, we all do.

At this point the mounted courier returned from the Golden House with the message denying Seneca's request for Lucan's company. I was called from the room to hear his report, and I returned to deliver the rebuff to Seneca, adding also, however, that Statius Annaeus was on his way.

Seneca then asked me for tablets on which to inscribe a new will, but I, hardened by Himself's refusal of the request about Lucan, and worried about a further postponement of the execution, denied this favor, too—and at once regretted it, because of Seneca's gracious, if conceited, reaction. He turned to Paulina and his friends and dependents, and:

SENECA: They deny me the right to readjust my repayments to you for all that you have done for me, so I must bequeath to you by word of mouth the only thing I have left to give— but anyway the noblest thing I have to give: my way of life. If you will accept that and live by it, my dearest ones, you will be known in time for your integrity and loyal friendship.

That put the policeman where he belonged—and did it the more firmly because Seneca included *me* with his eyes in this bequest. Uffa! I felt the way I feel when I get certain messages from you, Tigellinus, but I must say your messages are both less subtle and less powerful. In other words, I saw in Seneca in those moments, alongside the formidable sweetness and probity, also a flash of bitterness, hatred, and contempt. That raised right eyebrow!

But Seneca faced death; I faced only myself.

Now Seneca stood up and went to Paulina and took her in his arms, and he spoke to her as if they were alone together. He begged her to pay their past relationship the greatest possible compliment—of mourning only a short while, and then living proudly, thinking of the good life they had shared. In this speech to her he was wholly unaffected; these two must indeed have opened themselves to each other over the years. He invited her even to marry again soon, to some honorable and kindly widower—thus paying a further homage to their life together, as if to say, the married state suits me very well because I know how rich it can be.

But Paulina now surprised us. Her eyes were full to the brim with emotion but not, now, with tears, and she still clasped Seneca; she spoke in a steady, deep-throated voice.

PAULINA: I cannot do what you ask, dear man, because I am going with you. I cannot see you off on this journey; I cannot stay behind. I claim the right as your wife, a person partly given to you and partly taken from you, as the source myself of much of your strength and wisdom, and so really a part of you—a sharer in your crime, which is the crime of being too strong to submit either to a tyrant or to fear; as all this, I claim the right to the executioner's stroke alongside you.

Seneca accepted, perhaps too quickly and readily, certainly with no pause for thought, this claim of hers.

SENECA: I have tried to point out how you could live without me; you prefer to die with me. You know your worth, and I certainly cannot deny that you are the best part of my strength. All right, then let us show our strength together— and your courage, Paulina, will deserve much more fame than mine. I have no choice; you have.

I was so affected by the bravery of this quiet woman that I did not at first consider my own responsibility in the situation. At his acquiescence her face became radiant.

Now Seneca asked Marcellinus for a sharp knife and some basins. Marcellinus left the room and soon came back with a dagger, and a slave brought basins.

Paulina and Seneca, resolute and altogether steady, put two wrists side by side and with one motion of the dagger Seneca quite gently, if that word can apply, opened the veins of both. Then Paulina took the weapon and made a like common incision on their other wrists placed next to one another.

PAULINA, looking in Seneca's eyes: It does not hurt, Seneca.

I was suddenly greatly alarmed and hurried from the room to send a mounted courier to ask whether Himself wanted Paulina to die.

When I went back in the room, Seneca, bleeding very slowly because of his age and because his body had been so wasted by a frugal diet, was carefully opening some veins in his legs.

That done, he began speaking again to his friends and retinue, as if nothing out of the ordinary had happened. First he gave some advice about how they should mourn him.

SENECA: Your eyes shouldn't be dry when we have left you, but don't let them overflow, either. Weep, but don't wail. Do you want to know the reason for noisy lamentations? People want to give proof of their bereavement in their mourning; they don't succumb to sorrow, they root around in it and dress themselves in it. You know, my teacher Attalus used to say, "Remembering lost friends is pleasant in the same way that certain fruits are agreeably tart, or as in extremely old wines it is their edge that pleases us. Indeed, after some time has gone by, all that has given us pain burns out, and the pleasure comes to us pure."

Now there was some bustle as Statius Annaeus came in. Seneca greeted him as if he were a guest, and Statius deported himself well, showing the warm sympathy of a physician and hiding his grief. He examined the wounds of both Seneca and Paulina, declared them well incised and bleeding gently. He asked Marcellinus to have two cathedras brought in, and for their greater comfort he settled the two in these large chairs with their sloping backs.

Then Seneca went on talking—now to his slaves and servants.

SENECA: My dear friends, I've tried to treat you as I would wish to be treated by a master. I think we have respected each other. Respect means love; fear and love are oil and water to each other. We have lived together, talked together, planned together. Try to remember what I have given you tonight— the pattern of my life. And remember that I learned part of that pattern in humility from some of you.

In the midst of my anxiety lest Paulina should die before a message could come back from Himself, I was nevertheless able to perceive a certain false note in this speech of Seneca's to his slaves, and in their response—many came forward, fell to their knees, and kissed his and Paulina's hands. The tears of Cleonicus seemed to be, and may have been, perfectly sincere, but I was in a position to know that there was surely irony in them. And I remembered, against the background of Seneca's sentimental writings on slaves, his not knowing even of the existence of the scullery slave who might have poisoned him.

Nevertheless, his mien and gestures were magnificent; life was ebbing away. *This*, it struck me, was why Seneca had been dangerous. In the end it is a man's bearing, as much as his words, that have real meaning. Cowards talk bravely, brave men walk bravely. (Ah, Tigellinus, I hear you now: Paenus, you've listened to so many of Seneca's pompous epigrams that you've started mimicking them. But have you been paying attention to what I have written, Tigellinus?)

SENECA, to his stenographer: I want to dictate a letter to Lucan. . . . Are you ready? . . .

"Seneca to Lucan, greetings:

"If you are well, it is well. I also am well.

"This is how men used to start their letters to each other, and it is an appropriate salute from me to you at this moment.

"I asked permission to see you tonight, and it was denied me. I wanted to hold your hand, to look in your eyes. I have wanted a son.

"I understand that you are under arrest for the crime of having an independent mind. I congratulate you.

"You may be faced with more than house arrest—I pray not. If you are, get permission to have my dear friend Statius Annaeus attend you, and have him tell you how Seneca took his leave.

"But even my physician cannot tell you everything. I am at this instant afraid and very sad. Yes, Lucan, take anyone off his guard—young, old, or middle-aged—and you will find that all are equally afraid of death, and equally ignorant of life. After all I have written and said about not being afraid, I am afraid. I have loved my life, even though I feel as if I have merely groped my way through it, and suddenly I see the horror of leaving it. I am not really ready. No one has anything finished, because we have all kept putting off things we wanted to do. Your poem. My tragedies, my investigations of nature, my views on life—all incomplete, Lucan, in a way only just begun.

"I am still learning.

"It is too late for regrets. Back to our question: What is the responsibility of a writer? Be consoled, Lucan. You have done your duty as a writer as best you could, which was to be true to your gifts. The responsibility of a writer is to write. What more can be said? You have faithfully done this.

"But what, you have asked me all along, should a writer do about the evils of the world? I believe in philosophy —in living life as a constant search for wisdom, always in love with learning. I suppose the verdict against me, though totally arbitrary, is just. A philosopher, a writer: he is by definition one who wants to find a better way of doing things—less criminal, less violent, less rigid, less grasping, less cruel. A writer is a rebel. But, you see, as he is, so he would always be. Overthrowing a tyrant would not absolve him of the duty (the fate) of being a rebel. Systems change but men do not. Men have lived pretty much the same—with the same greeds, the same lusts, doing the same unforgivable wrongs to each other—under the democracy in Greece, under our Republic, now under the Principate whether the Emperor is Augustus or Nero, under tyrants, pharaohs, kings, satraps, chieftains, priests. If anything can save mankind from its darker side, dear Lucan, dear son, and dying I do not know if anything can, it will be the example of those who search—those few men in every setting who try to find and live by the rules of wisdom; and who write down what little they learn.

"I have tried to do this. You in your way have tried to do this. I salute you.

"Farewell."

It was in the pronunciation of this last word, as he dictated it, that for the very first time all night Seneca's voice trembled. He was growing weak. His head lolled back against the slope of the chair.

The messenger came with the order to save Paulina. I told Statius Annaeus, and he applied tourniquets. She was barely conscious, and was too weak to protest even if she realized what was happening. Seneca was still clear of mind, and when told of Nero's decision he feebly said he was really glad, for once, of a tyrant's command.

When the physician had finished with Paulina, Seneca told Statius that the force of life was too strong in him, and he asked his friend to administer to him a small vial of poison which he had long kept for an emergency; he sent Cleonicus —final irony—to get it. When the freedman came back, Statius helped Seneca to take it. But either the poison had lost its strength or Seneca's frame was closed to it; it had no effect.

Statius asked Marcellinus to prepare a warm and a hot bath. When the warm one was ready, Seneca was carried to it and was lowered into it. In a few moments he sprinkled some of his slaves with the water and blood.

SENECA: I offer this liquid as a libation to Jupiter the Deliverer.

Soon he was carried into the hot bath, where in the steam life left him, and he, life.

To PAENUS, Tribune of Secret Police, from TIGELLINUS

I am sorry to interrupt your earned sleep. Himself has read your report on Seneca. You are suddenly a trusted man, and he urgently wants you present at the series of interrogations we must conduct this morning. Come at once. Bring Natalis and Scaevinus.

INTERROGATION:
Cervarius Proculus

In the Presence of the Emperor. Attending: Tigellinus, Rufus, Paenus, Cassius; Natalis, Scaevinus, in confrontation; Felix, Stenographer.

The early part of the interrogation is summarized as follows: Cervarius, identified as belonging to the equestrian order, is questioned, principally by Tigellinus, about his relationship to Piso; at first Cervarius denies anything more than a casual acquaintanceship. At a certain point Co-Commander Rufus actively joins the questioning, treating Cervarius to fierce looks and brusque challenges. Natalis and Scaevinus, interested in their own skins, also press Cervarius, who begins to involve himself in damaging contradictions. Then:

SCAEVINUS: Do you remember, CERVARIUS, the evening of what we called "the test of Fate"—our debate over who should be the successor? Tell about your part in that discussion.

RUFUS now turned on SCAEVINUS, saying that SCAEVINUS seemed to know much more about this miserable affair than he had previously admitted to. SCAEVINUS, in his indifferent way, responded only with a languid smile, which caused RUFUS to become angry and to browbeat SCAEVINUS with a series of menacing questions.

TIGELLINUS: My dear RUFUS, we are here to question CERVARIUS.

SCAEVINUS, still smiling, and with an insolent calm: Perhaps we should be questioning RUFUS. After all, my dear RUFUS, no one knows more about this miserable affair, as you call it, than you do.

RUFUS opened his mouth, as if to roar at SCAEVINUS, but no sound emerged.

SCAEVINUS, insisting: Why don't you show your true gratitude to the Prince who has been so good to you, RUFUS? Why don't you tell him what *you* know?

Here CERVARIUS, the accused, brazenly intervened, perhaps seeing a chance to rescue himself: Yes, RUFUS, tell us about the position you took during "the test of Fate."

RUFUS began looking first at HIMSELF, then at SCAEVINUS and CERVARIUS, then at TIGELLINUS. He seemed to be choking. FAENUS RUFUS, Co-Commander of the Praetorian Guard, a man with a battle record of searing valor, was pallid, trembling, perspiring, and speechless.

A roar now did emerge, not from RUFUS but from the mouth of HIMSELF.

HIMSELF: Not *you*!

RUFUS now finally tried to protest, but his words were halting.

HIMSELF: CASSIUS! CASSIUS!

The giant at once leaped forward and caught RUFUS in his arms. RUFUS in terror struggled to free himself, but he was like a kitten in the paws of CASSIUS, who had very soon bound RUFUS's limbs in strong cord.

SCAEVINUS, even now imperturbable: Why don't you tell your Prince, RUFUS, about what you said about a successor?

It was now TIGELLINUS's turn to emit a bellow.

TIG.: It was *you* who went to Seneca!

Now there was great confusion—babbling of many voices.

Repeated loud shouts by HIMSELF brought the interrogation of CERVARIUS to an abrupt conclusion.

PAENUS AFRANIUS (Recorder)

To PAENUS, Tribune of Secret Police, from TIGELLINUS
Take over interrogation of civilian arrestees. Himself, Poppaea, Cassius, and I will question Rufus, the Tribune Subrius

Flavus, the Centurion Sulpicius Asper, and other military conspirators as uncovered.

Worried about Himself. What shocks! The Co-Commander of the Guard! My "colleague," I thank the stars, seems to be completely broken. I knew he had no bronze in him when I backed him down about the investigation of the Guard—but I shudder when I think of having entrusted that "purge" to him. No wonder nothing happened. We have had a narrow escape.

Carry on. Be alert. You will have to handle all arrests from now on.

To PAENUS, Tribune of Secret Police, from TIGELLINUS
We have sent Rufus, Flavus, and Asper to have their heads cut off.

Arrest the Tribune Gavius Silvanus. This is the "trusted" officer Rufus sent with you to Seneca! From Rufus we have learned that after Himself ordered Silvanus to carry the death sentence to Seneca, *Silvanus went to Rufus to ask whether he should deliver it*. Rufus's nerve was already gone then; he ordered Silvanus to carry out the mission. But as you reported, Silvanus could not bring himself to bear the message face-to-face to Seneca and left it to you.

Arrest also the Tribune Statius Proximus, the Centurions Maximus Scaurus and Venetus Paulus. There will be others.

[Omitted here: Numerous messages to Tigellinus from Paenus about interrogations of civilians; orders for further civilian arrests.]

April 30
To PAENUS, Tribune of Secret Police, from TIGELLINUS
Poppaea and I have had a bad night with Himself. He

needed us by his side. I held his hand for hours. In his other hand he held the girl-goddess, all night long. His skin was clammy, his eyes bloodshot with swollen lids as if he wanted to but could not weep.

The blows have been dreadful ones for him. Seneca's brave death—without a word of reproach of Himself, except for that brief reference to his cruelty. How much easier it would have been if Seneca had lost control and had poured out a loathing of his former pupil. Then yesterday, Paenus. The exposure of Rufus was bad enough. But those other soldiers!

First there was Subrius Flavus. When confronted he scoffed at the idea that such a rough man as he could join himself in *any* undertaking with dissipated, effeminate, and unarmed associates—our literary friends. But under pressure from a shameless Rufus, he took pride in a full confession. Himself was close to those elusive tears, believe me, and he asked what could possibly have driven a good soldier to forget his oath of allegiance.

Flavus looked Himself full in the face and said: I hated you.

Himself had no answer for that; the threatened tears did not come, only a sickly pallor.

Flavus went on: No soldier was more loyal to you than I was as long as you deserved the love of a Roman. I started to hate you when you killed your mother. My hate grew and grew when you murdered your wife, when you began racing chariots, when you started singing female parts in the theater, when you became an incendiary.

You can imagine that it did not take long then for the death sentence of decapitation to be pronounced.

But Flavus's words had stabbed Himself, and later in the day news came of the manner of Flavus's dying, and this news turned the knife in the wound. I had decided that we could trust the Tribune Veianus Niger to behead Flavus. Flavus ordered a pit dug in the field where he was to die. Seeing it, Flavus criticized it—too shallow, too narrow; and he turned to the soldiers around him and said: Even this is not according to regulations. Niger urged him to offer his neck like a man. I only hope, Flavus said in the firm voice of a commanding officer, that your stroke will be as manly. Niger trembled terribly at that, and could hardly do his duty. . . .

Asper dealt Himself another gut wound with words. When Himself asked why he had conspired to murder him, the centurion answered: I could not have done a greater service to your career than to bring it to an end.

This man died resolutely, too.

Last evening was bitter. Himself began to be convinced that everyone was plotting against him, even Poppaea and I. Finally he developed a firm conviction that the Consul Vestinus was a leader of the plot. I tried to point out that no one had accused Vestinus, that because of his stubbornness about his elegant private guard we had conducted careful investigations, which had absolved him to our satisfaction. But Himself was wild, and he sent the Tribune Gerellanus with a cohort of soldiers to "seize Vestinus's fort," to crush the bodyguard, and to do away with him. Vestinus was entertaining a dinner party. The moment the soldiers broke into his house and announced the verdict, he shut himself up in his private chamber, called a physician, opened his veins, and died without a word of self-pity.

When a messenger reported late at night that the soldiers were still holding Vestinus's guests and wished to know the Emperor's pleasure, Himself laughed and laughed, and said the guests had been punished long enough for having given the traitor Vestinus a good time; let them go home.

But after the bout of laughter Himself had chills. In the

night he started from sleep, drenched with sweat, and said that he had dreamed that he was sailing a vessel and suddenly the helm was wrenched out of his grasp and then disappeared —there was nothing to steer with as the wind increased. He said that Lucan was somewhere on the vessel, but that he could not see him. He looked everywhere—in the bows, in the compartments below decks, among the galley slaves, at the mast—but could not find Lucan. The sense of Lucan's presence was oppressive, the wind was hot and moist.

To PAENUS, *Tribune of Secret Police, from TIGELLINUS*
Himself orders Lucan sentenced to death.

You are to deliver the sentence, Paenus. Take a squad of agents with you. You had perhaps better also take an executioner, as Lucan may not have the courage to take his own life.

This decision has been the worst—almost tore Himself in two. The dream he had last night has weighed on him all morning; he says he cannot shake the feeling that Lucan is nearby and can actually look at him.

He commands that you pick up Statius Annaeus on your way and take him to Lucan's, and also that you carry with you the letter that Seneca dictated for Lucan.

Verify the death, and give us an exact account of it.

To TIGELLINUS *from PAENUS, Tribune of Secret Police*
By mounted courier.
Lucan is dead.

To TIGELLINUS *from PAENUS, Tribune of Secret Police*
The report on Lucan's death. Give me no more errands of this sort.

The Execution of Lucan

I posted the squad of agents and the executioner at the gate, and we entered.

As soon as Lucan recognized Statius Annaeus in my company, he knew why I had come, and he confounded my (and Himself's, and your) anxiety lest he react as a coward: He spoke to us quietly, before I could even pronounce the sentence of death:

LUCAN: I have been expecting this.

He led us to his writing room, seated us, and offered us wine in silver cups with his own hands. He poured himself a cupful too, and drank it straight off. I told Lucan that Seneca had wished for him to hear from Statius Annaeus an account of Seneca's departure.

Lucan sat quietly while Statius spoke about Seneca's death. Statius, you will remember, had arrived well after Seneca had opened his veins; he had afterwards questioned Marcellinus, Paulina, Cleonicus, and others about the earlier part of the evening. I now found myself intervening from time to time in Statius's narrative, to correct or offer details.

As Lucan listened he began to give out quick little reactive grunts, and he frowned and grimaced. Finally he stood up, poured himself another cup of wine, tossed if off at a gulp, and impatiently burst out:

LUCAN: A *Phaedo*! He was trying to make a *Phaedo* of it. Playing at the death of Socrates.

To my surprise I could not resist denying this.

PAENUS: No, no, you're wrong, Lucan. He was much more modest than that.

STATIUS: I agree, I agree.

PAENUS: To me this was the point of what he did. If he was

self-conscious, well, he was less so than I had ever seen him. There was no pose, he was himself—a man, a dying man.

Though obviously unappeased, Lucan poured more wine, set the carafe on the floor close by his chair, and sat down again, and Statius continued the narrative. When he came to Seneca's dictation of the letter, I reached forward to Lucan the copy I was carrying.

Lucan's face was pale and expressionless as he read. He sipped at his wine, refilled his glass, read, sipped, read. At the end he let the letter fall to the floor from his hands and sighed. Then he barked out a sarcastic little laugh.

LUCAN: Example, example! Oh, Seca!

For a time he seemed lost in thought, then:

LUCAN: I am not as afraid of dying as I thought I would be.

A pause, then:

LUCAN: The trouble with Seneca, Statius, was that he could never stop *improving* people. He always made you feel aware of your imperfections. It seems to me that love is forgiveness. Nero cannot love in this sense. Epicharis gave this kind of love to me—but then, she gave it to everyone, and I was always mad with jealousy when I was around her. Paulina was the only person Seneca loved, besides himself; oh, he forgave himself *everything*. I am trying to think what dying is about; what Seneca's death meant, what mine will mean. I haven't loved anyone. Not a single person. Perhaps I have loved Cato, but he was just a dead person who came to life in my dreams. A kind of man I yearned to be. Seneca kept saying he loved me, but he just wanted my "love" as something he would own, like one of those famous matching inlaid tables Suilius objected to.

STATIUS: Don't be so bitter, dear fellow.

LUCAN: It's too late for bitterness—or for forgiveness, or for idealism, or for conspiracy. My feelings mean nothing now. I

think we had better get on with what has to be done. . . .
Everything that matters in the household is in order.

STATIUS: Where is Polla?

LUCAN: She has gone off to visit Natalis's wife at the Alban
Lake. She is *never* here when I need her.

This complaint Lucan spoke petulantly, like a little boy, as
if Polla were needed in connection with some petty household
annoyance, or had left Lucan in the lurch on some distasteful
duty of entertainment with which he did not wish to be
bothered.

STATIUS: Do you want to say good-bye to . . . ?

Statius left the query unfinished. He obviously meant freedmen, slaves, perhaps even friends. But Lucan shook his head.

LUCAN: I have no taste for setting an example.

This was a cold attitude which I found disgusting. Whether
he felt love (forgiveness) or not, had he no feeling of any
kind for *any* of the people in his house? Lucan reached for the
carafe and poured himself yet another cup of wine.

STATIUS: We will need basins. And a cathedra.

In reply to this, Lucan spoke to us as if we were servants.

LUCAN: Get basins from the kitchen. Turn right at the door
of this room and go straight to the end. There is a cathedra
in the first room on the right.

Statius nodded to me, a gesture which had the effect of
making *me* the servant, and I started for the kitchen, hoping
I would not have to explain my presence to elderly slaves who
loved Lucan, whatever he may have felt, or not felt, for them.
As I left the room I heard this exchange:

STATIUS: We should have water heated for a bath.

LUCAN: We can dispense with that.

I found basins in the kitchen and took them to the writing
room, then dragged the cathedra there.

With great fortitude—this was not at all the craven creature you interrogated, Tigellinus—Lucan allowed Statius to open his veins.

He sat for a time with his head leaning back and his eyes closed, as if he were searching out the meaning of his death in physical sensations—in what his senses told him about losing blood and life.

Then his eyes opened and he looked at me.

LUCAN: You are one of Nero's policemen?

I nodded acknowledgment, smarting from his denial, at this important moment, of my identity. He had met me a hundred times at the palace, and it had used to annoy me there that I had had to be presented to him over and over, but finally he had "known" me and had used my name—over and over. But now, this blank word: policeman. I nodded.

LUCAN: Are you people pleased?

PAENUS: Pleased?

LUCAN: With your conspiracy?

PAENUS: Our conspiracy?

LUCAN: Your conspiracy. The one you imagined. Made out of shadows. There hasn't been any conspiracy, you know, except the one you people invented. Nero. Tigellinus. Poppaea. You clumsy policemen. It has all been in your minds. You fabricated it. Now you're destroying us to justify yourselves.

This made me furious, and I objected with a disrespectful vigor that very nearly left out of account the fact that Lucan was a dying man. I cited the testimony and confessions of many persons, including his own abject admissions, and I reminded him, with a thrust of cruelty which I could not suppress, that he had even accused his own mother of sharing in the plot.

LUCAN: Oh, yes, we've all fed Nero what he wanted. We've made things up to make him happy. We Romans are all Nero's trained circus animals. We know how to amuse him.

Life is like this—people playing their parts. People try to sense what others expect of them, they derive a picture of themselves from the clues they pick up from others, and then they are driven to oblige—sometimes without even knowing it. They tell themselves that the others' picture of them is not the picture they themselves see. But they oblige. We have obliged. . . . But, do you know, in destroying us, you people are destroying Nero—destroying yourselves. Maybe this was what you secretly wanted when you invented the conspiracy. Maybe you are the real conspirators.

He laughed—a feeble laugh, which seemed to hurt him inside.

LUCAN: Yes, your conspiracy, the one you people manufactured—it has succeeded. Nero withered one part of himself when he killed his mother. But killing Seneca, killing me—he'll never recover from this—what is your name?

PAENUS: Paenus.

LUCAN: Paenus. He'll never, never recover.

As Lucan said this he pulled himself forward in his chair with his slowly bleeding arms, smearing blood on the chair, and he fixed me with a terrible, exaggerated scowl. It seemed as if he was laying a curse on us, Tigellinus. I became for a moment very frightened. Then I was quickly relieved as I thought: How true a man is to his character at the very end! What vanity! What an absurd idea that Nero would suffer more from executing Seneca and Lucan than from the death of his mother. The vanity of it! As if killing a writer were a greater crime than matricide!

Lucan settled back in the chair, seeming to have made a great effort, and for a time he closed his eyes. Then, eyes still closed:

LUCAN: My hands and feet are getting cold.

STATIUS: Courage, my friend.

He opened his eyes and began speaking slowly and halt-
ingly, but in a strange steady flow, to no one in particular.

LUCAN: I remember the first time I saw Nero after he called
me back from Greece. Seneca was with us. I was, let me see,
nineteen, he was twenty-one. . . . I was fascinated by his huge
neck. He and Seneca quarreled about something. Seneca was
like a testy nursemaid, he had no fear of Nero's power. Finally
Nero got tired of the argument and began asking me about
the contests in Greece. He wanted to know about all the
arrangements. I said: It depends which festival . . . He said:
Nobody can ever tell me anything straight. I'll have to go
there myself. Ai, Seneca, I had a dream last night. I was
standing in front of a huge water-clock, it was the third hour,
but I couldn't tell whether it was day or night. Light and
darkness were the same. What does that mean? . . . Seneca
said it meant he was disrespectful of days and nights—that he
went into the streets at night, dined at noon. . . . Nero
snorted and said Seneca had a literal mind. *He* thought it
meant that life is gray, gray. Then, I remember, he began
talking about singing—he was just taking it up—something
about high tones. . . . I said: It seems to me that what matters in a voice is conviction—truth. . . . And he said: How
vain poets are! . . . Ah, I said, I was getting bold, it's the
sound you care about, not the meaning. . . . He gave me a
sudden look that shot fear into me, his eyes were the little
pig eyes of a charging wild boar—but his big lips smiled, and
he said: Exactly. Yes. I do. The sound is all that matters.

Suddenly tears were coursing down Lucan's pallid face. I
felt a begrudging pity for this little rooster of a man, all alone
at the end. Here he was with two strangers to whom he could
by no means bare his heart—a physician, not really his friend
but a friend of his dead uncle, and one of *Nero's policemen.*
His wife away. Not even any slaves standing by with servile

comforts. I wondered if he was crying out of self-pity. Or weeping for Epicharis—that she-leopard, so much stronger than he? Or was he thinking of Seneca's example? Or of Nero —a friendship squandered in prodigal bouts of vanity and envy?

But no! Nothing so human as any of that. Out came an unearthly groan, and:

LUCAN: My poem! Oh, Statius, I haven't been able to work. . . . It's all unfinished. . . .

He feebly sobbed.

I was struck very hard, Tigellinus, and very unexpectedly, by a sense of the uselessness, the ridiculousness, of my profession. Oh, yes, there had been a conspiracy, no doubt of that. I suppose there had been real danger. But we had been running around all these months, stealing bits of this man's privacy, that man's loneliness, sniffing, sniffing—and for what? Do you know something? I, "one of Nero's policemen," would like to be a poet. I hear your laughter. Laugh, Tigellinus. Laugh the laugh of a horse trader. I yearn for the life of a poet. As he wept I loved Lucan—I forgave him. Perhaps you will. Perhaps Himself will. Do you think we really are destroying ourselves?

Now Lucan stopped crying and began to recite a passage from his enormous poem. He *was*, at last, Cato. I remembered Curtius Marsus's astonishment at the vibrant power of Lucan's voice at the reading at Piso's banquet. Now the voice was barely comprehensible, weak, hazy, somehow doubting; the faint delivery seemed to drench these lines, which must have been intended to be unequivocal, in an agonized ambiguity:

What should be asked? Whether I'd rather die
Free and armed, or swallow tyranny?
Whether prolonging a life has any meaning,
Or if years make a difference at all? Or whether a man,

If he be good, can be hurt by any blow?
Does Fortune drop her threats at the sight of courage?
Is it not enough to try to do what's right?
Does fame fatten on virtue? We know the answers:
Jove cannot plant them deeper in our hearts.

But I thought: He is saying: We do *not* know the answers. He had delved in extremity under the surface of the poem, into a richness of meaning that even he may not have known was there. And now, in what happened next, I glimpsed some sort of desperate inner search, in these last moments, for other new and fluid meanings in all that he had done.

Lucan was weak. With his head leaning against the seat back he asked Statius in a whisper for an orange. Statius fetched one from a bowl of fruit on a side table, and first kneading it hard to loosen the juices within the skin, he then took a clean scalpel and with skillful thrusts cut a small hole in one end, and jabbed within, further to set free the juices. He then held the hole to Lucan's mouth.

At once Lucan began to suck, with the desperate, blind, ravenous strength of a newborn baby at its mother's breast. It was as if an infantile life force were at work—a refusal of chaos and darkness, a desire for energy, nourishment, health, new growth. I felt very strongly the presence in Lucan's weak frame of his poem, the deep, deep drive in him for completion. In the very moment when the last fatal drams of blood were taking their leave from his veins, he wanted more time. Most of his body was utterly slack, but that sucking mouth worked at the fruit with the full power of the muses. Those lips would gladly swallow tyranny for the hours, the days, the whatever time the work would take. What did Lucan care about *conspiracy?*

The lips moved long after it was clear that no more sweetness was left in the fruit. Then Statius gently removed the globe of life. The lips still moved, and a mumbling sound came from them.

The mumbling went on and on. It had a steady, slow, pulsing flow. In his withdrawal into the farthest reaches of the double mirrors, the poet was giving us a final, passionate reading of infinite layers of meaning. We could not make out the words, but we could see the pale, pale shadows of deep emotions flicker briefly on the face. It seemed that he must be unconscious, yet the rhythms, soundless now, went on and on. The poem was all that was left alive in him.

There was a stillness. Statius, waiting in decent respect for a long time, finally pronounced Lucan dead. One saw the salt on the poet's face where the tears had dried.

May 1

To PAENUS, Tribune of Secret Police, from TIGELLINUS

I cannot adequately describe to you the transformation of Himself since he read your account of the execution of Lucan. He is up and about, confident, has a look of a man who has just had a glowing report from his bailiff. He gives commands with assurance. He is, by the way, very pleased with you. Do not be astonished by a promotion.

Ai, Paenus, we can afford at last to congratulate ourselves. We have broken the back of this repulsive, many-legged monster.

To TIGELLINUS from PAENUS, Tribune of Secret Police

Please desist. At this moment congratulations make me sick to my stomach.

To PAENUS, Tribune of Secret Police, from TIGELLINUS

Come, come. Your last message was not worthy of so talented a *policeman*.

To PAENUS, Tribune of Secret Police, from TIGELLINUS

I have found a way to cheer you up: a series of delightful commands.

Sentences of death to Tullius Severus (another whom I trusted too much!), Quintianus the pederast, Scaevinus who may now close his sleepy eyes in a good rest.

Assign pretty (but very small) Aegean islands to Novius Priscus, Glitius Gallus, Annius Pollo, Verginius Flavus, Musonius Rufus, Cluvidienus Quietus, Julius Agrippa, Blitius Catulinus, Petronius Priscus, Julius Altinus.

Acquitted: Natalis (so great was his help in the interrogations—Scaevinus, by comparison, was too languid and insolent to all equally, including Himself and Myself!); Cervarius Proculus, for his aid in convicting Rufus; the Tribunes Gavius Silvanus and Statius Proximus.

To TIGELLINUS from PAENUS, Tribune of Secret Police

I see from the tone of your messages that you, too, have come out of your recent funk. You have adopted a charming designation for your dignified person, reminiscent of a designation you have long used for one somewhat more elevated: You now call yourself "Myself." Felicitations. I hope you do not suffer from vertigo.

To ABASCANTUS, Imperial Treasury, from TIGELLINUS

Himself commands:

A donative to the troops: Two thousand sesterces to each common soldier, with a supplement of a measure of free corn equal to the standard market-price ration.

To the SENATORS of ROME from TIGELLINUS

Nero Claudius Caesar Drusus Germanicus, Emperor, requires your presence at an extraordinary session of the Senate at the Capitol, at the seventh hour on May the fifth, at which he will address you on the recent deliverance of the Principate. Military Triumphal Honors to be awarded to Sofonius Tigellinus.

May 2

To SULPICIUS CASTOR, Sculptor by Appointment, from TIGELLINUS

Himself commands that you carve a full-length statue of me to be placed in the Forum, subsequent to Military Triumphal Honors to be awarded me in a few days. He also commands a bust, which will be displayed in the palace. Arrange appointments for sittings.

To CELER, Office of Planning and Construction, from TIGELLINUS

For an alfresco banquet in celebration of the suppression of the recent conspiracy, design and construct in the gardens of the Golden House various pavilions, belvederes, gazebos, and galleries. Use materials of the brightest colors. Be provided with many lanterns with tinted lights. Prepare a sanded ring about twenty paces in diameter, with six stakes with chains, as for the tethering of wild animals. We will also need a large cage on wheels, of the sort used for the most dangerous beasts; as well as a single tiger skin in excellent condition.

You have one week.

To IPPOLITE, Imperial Household, from TIGELLINUS

In utmost confidence.

Another delicate mission of the sort for which you have such sweet talent, Ippolite. This is a fancy of Himself himself, so requires especial tact and judgment. The idea is this (he is feeling mischievous): He wishes to chain to half a dozen stakes four beautiful young—and, it goes without saying, noble, rich, and naked—Roman women; one beautiful young (noble, etc.) man; and a female sheep that has come in season. It is his intention to cover his own bare body with the skin of a tiger, be released from a cage in the presence of guests, descend on these chained creatures, enjoy them one after another *in various ways*—and then allow his "wife," the eunuch Sporus, to drive him back in the cage in a display of mock jealousy. It is your task to enlist the four women and one man. Get Canus to provide the sheep.

I am afraid you have only one week.

May 4

To TIGELLINUS from PAENUS, Tribune of Secret Police

I do not seem to have heard anything more about a promotion.

May 5

To the SENATE and PEOPLE of ROME, from TIGEL-
LINUS, Commander, Praetorian Guard, by order of
NERO CLAUDIUS CAESAR DRUSUS GERMAN-
ICUS, EMPEROR:

A PROCLAMATION

Let there be observed, in gratitude for the deliverance of the Person of Nero Claudius Caesar Drusus Germanicus, Emperor, a suspension of all commerce and labor for a period of one week of unrestrained thanksgiving.

Let the benign month of April henceforth be named Neroneus.

Let there be special honors to the Sun in the ancient temple at the Circus Maximus—the great Sun who revealed by his brilliant power the secrets of those who would have used the Circus for their purposes.

Let Ceres be praised with additional chariot races in that same Circus—times to be announced.

Let a Temple of Safety be erected in the town of Farentum, whence was stolen the dagger that was to have been used for the imperatricide.

Let this dagger be inscribed, *To Jupiter the Avenger*, and let it be hung in the temple of the Capitol.

Let there be rejoicing in Rome. Let there be rejoicing in Rome. Let there be rejoicing in Rome.

AFTERWORD

It will have been especially clear to anyone who knows the time of the Roman Empire that this book has been intended as entertainment, not as history. I have gone to the obvious sources and have departed from them, too. One of the many glories of Tacitus is that under his sure hands time becomes something like a viscous amber fluid—clear, slow-moving, shot with iridescent glints and strange refractions; and Suetonius cares less for chronology than for kicks. Thus I seemed to have some scope in ordering things, and I have let myself use it. I have taken several casual liberties with the standard accounts—for a random example, the attribution to Lucan of a satirical line of verse that Suetonius ascribed to Persius. Rather more drastic is the assignment to Lucan, rather than to Natalis and Scaevinus, of the first important revelations of the plot. In giving such a large role to the secret police, I have anticipated the *Agentes in Rebus* of somewhat later years. To spare the reader even more confusion than he was bound to have as he encountered Roman names, I have changed two: the character here called Severus represents the Senecio of history; Valerius stands for Vatinius. Otherwise we would have had, on top of all the rest, Seneca and Senecio and Vestinus and Vatinius to keep straight.

A NOTE ABOUT THE AUTHOR

JOHN HERSEY was born in Tientsin, China, in 1914, and lived there until 1925, when his family returned to the United States. He was graduated from Yale in 1936 and attended Clare College, Cambridge University, for a year. He was private secretary to Sinclair Lewis during a subsequent summer and then worked as a journalist and war correspondent. His first novel, *A Bell for Adano*, won the Pulitzer Prize in 1945, and the next year he wrote *Hiroshima*, an account of the first atomic bombing. Since 1947 he has devoted his time mainly to fiction and has published *The Wall* (1950), *The Marmot Drive* (1953), *A Single Pebble* (1956), *The War Lover* (1959), *The Child Buyer* (1960), *White Lotus* (1965), *Too Far to Walk* (1966), and *Under the Eye of the Storm* (1967). *The Algiers Motel Incident*, an account of violence in the Detroit riot of 1967, was published in 1968. *Letter to the Alumni*, published in 1970, was the culmination of Mr. Hersey's five years as Master of Pierson College at Yale. Mr. Hersey spent the year 1970–71 as Writer in Residence at the American Academy in Rome.